W9-AKE-269

Smoke Bellew

Smoke Bellew

by JACK LONDON

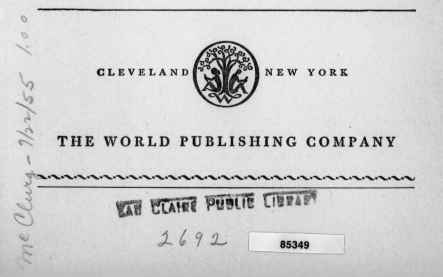

CLEVELAND · NEW YORK

THE WORLD PUBLISHING COMPANY

EAU CLAIRE PUBLIC LIBRARY

2692

85349

McClurg — 9/22/55 1.00

Library of Congress Catalog Card Number: 52-13236

HC 755

Copyright 1940 by Charmian K. London, Glen Ellen, California. Revised Edition 1953. All rights reserved. No part of this book may be reproduced in any form without written permission from the publisher, except for brief passages included in a review appearing in a newspaper or magazine. Manufactured in the United States of America.

CONTENTS

Smoke Bellew

CHAPTER 1

The Taste of the Meat

IN THE beginning he was Christopher Bellew. By the time he was at college he had become Chris Bellew. Later, in the Bohemian crowd of San Francisco, he was called Kit Bellew. And in the end he was known by no other name than Smoke Bellew. And this history of the evolution of his name is the history of his evolution. Nor would it have happened had he not had a fond mother and an iron uncle, and had he not received a letter from Gillet Bellamy in Paris.

"I have just seen a copy of *The Billow*," Gillet wrote. "Of course O'Hara will succeed with it. But he's missing some tricks." Here followed details for the improvement of the budding literary weekly. "Go down and see him. Let him think they're your own suggestions, don't let him know they're from me. If you do, he'll make me Paris correspondent, which I can't afford. I'm getting real money for my stuff from the big magazines. Above all, make him fire the dub who's doing the music and art criticism. Another thing. San Francisco has always had a literature of her own. But she hasn't any now. Tell him to look around and get someone who can turn out a live serial, and put into it the real romance and glamor and color of the place."

9

And down to the office of *The Billow* went Kit Bellew.
O'Hara listened. O'Hara debated. O'Hara agreed. O'Hara
fired the dub who wrote criticisms. Further, O'Hara had a
way with him, the very way that was feared by Gillet in
distant Paris. When O'Hara wanted anything, no friend
could deny him. He was sweetly and compellingly irre-
sistible. Before Kit Bellew could escape from the office, he
had become an associate editor, had agreed to write weekly
columns of criticism till some decent pen was found, and
had pledged himself to write a weekly installment of ten
thousand words on San Francisco—and all this without
pay. *The Billow* wasn't paying yet, O'Hara explained; and
just as convincingly stated that there was only one man in
San Francisco capable of writing the serial and that man
was Kit Bellew.

"Oh, Lord, I'm it!" Kit groaned to himself afterward on
the narrow stairway.

Thus began his servitude to O'Hara and the insatiable
columns of *The Billow*. Week after week he held down an
office chair, stood off creditors, wrangled with printers, and
turned out twenty-five thousand words of all sorts. Nor did
his labors lighten. *The Billow* was ambitious. It went in
for illustration. The processes were expensive. It never had
any money to pay Kit Bellew, and by the same token it
was unable to pay for any additions to the office staff.
Luckily for Kit, he had his own small income. Yet he was
always broke, for *The Billow*, in perennial distress, absorbed his cash as well as his brains. There were the illus-
trators, who periodically refused to illustrate; the printers,
who periodically refused to print; and the office-boy, who
frequently refused to officiate. At such times O'Hara looked
at Kit, and Kit did the rest.

When the steamship *Excelsior* arrived from Alaska in

July, bringing the news of the great Klondike strike that set the country mad, Kit made a purely frivolous proposition.

"Look here, O'Hara," he said. "This gold rush is going to be big—the days of '49 over again. Suppose I cover it for *The Billow?* I'll pay my own expenses."

O'Hara shook his head. "Can't spare you from the office, Kit. Besides, I saw Jackson less than an hour ago. He's starting for the Klondike tomorrow, and he's agreed to send a weekly letter and photos. I wouldn't let him get away till he promised. The beauty of it is that it won't cost us anything."

The next Kit heard of the Klondike was when he dropped into his club that afternoon and in an alcove off the library encountered his uncle.

"Hello, avuncular relative," Kit greeted, sliding into a leather chair and spreading out his legs. "May I join you?"

"What's the matter with you?" the other demanded. "You're pale. You're a wreck."

Kit's only answer was a groan.

"I'll have the pleasure of burying you. I can see that."

John Bellew came of the old hard and hardy stock that had crossed the plains by ox-team in the eighteen-fifties, and in him was this same hardness and the hardness of a childhood spent in conquering a new land. "You're not living right, Christopher. I'm ashamed of you."

"Primrose path, eh?" Kit chuckled.

The older man shrugged his shoulders.

"Shake not your gory locks at me, avuncular. I wish it *were* the primrose path. But that's all cut out. I have no time."

"Then what in—?"

"Overwork."

John Bellew laughed harshly and incredulously.

"Overwork! You never earned a cent in your life."

"You bet I have, only I never got it. I'm earning five hundred a week right now, and doing four men's work."

"Pictures that won't sell? Or—er—fancy work of some sort? Can you swim?"

"I used to."

"Sit a horse?"

"I've tried that adventure."

John Bellew snorted his disgust. "I'm glad your father didn't live to see you in all the glory of your gracelessness," he said. "Your father was a man, every inch of him. He'd have whaled all this tomfoolery out of you."

"Alas! these degenerate days," Kit sighed.

"I could understand it, and tolerate it," the other went on, "if you succeeded at it. But you've never earned a cent in your life, nor done a rap of man's work. What earthly good are you, anyway? You're certainly strong enough, yet even at the University you didn't play football. You didn't row. You didn't—"

"I boxed and fenced—some."

"When did you box last?"

"Not since, but I was considered an excellent judge of time and distance. Only I was—er—"

"Go on."

"Considered desultory."

"Lazy, you mean."

"I always imagined it was an euphemism."

"My father, sir, your grandfather, old Isaac Bellew, killed a man with a blow of his fist when he was sixty-nine years old."

"The man?"

"No, you graceless scamp! But you'll never kill a mosquito at sixty-nine."

"The times have changed, avuncular! They send men to prison for homicide now."

"Your father rode one hundred and eighty-five miles without sleeping, and killed three horses."

"Had he lived to-day he'd have snored over the same course in a Pullman."

The older man was on the verge of choking with wrath. "How old are you?"

"I have reason to believe—"

"I know. Twenty-seven. You finished college at twenty-two. You've dabbled and played and frilled for five years. Before God and man, of what use are you? When I was your age I had one suit of underwear. I was riding with the cattle in Coluso. I was hard as rocks, and I could sleep on a rock. I lived on jerked beef and bear-meat. And I'm a better man physically right now than you are. You weigh about one hundred and sixty-five. I can throw you right now, or thrash you with my fists."

"It doesn't take a physical prodigy to mop up cocktails or pink tea," Kit murmured. "Don't you see, my avuncular, times have changed. Besides, I wasn't brought up right. My dear fool of a mother—"

John Bellew started angrily.

"—as you once described her, was too good to me. Now, if when I was a youngster I had taken some of those intensely masculine vacations you go in for—I wonder why you didn't invite me sometimes? You took Hal and Robbie all over the Sierras and on that Mexico trip."

"I guess you were too Lord Fauntleroyish."

"Your fault, avuncular, and my dear mother's. How was I to know the hard life? I was only a chee-ild. What was there left but etchings and pictures and fans? Was it my fault that I never had to sweat?"

The older man looked at his nephew with unconcealed disgust. "Well, I'm going to take another one of those 'masculine' vacations. Suppose I asked you to come along?"

"Rather belated, I must say. Where is it?"

"Hal and Robert are going to the Klondike. I'm going to see them across the Pass and down to the lakes, then return—"

He got no further, for the young man had sprung forward and gripped his hand. "My preserver!"

John Bellew was immediately suspicious. He had not dreamed the invitation would be accepted. "You don't mean it?" he said.

"When do we start?"

"It will be a hard trip. You'll be in the way."

"No, I won't. I'll work. I've learned to work since I went on *The Billow*."

"Each man has to take a year's supplies in with him. There'll be such a jam the Indian packers won't be able to handle it. Hal and Robert will have to pack their outfits across themselves. That's what I'm going along for—to help them pack. If you come you'll have to do the same."

"Watch me."

"You can't pack," was the objection.

"When do we start?"

"Tomorrow."

"You needn't assume that your lecture on the hard life has done it," Kit said, at parting. "I just had to get away, somewhere, anywhere, from O'Hara."

"Who is O'Hara?"

"An Irishman, a slave-driver, and my best friend. He's

the editor and proprietor and all-round big boss of *The Billow*. What he says goes. He can make ghosts walk."

That night Kit Bellew wrote a note to O'Hara. "It's only several weeks' vacation," he explained. "You'll have to get some other guy to dope out installments for that serial. Sorry, old man, but my health demands it. I'll work twice as hard when I get back."

Kit Bellew landed through the madness of the Dyea beach congested with the thousand-pound outfits of thousands of men. This immense mass of luggage and food, flung ashore in mountains by the steamers, was beginning slowly to dribble up the Dyea Valley and across the Chilkoot Pass. It was a portage of twenty-eight miles, and could be accomplished only on the backs of men. Despite the fact that the Indian packers had jumped from eight cents a pound to forty, they were swamped with the work, and it was plain that winter would catch the major portion of the outfits on the wrong side of the divide.

Tenderest of the tenderfeet was Kit. Like many hundreds of others, he carried a big revolver swung on a cartridge belt. Of this his uncle, filled with memories of old lawless days, was likewise guilty. But Kit Bellew was romantic. He was fascinated by the froth and sparkle of the gold rush, and viewed its life and movement with an artist's eye. He did not take it seriously. As he said on the steamer, he was merely on vacation, and intended to peep over the top of the Pass for a "look see" and then return.

Leaving his party on the sand to wait for the putting ashore of the freight, he strolled up the beach toward the old trading post. He did not swagger, though he noticed that many of the be-revolvered individuals did. A strapping, six-foot Indian passed him, carrying an unusually large pack. Kit swung in behind, admiring the grace and ease with which he moved along under his burden. The Indian dropped his pack on the scales in front of the post, and Kit joined the group of admiring gold-rushers who surrounded him. The pack weighed one hundred and twenty-five pounds, which fact was uttered back and forth in tones of awe. Kit wondered if he could lift such a weight, much less walk off with it.

"Going to Lake Lindeman with it?" he asked.

The Indian grunted an affirmative.

"How much you make on that one pack?"

"Fifty dollars."

Here Kit slid out of the conversation. A young woman, standing in the doorway, had caught his eye. She was young and pretty. The bright beauty and color of her face held him, and he looked overlong—looked till she resented, and her own eyes, long lashed and dark, met his in cool survey. From his face, they traveled in evident amusement down to the big revolver at his thigh. Then her eyes came back to his, and in them was amused contempt. It struck him like a blow. She turned to the man beside her and indicated Kit. The man glanced him over with the same amused contempt.

"Cheechako," the girl said.

The man, who looked like a tramp in his cheap overalls and dilapidated woolen jacket, grinned dryly, and Kit felt withered. But anyway she was an unusually pretty girl, he decided, as the two moved off. He noted particularly the way of her walk.

"Did you see that man with the girl?" Kit's neighbor asked him excitedly. "Know who he is?"

Kit shook his head.

"Cariboo Charley. He was just pointed out to me. He struck it big on Klondike. Old-timer. Been on the Yukon a dozen years. He's just come out."

"What does 'cheechako' mean?" Kit asked.

"You're one; I'm one," was the answer.

"Maybe I am, but what does it mean?"

"Tenderfoot."

On his way back to the beach, Kit turned the phrase over and over. It rankled him to be called tenderfoot by a woman. Going into a corner among the heaps of freight, his mind filled with the vision of the Indian with the re- doubtable pack, Kit essayed to learn his own strength. He picked out a sack of flour which he knew weighed an even hundred pounds. He stepped astride it, reached down, and strove to get it on his shoulder. His first conclusion was that one hundred pounds were really heavy. His next was that his back was weak. His third was an oath, and it oc- curred at the end of five futile minutes, when he collapsed on top of the burden with which he was wrestling. He mopped his forehead, and across a heap of grub sacks saw John Bellew gazing at him, wintry amusement in his eyes.

"God! Out of our loins has come a race of weaklings. When I was sixteen I toyed with things like that."

"You forget, avuncular," Kit retorted, "that I wasn't raised on bear-meat."

"And I'll toy with it when I'm sixty."

"You've got to show me."

John Bellew did. He was forty-eight, but he bent over the sack, applied a tentative, shifting grip that balanced it, and with a quick heave stood erect, the sack of flour on his shoulder.

"Knack, my boy, knack—and a spine."

Kit took off his hat reverently. "You're a wonder, avuncular, a shining wonder. You think I can learn the knack?"

John Bellew shrugged his shoulders. "You'll be hitting the trail home before we even get started."

"Never you fear," Kit groaned. "There's O'Hara, the roaring lion, down there. I'm not going back till I have to."

Kit's first pack was a success. Up to Finnegan's Crossing they had managed to get Indians to carry the twenty-five-hundred-pound outfit. From that point their own backs must do the work. They planned to move forward at the rate of a mile a day. It looked easy—on paper. Since John Bellew was to stay in camp and do the cooking, he would be unable to make more than an occasional pack; so to each of the three young men fell the task of carrying eight hundred pounds one mile each day. If they made fifty-pound packs, it meant a daily walk of sixteen miles loaded and of fifteen miles light. Eighty-pound packs meant nineteen miles travel each day; and hundred-pound packs meant only fifteen miles.

"I don't like walking," said Kit. "Therefore I shall carry a hundred pounds." He caught the grin of incredulity on his uncle's face, and added hastily: "Of course I shall work up to it. A fellow's got to learn the ropes and tricks. I'll start with fifty."

He did, and ambled gaily along the trail. He dropped the sack at the next camp-site and ambled back. It was easier than he had thought. But two miles had rubbed off the velvet of his strength and exposed the underlying softness. His second pack was sixty-five pounds. It was more difficult, and he no longer ambled. Several times, following the custom of all packers, he sat down on the ground, resting the pack behind him on a rock or stump. With the third pack he became bold. He fastened the straps to a ninety-five-pound sack of beans and started. At the end of a hundred yards he felt that he must collapse. He sat down and mopped his face.

"Short hauls and shirt rests," he muttered. "That's the trick."

Sometimes he did not make a hundred yards, and each time he struggled to his feet for another short haul the pack became undeniably heavier. He panted for breath, and the sweat streamed from him. Before he had covered a quarter of a mile he stripped off his woolen shirt and hung it on a tree. A little later he discarded his hat. At the end of half a mile he decided he was finished. He had never exerted himself so in his life, and he knew that he was finished. As he sat and panted, his gaze fell upon the big revolver and the heavy cartridge belt.

"Ten pounds of junk!" he sneered. He unbuckled it and flung it into the underbrush. And as the steady tide of packers flowed by him, up trail and down, he noted that the other tenderfeet were beginning to shed their shooting irons.

His short hauls decreased still more. At times a hundred feet was all he could stagger, and then the ominous pounding of his heart against his eardrums and the sickening tottering of his knees compelled him to rest. And his rests grew longer. But his mind was busy. It was a twenty-eight-mile portage, which represented as many days, and this by all accounts was the easiest part of it. "Wait till you get to Chilkoot," others told him as they rested and talked, "where you climb with hands and feet."

"There ain't going to be no Chilkoot," was his answer. "Not for me. Long before that I'll be at peace beneath the moss."

A slip and a violent, wrenching effort at recovery frightened him. He felt that everything inside him had been torn asunder.

"If ever I fall down with this on my back, I'm a goner," he told another packer.

"That's nothing," came the answer. "Wait till you hit the Canyon. You'll have to cross a raging torrent on a sixty-foot pine tree. No guide ropes, nothing, and the water boiling. If you fall with a pack on your back, there's no getting out of the straps. You just stay there and drown."

"Sounds great," he retorted; and out of the depths of his exhaustion he almost meant it.

"They drown three or four a day there," the man assured him.

"Cheerful, I must say," said Kit, battling his way to his feet and stumbling on.

He and the sack of beans became a perambulating tragedy. It reminded him of the old man of the sea who sat on Sindbad's neck. And this was a vacation, he meditated. Compared with it, servitude to O'Hara was sweet. Again and again he was nearly seduced by the thought of abandoning the sack of beans in the brush, sneaking around the camp to the beach, and catching a steamer for civilization.

But he didn't. Somewhere in him was the strain of the hard life, and he repeated over and over to himself that what other men could do he could. It became a nightmare chant, and he gibbered it to those who passed him on the trail. At other times, resting, he watched and envied the stolid, mule-footed Indians who plodded by under heavier packs. They never seemed to rest, but went on and on with a steadiness and certitude that were to him appalling.

He sat and cursed, fighting the temptation to sneak back

to San Francisco. Before the mile was ended he ceased cursing and took to crying. The tears were tears of exhaustion and of disgust with self. If ever a man was a wreck, he was. As the end of the pack came in sight, he strained himself in desperation, gained the camp site, and pitched forward on his face, the beans on his back. It did not kill him, but he lay for fifteen minutes before he could summon sufficient strength to release himself from the straps. Then he became deathly sick, and was so found by Robbie, who had similar troubles of his own. It was this sickness of Robbie that braced Kit up.

"What other men can do we can do," he told Robbie, though down in his heart he wondered whether or not he was bluffing.

"And I am twenty-seven years old and a man," he privately assured himself many times in the days that followed. There was need for it. At the end of a week, though he had succeeded in moving his eight hundred pounds a mile a day, he had lost fifteen pounds of his own weight. His face was lean and haggard. All resilience had gone out of his body and mind. He no longer walked, but plodded. And on the back trips, traveling light, his feet dragged almost as much as when he was loaded.

He had become a work animal. He fell asleep over his food, and his sleep was heavy and beastly, save when he was aroused, screaming with agony, by the cramps in his legs. Every part of him ached. He tramped on raw blisters; yet even this was easier than the fearful bruising his feet received on the water-rounded rocks of the Dyea Flats, across which the trail led for two miles. These two miles represented thirty-eight miles of traveling. His shoulders

and chest, galled by the pack straps, made him think, and
for the first time with understanding, of the horses he
had seen on city streets.

When they had moved the outfit across the footlogs at
the mouth of the Canyon, they made a change in their
plans. Word had come across the Pass that at Lake Lindeman the last available trees for building boats were now
being cut. The two cousins, with tools, whipsaw, blankets,
and grub on their backs, went on, leaving Kit and his uncle
to hustle along the outfit. John Bellew now shared his cooking with Kit, and both packed shoulder to shoulder. Time
was flying, and on the peaks the first snow was falling. To
be caught on the wrong side of the Pass meant a delay of
nearly a year. The older man put his iron back under a
hundred pounds. Kit gritted his teeth and fastened his own
straps to a hundred pounds. It hurt, but he had begun to
learn the knack, and his body, purged of softness and fat,
was hardening up with lean and bitter muscle. Also, he observed and devised. He took note of the head-straps worn
by the Indians and manufactured one for himself which
he used in addition to the shoulder-straps. It made things
easier, so that he began the practice of piling any light,
cumbersome piece of luggage on top. Thus he was soon
able to move along with a hundred pounds in the straps,
fifteen or twenty more lying loosely atop the pack and
against his neck, an ax or a pair of oars in one hand, and in
the other the nested cooking-pails of the camp.

But work as they would, the toil increased. The trail
grew more rugged; their packs grew heavier; and each day
saw the snow line dropping down the mountains, while
freight jumped to sixty cents. No word came from the
cousins beyond, so they knew they must be at work chopping down the trees and whipsawing them into boat

planks. John Bellew grew anxious. Capturing a bunch of Indians back-tripping from Lake Lindeman, he persuaded them to put their straps on the outfit. They charged thirty cents a pound to carry it to the summit of Chilkoot, and it nearly broke him. As it was, some four hundred pounds were not handled. He remained behind to move it alone, despatching Kit with the Indians. At the summit Kit was to remain, slowly moving his ton until overtaken by the four hundred pounds with which his uncle guaranteed to catch him.

Kit plodded along the trail with his Indian packers. In recognition of the fact that it was to be a long pack, straight to the top of Chilkoot, his own load was only eighty pounds. The Indians plodded under their loads, but it was a quicker gait than he had practiced. Yet he felt no apprehension, and by now had come to deem himself almost the equal of an Indian.

At the end of a quarter-mile he desired to rest. But the Indians kept on. He stayed with them and kept his place in the line. At the half-mile he was convinced that he was incapable of another step, yet he gritted his teeth, kept his place, and at the end of the mile was amazed that he was still alive. Then, in some strange way, came the thing called second wind, and the next mile was almost easier than the first. The third mile nearly killed him, but, though half-delirious with pain and fatigue, he never whimpered. And then, when he felt he must surely faint, came the rest. Instead of sitting in the straps, as was the custom of the white packers, the Indians slipped out of the shoulder- and head-straps and lay at ease, talking and smoking. A full half-hour passed before they made another start. To Kit's surprise, he found himself a fresh man, and "long hauls and long rests" became his newest motto.

The pitch of Chilkoot was all he had heard of it, and many were the occasions when he climbed with hands as well as feet. But when he reached the crest of the divide in the thick of a driving snow squall, it was in the company of his Indians, and his secret pride was that he had come through with them and never squealed and never lagged. To be almost as good as an Indian was a new ambition to cherish.

When he had paid off the Indians and seen them depart, a stormy darkness was falling, and he was left alone, a thousand feet above timber line, on the backbone of a mountain. Wet to the waist, famished and exhausted, he would have given a year's income for a fire and a cup of coffee. Instead, he ate half a dozen cold flapjacks and crawled into the folds of the partly unrolled tent. As he dozed off he had time for only one fleeting thought, and he grinned with pleasure at the picture of John Bellew in the days to follow, masculinely trudging his four hundred pounds up Chilkoot. As for himself, even though burdened with two thousand pounds, he was bound downhill.

In the morning, stiff from his labors and numb with frost, he rolled out of the canvas, ate a couple of pounds of uncooked bacon, buckled the straps on a hundred pounds, and started down the rocky way. Several hundred yards beneath, the trail led across a small glacier and down to Crater Lake. Other men packed across the glacier. All that day, Kit, however, dropped his packs at the glacier's upper edge. By virtue of the shortness of the pack, he put his straps on one hundred and fifty pounds each load. His astonishment at being able to do it never abated. For two dollars he bought from an Indian three leathery sea-biscuits, and out of these, and a huge quantity of raw bacon, made several meals. Unwashed, unwarmed, his clothing wet with sweat, he slept another night in the canvas.

In the early morning he spread a tarpaulin on the ice, loaded it with three-quarters of a ton, and started to pull. Where the pitch of the glacier increased, his load accelerated, overran him, scooped him in on top, and ran away with him.

A hundred packers, bending under their loads, stopped to watch. He yelled frantic warnings, and those in his path stumbled and staggered clear. Below, at the edge of the glacier, a small tent seemed to leap toward him. He left the beaten track where the packers' trail swerved, and struck a patch of fresh snow. This rose about him in frosty smoke, while it reduced his speed. He saw the tent the instant he struck it, carrying away the corner guys, bursting in the front flaps, and ending up inside, still on top of the tarpaulin and in the midst of his grub sacks. The tent rocked drunkenly, and in the frosty vapor he found himself face to face with a startled young woman who was sitting up in her blankets—the very one who had called him a tenderfoot at Dyea.

"Did you see my smoke?" he queried cheerfully.

"Smoke?" She regarded him with disapproval.

"Talk about magic carpets!" he went on.

Her coolness was a challenge. "It was lucky you didn't overturn the stove," she said.

He followed her glance and saw a sheet-iron stove and a coffeepot, attended by a young squaw. He sniffed the coffee and looked back to the girl.

"I'm still a cheechako, but I've shed my shooting-irons."

Then she recognized him, and her eyes lit up. "I never thought you'd get this far."

Again, and greedily, he sniffed the air. "As I live, coffee! I'll do anything if you'll give me a cup out of that pot."

And over the coffee he gave his name and learned hers —Joy Gastell. Also, he learned that she was an old-timer in the country. She had been born in a trading post on Great Slave Lake, and as a child had crossed the Rockies with her father and come down the Yukon. She was going back in, she said, with her father, who had been delayed by business in Seattle and who had then been wrecked on the ill-fated *Chanter* and carried back to Puget Sound by the rescuing steamer.

In view of the fact that she was still in her blankets, he did not make it a long conversation, and, heroically declining a second cup of coffee, removed himself and his heaped and shifted baggage from her tent. Further, he took several conclusions away with him: she had a fetching name and fetching eyes; could not be more than twenty, or twenty-one or two; her father must be French; she had a will of her own; temperament to burn; and she had been educated elsewhere than on the frontier.

Over the ice-scoured rocks and above the timber line, the trail ran around Crater Lake and gained the rocky defile that led toward Happy Camp and the first scrub pines. To pack his heavy outfit around would take days of heartbreaking toil. On the lake was a canvas boat employed in freighting. Two trips with it, in two hours, would see him and his ton across. But he was broke, and the ferryman charged forty dollars a ton.

"You've got a gold mine, my friend, in that dinky boat," Kit said to the ferryman. "Do you want another gold mine?"

"Show me," was the answer.

"I'll sell it to you for the price of ferrying my outfit. It's

an idea, not patented, and you can jump the deal as soon as
I tell you it. Are you game?"

The ferryman said he was.

"Very well. You see that glacier. Take a pick-ax and
wade into it. In a day you can have a decent groove from
top to bottom. See the point? The Chilkoot and Crater Lake
Consolidated Chute Corporation, Limited. You can charge
fifty cents a hundred, get a hundred tons a day, and have
no work to do but collect the coin."

Two hours later, Kit's ton was across the lake, and he
had gained three days on himself. And when John Bellew
overtook him, he was well along toward Deep Lake, another volcanic pit filled with glacial water.

The last pack, from Long Lake to Lindeman, was three
miles, and the trail, if trail it could be called, rose up over
a thousand-foot hogback, dropped down a scramble of slippery rocks, and crossed a wide stretch of swamp. John Bellew remonstrated when he saw Kit rise with a hundred
pounds in the straps and pick up a fifty-pound sack of flour
and place it on top of the pack against the back of his neck.

"Come on," Kit retorted. "What about your bear-meat
fodder and your one suit of underwear?"

John Bellew shook his head. "I'm afraid I'm getting old,
Christopher."

"You're only forty-eight. Do you realize that my grandfather, sir, your father, old Isaac Bellew, killed a man with
his fist when he was sixty-nine years old?"

John Bellew grinned and swallowed his medicine.

"Avuncular, I want to tell you something important. I
was raised a Lord Fauntleroy, but I can outpack you, out-
walk you, put you on your back, or lick you with my fists
right now."

John Bellew thrust out his hand and spoke solemnly.

"Christopher, my boy, I believe you can do it. I believe you can do it with that pack on your back at the same time. You've made good, boy."

Kit made the round trip of the last pack four times a day, which is to say that he daily covered twenty-four miles of mountain climbing, twelve miles of it under one hundred and fifty pounds. He was proud, hard, and tired, but in splendid physical condition. He ate and slept as he had never eaten and slept in his life, and as the end of the work came in sight, he was almost half-sorry.

One problem bothered him. He had learned that he could fall with a hundred pounds on his back and survive; but he was confident that if he fell with that additional fifty pounds across the back of his neck, it would break it clean. Each trail through the swamp was quickly churned into a morass by the thousands of packers, who were compelled continually to make new trails. It was while pioneering such a new trail that he solved the problem of the extra fifty.

The soft, lush surface gave way under him, he floundered, and pitched forward on his face. The fifty pounds crushed his face into the mud and went clear without snapping his neck. With the remaining hundred pounds on his back, he arose on hands and knees. But he got no farther. One arm sank to the shoulder, pillowing his cheek in the slush. As he drew this arm clear, the other sank to the shoulder. In this position it was impossible to slip the straps, and the hundred-weight on his back would not let him rise. On hands and knees, sinking first one arm and then the other, he made an effort to crawl to where the small sack of flour had fallen. But he exhausted himself without advancing, and so churned and broke the grass surface that a tiny pool of water began to form in perilous proximity to his mouth and nose.

He tried to throw himself on his back with the pack underneath, but this resulted in sinking both arms to the shoulders and gave him a foretaste of drowning. With exquisite patience, he slowly withdrew one sucking arm and then the other and rested them flat on the surface for the support of his chin. Then he began to call for help. After a time he heard the sound of feet sucking through the mud as some one advanced from behind.

"Lend a hand, friend," he said. "Throw out a life line or something."

It was a woman's voice that answered, and he recognized it.

"If you'll unbuckle the straps I can get up," he said.

The hundred pounds rolled into the mud with a soggy noise, and he slowly gained his feet.

"A pretty predicament," Miss Gastell laughed, at sight of his mud-covered face.

"Not at all," he replied airily. "My favorite setting-up exercise. Try it some time. It's great for the pectoral muscles and the spine." He wiped his face, flinging the slush from his hand with a jerk.

"Oh!" she cried in recognition. "It's Mr.—ah—Mr. 'Smoke' Bellew."

"I thank you gravely for your timely rescue and for that name," he answered. "I have been doubly baptized. Henceforth I shall insist always on being called Smoke Bellew. It's a strong name, and not without significance."

The arctic winter came down. Snow lay six inches on the ground, and ice was forming in quiet ponds, despite the fierce gales that blew. It was in the late afternoon, dur-

ing a lull in such a gale, that Kit and John Bellew helped
the cousins load the boat and watched it disappear down
the lake in a snow squall.

"And now a night's sleep and an early start in the morning," said John Bellew. "If we aren't stormbound at the
summit we'll make Dyea tomorrow night, and with luck
catching a steamer we'll be in San Francisco in a week."

Their camp for that last night at Lindeman was a melancholy remnant. Everything of use, including the tent,
had been taken by the cousins. A tattered tarpaulin,
stretched as a windbreak, partially sheltered them from the
driving snow. Supper was cooked on an open fire in a
couple of battered and discarded camp utensils. All that
was left them were their blankets and food for several
meals.

Only once during supper did Kit speak. "Avuncular,"
he said, "after this I wish you'd call me Smoke. I've made
some smoke on this trail, haven't I?"

A few minutes later he wandered away in the direction
of the village of tents that sheltered the gold-rushers who
were still packing or building their boats. He was gone
several hours, and when he returned and slipped into his
blankets John Bellew was asleep.

In the darkness of a gale-driven morning, Kit crawled
out, built a fire in his stocking feet, by which he thawed
out his frozen shoes, then boiled coffee and fried bacon. It
was a chilly, miserable meal. As soon as it was finished,
they strapped their blankets. As John Bellew turned to
lead the way toward the Chilkoot Trail, Kit held out his
hand.

"Good-by, avuncular," he said.

John Bellew looked at him and swore in surprise.

"Don't forget, my name's Smoke," Kit chided.

"But what are you going to do?"

Kit waved his hand in a general direction northward over the lake. "What's the good of turning back after getting this far?" he asked. "Besides, I've got my taste of meat, and I like it. I'm going on."

"You're broke," protested John Bellew. "You have no outfit."

"I've got a job. Behold your nephew, Christopher Smoke Bellew! He's got a job. He's a gentleman's man. He's got a job at a hundred and fifty per month and grub. He's going down to Dawson with a couple of dudes and another gentleman's man—camp cook, boatman, and general all-round hustler. And O'Hara and *The Billow* can go to the devil."

John Bellew was dazed, and could only mutter, "I don't understand."

"They say the bald-face grizzlies are thick in the Yukon Basin," Kit explained. "Well, I've got only one suit of underwear, and now I'm going after the bear-meat, that's all."

CHAPTER 2

The Meat

HALF THE time the wind blew a gale, and Smoke Bellew staggered against it along the beach. In the gray of dawn a dozen boats were being loaded with the precious outfits packed across Chilkoot. They were clumsy homemade boats, put together out of planks sawed by hand from green spruce trees. One boat, already loaded, was just starting, and Kit paused to watch.

The wind blew in squarely on the beach, kicking up a nasty sea in the shallows. The men of the departing boat waded in high rubber boots as they shoved it out toward deeper water. Twice they did this. Clambering aboard but failing to row clear, the boat was swept back and grounded. Kit noticed that the spray on the sides of the boat quickly turned to ice. The third attempt was a partial success. The last two men to climb in were wet to their waists, but the boat was afloat. They struggled awkwardly at the heavy oars, and slowly worked off shore. Then they hoisted a sail made of blankets, had it quickly carried away in a gust, and were swept a third time back on the freezing beach.

Kit grinned to himself and went on. This was what he must expect to encounter, for he, too, in his new role of gentleman's man, was to start from the beach in a similar boat that very day.

Everywhere men were at work, and at work desperately, for the closing down of winter was so imminent that it was a gamble whether or not they would get across the great chain of lakes before the great freeze-up. Yet, when Kit arrived at the tent of Messrs. Sprague and Stine, he did not find them stirring.

By a fire, under the shelter of a tarpaulin, squatted a short, thick man, smoking a brown-paper cigarette. "Hello," he said. "Are you Mister Sprague's new man?"

As Kit nodded, he thought he had noted a shade of emphasis on the *Mister* and the *man*, and he was sure of a twinkle in the corner of the eye.

"Well, I'm Doc Stine's man," the other went on. "I'm five feet two inches long, and my name's Shorty, Jack Short for short, and sometimes known as Johnny-on-the-Spot."

Kit put out his hand and shook. "Were you raised on bear-meat?" he queried.

"Sure," was the answer; "though my first feedin' was buffalo milk as near as I can remember. Sit down an' have some grub. The bosses ain't turned out yet."

And despite the one breakfast with John Bellew, Kit sat down under the tarpaulin and ate a second breakfast thrice as hearty. The heavy, purging toil of weeks had given him the stomach and appetite of a wolf. He could eat anything, in any quantity, and be unaware that he possessed a digestion. Shorty he found voluble and pessimistic, and from him he received surprising tips concerning their bosses and ominous forecasts of the expedition. Thomas Stanley Sprague was a budding mining engineer and the son of a millionaire. Doctor Adolph Stine was also the son of a wealthy father. And, through their fathers, both had been backed by an investing syndicate in the Klondike adventure.

"Oh, they're sure made of money," Shorty expounded. "When they hit the beach at Dyea freight was seventy cents, but no Indians. There was a party from eastern Oregon, real miners, that'd managed to get a team of Indians together at seventy cents. Indians had the straps on the outfit, three thousand pounds of it, when along comes Sprague and Stine. They offered eighty cents and ninety, and at a dollar a pound the Indians jumped the contract and took off their straps. Sprague and Stine came through, though it cost them three thousand, and the Oregon bunch is still on the beach. They won't get through till next year.

"Oh, they are real humdingers, your boss and mine, when it comes to sheddin' dough an' never mindin' other folks' feelin's. What did they do when they hit Lindeman? The carpenters was just putting in the last licks on a boat they'd contracted to a 'Frisco bunch for six hundred. Sprague and Stine slipped 'em an even thousand, and they jumped their contract. The other bunch has got their outfit right here, but no boat. And they're stuck till next year. Have another cup of coffee, and take it from me I wouldn't travel with no such outfit if I didn't want to get to Klondike so blamed bad. They ain't hearted right. They'd take the crape off the door of a house in mourning if they needed it. Did they sign a contract to feed you?"

Kit shook his head.

"Then I'm sorry for you, pardner. They ain't no grub in the country, and they'll drop you cold as soon as they hit Dawson. Men are going to starve there this winter."

"They agreed—" Kit began.

"Verbal," Shorty snapped him short. "It's your say-so

against theirs, that's all. Well, anyway, what's your name, pardner?"

"Call me Smoke," said Kit.

"Well, Smoke, you'll have a run for your verbal contract just the same. This is a plain sample of what to expect. They can sure shed dough, but they can't work, or turn out of bed in the morning. We should have been loaded and started an hour ago. It's you an' me for the big work. Pretty soon you'll hear 'em shoutin' for their coffee— in bed, mind you, and them grown men. What d'ye know about boatin' on the water? I'm a cowman and a prospector, but I'm sure tenderfooted on water, an' they don't know punkins. What d'ye know?"

"Search me," Kit answered, snuggling in closer under the tarpaulin as the snow whirled before a fiercer gust. "I haven't been on a small boat since a boy. But I guess we can learn."

A corner of the tarpaulin tore loose, and Shorty received a jet of driven snow down the back of his neck.

"Oh, we can learn all right," he muttered wrathfully. "Sure we can. A child can learn. But it's dollars to doughnuts we don't even get started today."

It was eight o'clock when the call for coffee came from the tent, and nearly nine before the two employers emerged.

"Hello," said Sprague, a rosy-cheeked, well-fed young man of twenty-five. "Time we made a start, Shorty. You and—" Here he glanced interrogatively at Kit. "I didn't quite catch your name last evening."

"Smoke."

"Well, Shorty, you and Mr. Smoke had better begin loading the boat."

"Plain Smoke—cut out the Mister," Kit suggested.

Sprague nodded curtly and strolled away among the tents, followed by Doctor Stine, a slender, pallid young man.

Shorty looked significantly at his companion. "Over a ton and a half of outfit, and they won't lend a hand. You'll see."

"We're paid to do the work," Kit answered cheerfully, "and we might as well pitch in."

To move three thousand pounds on the shoulders a hundred yards was no slight task, and to do it in half a gale, slushing through the snow in heavy rubber boots, was exhausting. In addition there was taking down the tent and packing the small camp equipment. Then came the loading. As the boat settled it had to be shoved farther and farther out, increasing the distance they had to wade. By two o'clock it had all been accomplished, and Kit, despite his two breakfasts, was weak with the faintness of hunger. His knees were shaking under him. Shorty, in similar predicament, foraged through the pots and pans, and drew forth a big pot of cold boiled beans in which were imbedded large chunks of bacon. There was only one spoon, a long-handled one, and they took turns dipping into the pot. In all his life Kit had never tasted anything so good.

"Man," he mumbled between chews, "I never knew what appetite was till I hit the trail."

Sprague and Stine arrived in the midst of this pleasant occupation.

"What's the delay?" Sprague complained. "Aren't we ever going to get started?"

Shorty dipped in turn, and passed the spoon to Kit. Nor did either speak till the pot was empty and the bottom scraped.

"Of course we ain't been doin' nothing," Shorty said, wiping his mouth with the back of his hand. "We ain't been doin' nothing at all. And of course you ain't had nothing to eat. It was sure careless of me."

"We ate at one of the tents—friends of ours," Stine said quickly.

"Thought so," Shorty grunted.

"But now that you're finished, let us get started," Sprague urged.

"There's the boat," said Shorty. "She's sure loaded. Now just how might you be goin' about gettin' started?"

"By climbing aboard and shoving off. Come on."

They waded out, and the employers got on board, while Kit and Shorty shoved clear. When the waves lapped the tops of their boots they clambered in. The other two men were not prepared with the oars, and the boat swept back and grounded. Half a dozen times, with a great expenditure of energy, this was repeated.

Shorty sat down disconsolately on the gunwale, took a chew of tobacco, and questioned the universe, while Kit baled the boat and the other two exchanged unkind remarks.

"If you'll take my orders, I'll push her off," Sprague finally said.

The attempt was well intended, but before he could clamber on board he was wet to the waist.

"We've got to camp and build a fire," he said, as the boat grounded again. "I'm freezing."

"Don't be afraid of a wetting," Stine sneered. "Other men have gone off today wetter than you. Now I'm going to push her out."

This time it was he who got the wetting and who announced with chattering teeth the need of a fire.

"A little splash like that!" Sprague chattered spitefully. "We'll go on."

"Shorty, dig out my clothes bag and make a fire," the other commanded.

"You'll do nothing of the sort," Sprague cried.

Shorty looked from one to the other, expectorated, but did not move.

"He's working for me, and I guess he obeys my orders," Stine retorted. "Shorty, take that bag ashore."

Shorty obeyed, and Sprague shivered in the boat. Kit, having received no orders, remained inactive, glad for the rest.

"A boat divided against itself won't float," he soliloquized.

"What's that?" Sprague snarled at him.

"Talking to myself—habit of mine," he answered.

His employer favored him with a hard look, and sulked several minutes longer. Then he surrendered. "Get out my bag, Smoke," he ordered, "and lend a hand with that fire. We won't get off till morning now."

Next day the gale still blew. Lake Lindeman was no more than a narrow mountain gorge filled with water. Sweeping down from the mountains through this funnel, the wind was irregular, blowing great gusts at times and at others dwindling to a strong breeze.

"If you give me a shot at it, I think I can get her off," Kit said, when all was ready for the start.

"What do you know about it?" Stine snapped at him.

"Search me," Kit answered, and subsided.

It was the first time he had worked for wages in his life, but he was learning the discipline fast. Obediently and cheerfully he joined in various vain efforts to get clear of the beach.

"How would you go about it?" Sprague finally half-panted, half-whined at him.

"Sit down and get a good rest till a lull comes in the wind, and then buck in for all we're worth."

Simple as the idea was, he had been the first to evolve it; the first time it was applied it worked, and they hoisted a blanket to the mast and sped down the lake. Stine and Sprague immediately became cheerful. Shorty, despite his chronic pessimism, was always cheerful, and Kit was too interested to be otherwise. Sprague struggled with the steering sweep for a quarter of an hour, and then looked appealingly at Kit, who relieved him.

"My arms are broken," Sprague muttered apologetically.

"You never ate bear-meat, did you?" Kit asked sympathetically.

"What the devil do you mean?"

"Oh, nothing; I was just wondering." But behind the employer's back Kit caught the approving grin of Shorty, who had already caught the point of his metaphor.

Kit steered the length of Lindeman, displaying an aptitude that caused both young men of money and disinclination for work to name him boat steerer. Shorty was no less pleased, and volunteered to continue cooking and leave the boat work to the other.

Between Lindeman and Lake Bennett was a portage. The boat, lightly loaded, was lowered with lines down the small but violent connecting stream, and here Kit learned a lot more about boats and water. But when it came to packing the outfit, Stine and Sprague disappeared, and their men spent two days of backbreaking toil getting the outfit across. And this was the history of many miserable days of the trip—Kit and Shorty working to exhaustion, while their masters demanded only to be waited upon.

The iron-bound arctic winter continued to close down, and they were held back by numerous and unavoidable delays. At Windy Arm Stine arbitrarily dispossessed Kit of the steering sweep and within the hour had wrecked the boat on a wave-beaten lee shore. Two days were lost making repairs, and on the morning of the fresh start, as they came down to embark, on stern and bow, in large letters, was charcoaled "The Cheechako."

Kit grinned at the appropriateness of the word.

"Huh!" said Shorty, when accused by Stine. "I can sure read and spell, an' I know that 'cheechako' means tender-foot, but my education never went high enough to learn me to spell a jawbreaker like that."

Both employers looked daggers at Kit, for the insult rankled; but he did not mention that the night before Shorty had besought him for the spelling of that particular word.

"That's 'most as bad as your bear-meat slam," Shorty confided later.

Kit chuckled. Along with the continuous discovery of his own powers had come an ever-increasing disapproval of the two masters. It was not so much irritation, which was always present, as disgust. He had got his taste of the meat, and liked it; but these two were spoiling his meal. He came to dislike them to a degree that bordered on hatred. Their malingering bothered him less than their inefficiency. Somewhere in him old Isaac Bellew and all the rest of the hardy Bellews were beginning to show themselves.

"Shorty," he said one day, in the usual delay of getting

started, "I could almost fetch them a rap over the head with an oar and bury them in the river."

"Same here," Shorty agreed. "They're not meat-eaters. They're fish-eaters, and they sure stink."

They came to the rapids; first, the Box Canyon. It was adequately named. It was a box, a trap. Once in, the only way out was through. On either side rose perpendicular walls of rock. The river narrowed to a fraction of its width and roared through this gloomy passage in a madness of motion that heaped the water in the center into a ridge fully eight feet higher than at the rocky sides. This ridge, in turn, was crested with stiff, upstanding waves that curled over yet remained each in its unvarying place. The canyon was well feared, for it had collected its toll of dead from the passing gold-rushers.

Tying to the bank above, where lay a score of other anxious boats, Kit and his companions went ahead on foot to investigate. They crept to the brink and gazed down at the swirl of water. Sprague drew back, shuddering.

"My God!" he exclaimed. "A swimmer hasn't a chance in that."

Shorty touched Kit significantly with his elbow and said in an undertone:

"Cold feet. Dollars to doughnuts they don't go through."

Kit scarcely heard. From the beginning of the boat trip he had been learning the stubbornness and inconceivable viciousness of the elements, and this glimpse of what was below him acted as a challenge. "We've got to ride that ridge," he said. "If we get off it we'll hit the walls."

"And never know what hit us," was Shorty's verdict. "Can you swim?"

"I'd wish I couldn't if anything went wrong in there."

"That's what I say," a stranger, standing alongside and peering down into the canyon, said mournfully. "I wish I were through it."

"I wouldn't sell my chance to go through," Kit answered.

He spoke honestly, but also with the idea of heartening the man. He turned to go back to the boat.

"Are you going to tackle it?" the man asked.

Kit nodded.

"I wish I could get the courage to," the other confessed. "My name is Breck. I've been here for hours. The longer I look the more afraid I am. I'm no boatman, and I have with me only my nephew, a young boy, and my wife. If you get through safely, will you run my boat through?"

Kit looked at Shorty, who delayed to answer.

"He's got his wife with him," Kit suggested.

Nor had he mistaken his man. "Sure," Shorty affirmed. "That's just what I was stopping to think about. I knew there was some reason I ought to do it."

They turned to go, but Sprague and Stine made no movement.

"Good luck, Smoke," Sprague called to him. "I'll—er—" He hesitated. "I'll just stay here and watch you."

"We need three men in our boat, two at the oars and one at the steering sweep," Kit said quietly.

Sprague looked at Stine.

"I'm cursed if I do," said that gentleman. "If you're not afraid to stand here and look on, I'm not."

"Who's afraid?" Sprague demanded hotly. Stine retorted in kind, and their two men left them in the thick of a squabble.

"We can do without them," Kit said to Shorty. "You take the bow with a paddle, and I'll handle the steering sweep. All you'll have to do is just help keep her straight. Once we're started, you won't be able to hear me, so just keep on keeping her straight."

They cast off and worked out to the middle in the quickening current. From the canyon came an ever-growing roar. The river sucked in to the entrance with the smoothness of molten glass, and here, as the darkening walls received them, Shorty took a chew of tobacco and dipped his paddle. The boat leaped on the first crests of the ridge, and they were deafened by the uproar of wild water that reverberated from the narrow walls and multiplied itself. They were half-smothered with flying spray. At times Kit could not see his comrade at the bow. It was only a matter of two minutes, in which time they rode the ridge three-quarters of a mile and emerged in safety and tied to the bank in the eddy below.

Shorty emptied his mouth of tobacco juice he had forgotten to spit, and spoke. "That was bear-meat," he exulted, "the real bear-meat. Say, we went a few, didn't we? Smoke, I don't mind tellin' you that before we started I was the gosh-dangdest scaredest man this side of the Rocky Mountains. Now I'm a bear-eater. Come on an' we'll run that other boat through."

Midway back, on foot, they encountered their employers, who had watched the passage from above.

"There comes the fish-eaters," said Shorty. "Keep to win'ward."

After running the stranger's boat through, Kit and Shorty met his wife, a slender, girlish woman whose blue eyes were moist with gratitude. Breck himself tried to hand Kit fifty dollars, and then attempted it on Shorty.

"Stranger," was the latter's rejection, "I come into this

country to make money outa the ground, not outa my fellow critters."

Breck rummaged in his boat and produced a demijohn
of whiskey. Shorty's hand half went out to it and stopped
abruptly. He shook his head.

"There's that blamed White Horse right below, an'
they say it's worse than the Box. I reckon I don't dast
tackle any lightning."

Several miles below they ran in to the bank, and all four
walked down to look at the bad water. The river, a succession of rapids, was here deflected toward the right bank
by a rocky reef. The whole body of water, rushing crook-
edly into the narrow passage, accelerated its speed fright-
fully and was flung up in huge waves, white and wrathful.
This was the dread Mane of the White Horse, and here an
even heavier toll of dead had been exacted. On one side of
the Mane was a corkscrew curl-over and suck-under, and
on the opposite side was the big whirlpool. To go through,
the Mane itself must be ridden.

"This plumb rips the strings outa the Box," Shorty concluded.

As they watched, a boat took the head of the rapids
above. It was a large boat, fully thirty feet long, laden
with several tons of outfit, and handled by six men. Before it reached the Mane it was plunging and leaping, at
times almost hidden by the foam and spray.

Shorty shot a slow, sidelong glance at Kit and said:
"She's fair smoking, and she hasn't hit the worst. They've
hauled the oars in. There she takes it now. God! She's
gone! No; there she is!"

Big as the boat was, it had been buried from sight in
the flying smother between crests. The next moment, in

the thick of the Mane, the boat leaped up a crest and into view. To Kit's amazement he saw the whole long bottom clearly outlined. The boat, for a fraction of an instant, was in the air, the men sitting idly in their places, all save one in the stern, who stood at the steering sweep. Then came the downward plunge into the trough and a second disappearance. Three times the boat leaped and buried itself, then those on the bank saw its nose take the whirlpool as it slipped off the Mane. The steersman, vainly opposing with full weight on the steering gear, surrendered to the whirlpool and help the boat to take the circle.

Three times it went around, each time so close to the rocks on which Kit and Shorty stood that either could have leaped on board. The steersman, a man with a reddish beard of recent growth, waved his hand to them. The only way out of the whirlpool was by the Mane, and on the third round the boat entered the Mane obliquely at its upper end. Possibly out of fear of the draw of the whirlpool, the steersman did not attempt to straighten out quickly enough. When he did, it was too late. Alternately in the air and buried, the boat angled the Mane and was sucked into and through the stiff wall of the corkscrew on the opposite side of the river. A hundred feet below, boxes and bales began to float up. Then appeared the bottom of the boat and the scattered heads of six men. Two managed to make the bank in the eddy below. The others were drawn under, and the general flotsam was lost to view, borne on by the swift current around the bend.

There was a long minute of silence. Shorty was the first to speak.

"Come on," he said. "We might as well tackle it. My feet'll get cold if I stay here any longer."

"We'll smoke some," Kit grinned at him.

"And you'll sure earn your name." Shorty turned to their employers. "Comin'?" he queried.

Perhaps the roar of the water prevented them from hearing the invitation.

Shorty and Kit tramped back through a foot of snow to the head of the rapids and cast off the boat.

"You've sure got to keep the top of the ridge," Shorty shouted at him, the plug of tobacco lifting to his mouth as the boat quickened in the current and took the head of the rapids.

Kit nodded, swayed his strength and weight tentatively on the steering gear, and headed the boat for the plunge.

Several minutes later, half-swamped and lying against the bank in the eddy below the White Horse, Shorty spat out a mouthful of tobacco juice and shook Kit's hand.

"Meat! Meat!" Shorty chanted. "We eat it raw! We eat it alive!"

At the top of the bank they met Breck. His wife stood at a little distance. Kit shook his hand.

"I'm afraid your boat can't make it," he said. "It's smaller than ours and a bit cranky."

The man pulled out a roll of bills. "I'll give you each a hundred if you run it through."

Kit looked out and up the tossing Mane of the White Horse. A long, gray twilight was falling, it was turning colder, and the landscape seemed taking on a savage bleakness.

"It ain't that," Shorty was saying. "We don't want your money. Wouldn't touch it nohow. But my pardner is the real meat with boats, and when he says yourn ain't safe I reckon he knows what he's talkin' about."

Kit nodded affirmation, and chanced to glance at Mrs.

Breck. Her eyes were fixed upon him, and he knew that if ever he had seen prayer in a woman's eyes he was seeing it then. Shorty followed his gaze. They looked at each other in confusion and did not speak. Moved by a common impulse, they nodded to each other and turned to the trail that led to the head of the rapids. They had not gone a hundred yards when they met Stine and Sprague coming down.

"Where are you going?" the latter demanded.

"To fetch that other boat through," Shorty answered.

"No, you're not. It's getting dark. You two are going to pitch camp."

So huge was Kit's disgust that he forebore to speak.

"He's got his wife with him," Shorty said.

"That's his worry," Stine contributed.

"And Smoke's and mine," was Shorty's retort.

"I forbid you," Sprague said harshly. "Smoke, if you go another step I'll discharge you."

"And you, too, Shorty," Stine added.

"And a devil of a pickle you'll be in with us fired," Shorty replied. "How'll you get your blamed boat to Dawson? Who'll serve you coffee in your blankets and manicure your fingernails? Come on, Smoke. They don't dast fire us."

Barely had they shoved Breck's boat out from the bank and caught the first rough water, when the waves began to lap aboard. They were small waves, but it was a token of what was to come. Shorty cast back a quizzical glance as he gnawed at his inevitable plug, and Kit felt a strange rush of warmth at his heart for this man who couldn't swim and who couldn't back out.

The rapids grew stiffer, and spray began to fly. In the gathering darkness, Kit glimpsed the Mane and the crooked fling of the current into it. He worked into this crooked current, and felt a glow of satisfaction as the boat hit the head of the Mane squarely in the middle. After that, in the smother, leaping and burying and swamping, he had no clear impression of anything save that he swung his weight on the steering oar and wished his uncle were there to see. They emerged, breathless, wet through, the boat filled with water almost to the gunwale. Lighter pieces of baggage and outfit were floating inside the boat. A few careful strokes on Shorty's part worked the boat into the draw of the eddy, and the eddy did the rest till the boat softly touched the bank. Looking down from above was Mrs. Breck, tears streaming down her cheeks.

"You boys have got to take the money," Breck called down to them.

Shorty stood up, slipped, and sat down in the water, while the boat dipped one gunwale under and righted again.

"Damn the money," said Shorty. "Fetch out that whiskey. Now that it's over I'm getting cold feet, an' I'm sure likely to have a chill."

In the morning, as usual, they were among the last of the parties to start. Breck, despite his boating inexperience, and with only his wife and nephew for crew, had broken camp, loaded his boat, and pulled out at the first streak of day. But there was no hurrying Stine and Sprague, who seemed incapable of realizing that the freeze-up might come at any time. They malingered, got in the way, delayed, and doubled the work of Kit and Shorty.

"I'm sure losing my respect for God, seein' as he made them two mistakes in human form," was the latter's blasphemous way of expressing his disgust.

"Well, you're the real goods, at any rate," Kit grinned back at him. "It makes me respect God the more just to look at you."

"He was sure goin' some, eh?" was Shorty's fashion of overcoming the embarrassment of the compliment.

The trail by water crossed Lake Lebarge. Here was no fast current, but a tideless stretch of forty miles which must be rowed unless a fair wind blew. But the time for fair wind was past, and an icy gale blew in their teeth out of the north. This made a rough sea, against which it was almost impossible to pull the boat. Added to their troubles was driving snow; also, the freezing of the water on their oar-blades kept one man occupied in chopping it off with a hatchet. Compelled to take their turn at the oars, Sprague and Stine patiently loafed. Kit learned how to throw his weight on an oar, but he noted that his employers made only a pretense of throwing their weights and that they dipped their oars at a cheating angle.

At the end of three hours, Sprague pulled his oar in and said they would run back into the mouth of the river for shelter. Stine seconded him, and the several hard-won miles were lost. A second day, and a third, the same fruitless attempt was made. In the river mouth, the continually arriving boats from White Horse made a flotilla of over two hundred. Each day forty or fifty arrived, and only two or three won to the northwest shore of the lake and did not come back. Ice was now forming in the eddies and connecting from eddy to eddy in thin lines around the points. The freeze-up was imminent.

"We could make it if they had the souls of clams," Kit told Shorty, as they dried their moccasins by the fire on the evening of the third day. "We could have made it today if they hadn't turned back. Another hour's work would have fetched that west shore. They're—they're babes in the woods."

"Sure," Shorty agreed. He turned his moccasin to the flame and debated a moment. "Look, Smoke. It's hundreds of miles to Dawson. If we don't want to freeze in here, we've got to do something. What d'ye say?"

Kit looked at him, and waited.

"We've got the drop on them two," Shorty expounded. "They can give orders an' shed dough, but as you say, they're plumb babes. If we're going to Dawson, we got to take charge of this here outfit."

They looked at each other.

"It's a go," said Kit, and his hand went out in ratification.

In the morning, but long before daylight, Shorty issued his call. "Come on!" he roared. "Tumble out, sleepers! Here's your coffee! Kick into it! We're goin' to make a start!"

Grumbling and complaining, Stine and Sprague were forced to get under way two hours earlier than ever before. If anything, the gale was stiffer, and in a short time every man's face was iced up, while the oars were heavy with ice. Three hours they struggled, and four, one man steering, one chopping ice, two toiling at the oars, and each taking his various turns. The northwest shore loomed nearer and nearer. The gale blew ever harder, and at last Sprague pulled in his oar in token of surrender. Shorty sprang to it, though his relief had only begun.

"Chop ice," he said, handing Sprague the hatchet.

"What's the use?" the other whined. "We can't make it. We're going to turn back."

"We're going on," said Shorty. "Chop ice. An' when you feel better you can spell me."

It was heartbreaking toil, but they gained the shore, only to find it composed of surge-beaten rocks and cliffs, with no place to land.

"I told you so," Sprague whimpered. "We're going back."

Nobody spoke, and Kit held the boat into the waves as they skirted the forbidding shore. Sometimes they gained no more than a foot to the stroke, and there were times when two or three strokes no more than enabled them to hold their own. He did his best to hearten the two weaklings. He pointed out that the boats which had won this shore had never come back. Undoubtedly, he argued, they had found shelter somewhere ahead. Another hour they labored, and a second.

"If you fellows'd put into your oars some of that coffee you swig in your blankets, we'd make it," was Shorty's encouragement. "You're just goin' through the motions an' not pullin' a pound."

A few minutes later, Sprague drew in his oar again. "I'm finished," he said, and there were tears in his voice.

"So are the rest of us," Kit answered, himself ready to cry or to commit murder, so great was his exhaustion. "But we're going on just the same."

"We're going back. Turn the boat around."

"Shorty, if he won't pull, take that oar yourself," Kit commanded.

"Sure," was the answer. "He can chop ice."

But Sprague refused to give over the oar; Stine had ceased rowing, and the boat was drifting backward.

"Turn around, Smoke," Sprague ordered.

And Kit, who never in his life had cursed any man, astonished himself. "I'll see you in hell first," he replied. "Take hold of that oar and pull."

Each man had reached the breaking point. Sprague jerked off a mitten, drew his revolver, and turned it on his steersman. This was a new experience to Kit. He had never had a gun held on him in his life. Now, to his surprise, it seemed to mean nothing at all. It was the most natural thing in the world.

"If you don't put that gun up," he said, "I'll take it away and rap you over the head with it."

"If you don't turn the boat around, I'll shoot," Sprague threatened.

Then Shorty took a hand. He ceased chopping ice and stood up behind Sprague. "Go on an' shoot," said Shorty, wiggling the hatchet. "I'm just aching for a chance to brain you. Go on an' start the festivities."

"This is mutiny," Stine broke in. "You were engaged to obey orders."

Shorty turned on him. "You'll get yours as soon as I finish with your pardner, you little hog-wallopin' snooper, you."

"Sprague," Kit said, "I'll give you just thirty seconds to put away that gun and get that oar out."

Sprague hesitated, gave a short hysterical laugh, put the revolver away, and bent his back to the work.

For two hours more, inch by inch, they fought their way along the edge of the foaming rocks, until Kit feared he had made a mistake. And then, on the verge himself of turning back, they came abreast of a narrow opening, not twenty feet wide, which led into a landlocked enclosure where the fiercest gusts scarcely flawed the surface. It was the haven gained by the boats of previous days. They landed on a shelving beach, and the two employers lay in collapse in the boat, while Kit and Shorty pitched the tent, built a fire, and started the cooking.

"What is a hog-walloping snooper, Shorty?" Kit asked.

"Blamed if I know," was the answer; "but he *is* one, just the same."

The gale, which had been dying, ceased at nightfall, and it turned clear and cold. A cup of coffee, set aside to cool and forgotten, a few minutes later was found coated with half an inch of ice. At eight o'clock, when Sprague and Stine, already rolled in their blankets, were sleeping the sleep of exhaustion, Kit came back from a look at the boat.

"It's the freeze-up, Shorty," he announced. "There's a skin of ice over the whole inlet already."

"What are you going to do?"

"There's only one thing. The lake freezes first, but the rapid current of the river may keep it open for days. This time tomorrow any boat in Lake Lebarge remains there until next year!"

"You mean we got to get out tonight? Now?"

Kit nodded.

"Tumble out, sleepers!" was Shorty's answer, couched in a roar.

The other two awoke, groaning with the pain of stiffened muscles and the pain of rousing from the sleep of exhaustion.

"What time is it?" Stine asked.

"Half-past eight."

"It's dark yet," was the objection.

Shorty jerked out a couple of guys, and the tent began to sag. "Not morning," he said. "Evening. Come on. The lake's freezin'. We got to get acrost."

Stine sat up, his face bitter and wrathful. "Let it freeze. We're not going to stir."

"All right," said Shorty. "We're goin' on with the boat."

"You were engaged—"

"To take your outfit to Dawson," Shorty caught him up. "Well, we're takin' it, ain't we?" He punctuated his query by bringing half the tent down on top of them.

They broke their way through the thin ice in the little harbor, and came out on the lake, where the water, heavy and glassy, froze on their oars with every stroke. The water soon became like mush, clogging the stroke of the oars and freezing in the air even as it dripped. Later the surface began to form a skin, and the boat proceeded slower and slower.

Often afterward, when Kit tried to remember that night and failed to bring up anything but nightmare recollections, he wondered what must have been the sufferings of Stine and Sprague. His own impression was that he struggled through biting frost and intolerable exertion for a thousand years.

Morning found them stationary. Stine complained of frosted fingers, and Sprague of his nose, while the pain in Kit's cheeks and nose told him that he, too, had been touched. A hundred yards away was the shore of the north end. Shorty insisted that it was the opening of the river and that he could see water. He and Kit alone were able to work, and with their oars they broke the ice and forced the boat along. And at the last gasp of their strength they made the suck of the river. One look back showed them several boats which had also fought through the night and were hopelessly frozen in; then they whirled around a bend in a current running six miles an hour.

Day by day they floated down the swift river, and day by day the ice extended farther out. When they made camp at nightfall, they chopped a space in the ice in which to lay the boat and carried the camp outfit hundreds of feet to shore. In the morning they chopped the boat out through the new ice and caught the current. Shorty set up the sheet-iron stove in the boat, and over this Stine and Sprague hung through the long drifting hours. They had surrendered and no longer gave orders. Their one desire was to gain Dawson. Shorty, pessimistic, indefatigable, and joyous, at frequent intervals roared out three lines of a song he had forgotten. The colder it got the oftener he sang:

> *"Like Argus of the ancient times,*
> *We leave this Modern Greece,*
> *Tum-tum, tum-tum, tum-tum, tum-tum,*
> *To shear the Golden Fleece."*

As they passed the mouths of the Hootalinqua and the Big and Little Salmon, they found these streams throwing mush-ice into the main Yukon. This gathered about the boat and attached itself, and at night they found themselves compelled to chop the boat out of the current. In the morning they chopped the boat back into the current.

The last night ashore was spent between the mouths of the White River and the Stewart. At daylight they found the Yukon, half a mile wide, running white from ice-rimmed bank to ice-rimmed bank. Shorty cursed the universe with less geniality than usual, and looked at Kit.

"We'll be the last boat this year to make Dawson," Kit said.

"But they ain't no water, Smoke."

"Then we'll ride the ice down. Come on."

Futilely protesting, Sprague and Stine were bundled on board. For half an hour, with axes, Kit and Shorty struggled to cut a way into the swift but solid stream. When they did succeed in clearing the shore ice, the floating ice forced the boat along the edge for a hundred yards, tearing away half of one gunwale and making a partial wreck of it. Then, at the lower end of the bend, they caught the current that flung offshore. They proceeded to work farther toward the middle. The stream was no longer composed of mush-ice, but hard cakes. In between the cakes mush-ice froze solidly as they looked at it. Shoving with the oars against the cakes, sometimes climbing out on the cakes in order to force the boat along, after an hour they gained the middle. Five minutes after they ceased their exertions, the boat was frozen in. The whole river was coagulating as it ran. Cake froze to cake, until at last the boat was the center of a cake seventy-five feet in diameter. Sometimes they floated sidewise, sometimes stern first, while friction tore asunder the forming fetters in the moving mass, only to be manacled by faster-forming ones. While the hours passed, Shorty stoked the stove, cooked meals, and chanted his war song.

Night came, and after many efforts they gave up the attempt to force the boat to shore. Through the darkness they swept helplessly onward.

"What if we pass Dawson?" Shorty queried.

"We'll walk back," Kit answered, "if we're not crushed in a jam."

The sky was clear, and in the light of the cold, leaping stars they caught occasional glimpses of the loom of mountains on either hand. At eleven o'clock, from below, came a dull grinding roar. Their speed began to diminish and cakes of ice to up-end and crash and smash about them. The river was jamming. One cake, forced upward, slid across and carried one side of the boat away. It did not sink, but they saw dark water show for an instant within a foot of them. Then all movement ceased. At the end of half an hour the whole river picked itself up and began to move. This continued for an hour, when again it was brought to rest by a jam. Once again it started, running swiftly and savagely, with a great grinding. Then they saw lights ashore, and, when abreast, gravity and the Yukon surrendered, and the river ceased for six months.

On the shore at Dawson, curious ones gathered to watch the river freeze heard from out of the darkness the war song of Shorty:

> *"Like Argus of the ancient times,*
> *We leave this Modern Greece,*
> *Tum-tum, tum-tum, tum-tum, tum-tum,*
> *To shear the Golden Fleece."*

For three days Kit and Shorty labored, carrying the ton and a half of outfit from the middle of the river to a log cabin Stine and Sprague bought on the hill overlooking Dawson. This work finished, in the warm cabin, as twilight was falling, Sprague motioned Kit to him. Outside the thermometer registered sixty-five below zero.

"Your full month isn't up, Smoke," Sprague said. "But here's your money in full. I wish you luck."

"How about our agreement on food?" Kit asked. "You know there's a famine here. A man can't get work in the mines even unless he has his own grub. You agreed—"

"I know of no agreement," Sprague interrupted. "Do you, Stine? We engaged you by the month. There's your pay. Will you sign the receipt?"

Kit's hands clenched, and for the moment he saw red. Both men shrank away from him.

Shorty interposed.

"Look here, Smoke, I aint' travelin' no more with a ornery outfit like this. Right here's where I sure jump it. You an' me stick together. Savvy? Now you take your blankets an' hike down to the Elkhorn Saloon. Wait for me. I'll settle up, collect what's comin', an' *give* what's comin'. I ain't no good on the water, but my feet's on terry-firmy now, an' *I'm* goin' to make smoke."

Half an hour afterward Shorty appeared at the Elkhorn. From his bleeding knuckles and the skin off one cheek, it was evident that he had given Stine and Sprague what was coming.

"You ought to see that cabin," he chuckled, as they stood at the bar. "Roughhouse ain't no name for it. Dollars to doughnuts nary one of 'em shows up on the street for a week. An' now it's all figgered out for you an' me. They ain't no work for wages without you have your own grub. Moose-meat's sellin' for two dollars a pound, an' they ain't none. We got enough money for a month's grub an' ammunition, an' we hike up the Klondike to the back country. If they ain't no moose, we go an' live with the Indians. But if we ain't got five thousand pounds of meat six weeks from now, I'll sure go back an' apologize to our bosses. Is it a go?"

Kit's hand went out, and they shook. Then he faltered. "I don't know anything about hunting," he said.

Shorty lifted his glass. "But you're sure a meat-eater, an' I'll learn you."

CHAPTER 3

The Stampede to Squaw Creek

TWO MONTHS after Smoke Bellew and Shorty went after moose for a grubstake, they were back in the Elkhorn Saloon at Dawson. The hunting was done, the meat hauled in and sold for two dollars and a half a pound, and between them they possessed three thousand dollars in gold dust and a good team of dogs. They had been in luck. Despite the fact that the gold rush had driven game a hundred miles or more into the mountains, they had within half that distance bagged four moose in a narrow canyon.

The mystery of the strayed animals was no greater than the luck of their killers, for within the day four famished Indian families, reporting no game in three days' journey back, camped beside them. Meat was traded for starving dogs, and after a week of feeding Smoke and Shorty harnessed the animals and began freighting the meat to the eager Dawson market.

The problem of the two men now was to turn their gold dust into food. The current price for flour and beans was a dollar and a half a pound, but the difficulty was to find a seller. Dawson was in the throes of famine. Hundreds of

60

men, with money but no food, had been compelled to leave
the country. Many had gone down river on the last water,
and many more, with barely enough food to last, had
walked the six hundred miles back over the ice to Dyea.

Smoke met Shorty in the warm saloon, and found the
latter jubilant.

"Life ain't no punkins without whiskey an' sweetenin',"
was Shorty's greeting, as he pulled lumps of ice from his
thawing mustache and flung them rattling onto the floor.
"An' I sure just got eighteen pounds of that same sweetenin'. The geezer only charged three dollars a pound for
it. What luck did you have?"

"I bought fifty pounds of flour. And there's a man up on
Adam Creek who says he'll let me have fifty pounds more
tomorrow."

"Great! We'll sure live till the river opens. Say, Smoke,
them dogs of ourn is the goods. A dog-buyer offered me
two hundred apiece for the five of them. I told him nothin'
doin'. They sure took on class when they got meat to get
outside of; but it goes against the grain, feedin' dog-crit-
ters on grub that's worth two an' a half a pound. Come on
an' have a drink. I just got to celebrate them eighteen
pounds of sweetenin'."

Several minutes later, as he weighed in on the gold-
scales for the drinks, he gave a start of recollection.

"I plumb forgot that man I was to meet in the Tivoli.
He's got some spoiled bacon he'll sell for a dollar an' a
half a pound. We can feed it to the dogs an' save a dollar
a day on each's board bill. So long."

Hardly had Shorty left the place, when a fur-clad man
entered through the double storm doors. His face lit up
at sight of Smoke. It was Breck, the man whose boat they
had run through Box Canyon and White Horse Rapids.

"I heard you were in town," Breck said hurriedly, as they shook hands. "Been looking for you for half an hour. Come outside, I want to talk with you."

Smoke looked regretfully at the roaring, red-hot stove. "Won't this place do?"

"No. Come outside."

As they emerged, Smoke drew off one mitten, lit a match, and glanced at the thermometer that hung beside the door. He remittened his naked hand hastily, as if the frost had burned him. Overhead arched the flaming aurora borealis, while from all Dawson arose the mournful howl-ing of thousands of wolf dogs.

"What did it say?" Breck asked.

"Sixty below." Kit spat experimentally, and the spittle crackled in the air. "And the thermometer is certainly working. It's falling all the time. An hour ago it was only fifty-two. Now, what's on your mind? Don't tell me it's a stampede."

"Yes," Breck whispered back cautiously, casting anx-ious eyes about in fear of some other listener. "You know where Squaw Creek empties in on the other side the Yukon thirty miles up?"

"Nothing doing there. It was prospected years ago."

"So were all the other rich creeks. Listen! It's big. Only eight to twenty feet to bedrock. There won't be a claim that don't run to half a million. It's a dead secret. Two or three of my close friends let me in on it. I told my wife right away that I was going to find you before I started. My pack's hidden down the bank. In fact, when they told me they made me promise not to pull out until Dawson was asleep. You know what it means if you're seen with a stampeding outfit. Get your partner and follow. You ought to stake fourth or fifth claim from *Discovery*. Don't forget—Squaw Creek. It's the third after you pass Swede Creek."

When Smoke entered the little cabin on the hillside back of Dawson, he heard a heavy familiar breathing.

"Ah, go to bed," Shorty mumbled, as Smoke shook his shoulder. "I'm not on the night shift," was his next remark, as the rousing hand became more vigorous. "Tell your troubles to the barkeeper."

"Kick into your clothes," Smoke said. "We've got to stake a couple of claims."

Shorty sat up and started to explode, but Smoke's hand covered his mouth.

"Ssh!" Smoke warned. "It's a big strike. Don't wake the neighborhood. Dawson's asleep."

"Huh! You got to show me. Nobody tells anybody about a strike, of course not. But ain't it plumb amazin' the way everybody hits the trail just the same?"

"Squaw Creek," Smoke whispered. "Breck gave me the tip. Shallow bedrock. Gold from the grass roots down. Come on. We'll sling a couple of light packs together and pull out."

Shorty's eyes closed as he lapsed back into sleep. The next moment his blankets were swept off him.

"I'll need them more than you," Smoke explained.

Shorty followed the blankets and began to dress. "Take the dogs?" he asked.

"No. The trail up the creek is probably unbroken, and we can make better time without them."

"I'll throw 'em a meal which'll have to last till we get back. Be sure you take some birchbark and a candle."

Shorty opened the door, felt the bite of the cold, and shrank back to first pull down his ear flaps and mitten his hands. Five minutes later he returned, sharply rubbing his nose. "Smoke, I'm sure opposed to makin' this stampede. It's colder than the hinges of hell a thousand years before the first fire was lighted. Besides, it's Friday the thirteenth, an' we're goin' to trouble sure as sparks fly upward."

With small stampeding-packs on their backs, they closed the door behind them and started down the hill. Shorty floundered off a turn of the trail into deep snow, and raised his voice in blessing of the date of the week and month and year.

"Can't you keep still?" Smoke chided. "You'll have all Dawson awake and after us."

"Huh! See the light in that cabin? An' in that one over there? An' hear that door slam? Oh, sure Dawson's asleep. Them lights? Just buryin' their dead. They ain't stampedin', betcher life they ain't."

By the time they reached the foot of the hill in Dawson, lights were springing up in the cabins, doors were slamming, and from behind came the sound of many moccasins on the hard-packed snow. Again Shorty delivered himself.

"It beats the devil the amount of mourners they is."

They passed a man who stood by the path and was calling anxiously in a low voice, "Charley, get a move on."

"See that pack on his back, Smoke? The graveyard's sure a long ways off when the mourners got to pack their blankets."

By the time they reached the main street a hundred men were in line behind them, and while they sought in the deceptive starlight for the trail that dipped down the bank to the river, more men could be heard arriving.

Shorty slipped and shot down the thirty-foot chute into soft snow. Smoke followed, knocking him over as he was rising to his feet.

"I found it first," he gurgled, taking off his mittens to shake the snow out of the gauntlets.

The next moment they were scrambling wildly out of the way of the hurtling bodies that followed. At the time of the freeze-up, a jam had occurred at this point, and cakes of ice were up-ended in snow-covered confusion. After several hard falls, Smoke drew out his candle and lighted it. Those in the rear hailed it with acclaim. In the windless air it burned easily, and he led the way more quickly.

"It's a sure stampede," Shorty decided. "Or might all them be sleepwalkers?"

"We're at the head of the procession at any rate," was Smoke's answer.

"Oh, I don't know. Mebbe that's a firefly ahead there. Mebbe they're all fireflies—that one, an' that one. Look at 'em! Believe me, they is a whole string of processions ahead."

It was a mile across the jams to the west bank of the Yukon, and candles flickered the full length of the twisting trail. Behind them, clear to the top of the bank they had descended, were more candles.

"Say, Smoke, this ain't no stampede. It's a exode-us. They must be a thousand men ahead of us an' ten thousand behind. Now you listen to your uncle. My medicine's good. When I get a hunch it's sure right. An' we're in wrong on this stampede. Let's turn back an' hit the sack."

"You'd better save your breath if you intend to keep up," Smoke retorted gruffly.

"Huh! My legs is short, but I slog along slack at the knees an' don't worry my muscles none. I can sure walk every piker off the ice an' I'm plumb troddin' on your heels. If you can't do better, let me go ahead and set pace."

Smoke quickened, and was soon at the rear of the nearest bunch of stampeders.

"Hike along, Smoke," the other urged. "Walk over them unburied dead. This ain't no funeral. Hit the frost like you was goin' somewheres."

Smoke counted eight men and two women in this party, and before the way across the ice was won, he and Shorty had passed another party twenty strong. Within a few feet of the west bank, the trail swerved to the south, emerging from the jam upon smooth ice. The ice, however, was buried under several feet of fine snow. Through this the sled trail ran, a narrow ribbon of packed footing barely two feet in width. On either side one sank to his knees deep in the snow. The stampeders they overtook were reluctant to give way, and often Smoke and Shorty had to plunge into the deep snow and by supreme efforts flounder past.

Shorty was irrepressible. When the stampeders resented being passed, he retorted in kind.

"What's your hurry?" one of them asked.

"What's yours?" he answered. "A stampede come down from Indian River yesterday afternoon an' beat you to it. They ain't no claims left."

"So, I repeat, what's your hurry?"

"*Who?* Me? I'm workin' for the government. I'm on official business. I'm just trapesin' along to take the census of Squaw Creek."

To another, who hailed him with: "Where away, little one? Do you really expect to stake a claim?" Shorty answered:

"Me? I'm the discoverer of Squaw Creek. I'm already comin' back from recordin' so as to see no blamed chee-chako jumps my claim."

The average pace of the stampeders on the smooth going was three and a half miles an hour. Smoke and Shorty were doing four and a half, though sometimes they broke into short runs and went faster.

"I'm going to travel your feet clean off, Shorty," Smoke challenged.

"Huh! I can hike along on the stumps an' wear the heels off your moccasins. Though it ain't no use. I've been figgerin'. Creek claims is five hundred feet. Call 'em ten to the mile. They's a thousand stampeders ahead of us, an' that creek ain't no hundred miles long. Some-body's goin' to get left, an' it makes a noise like you an' me."

Smoke laughed. "Shorty, I've got you skinned to death. I've reconstructed every cell in my body since I hit the beach at Dyea. My flesh is as stringy as whipcord, and as mean as the bite of a rattlesnake. I'm the real, bitter, sting-ing goods, and no scrub of a mountaineer can put any-thing over on me without getting it back double. Now go ahead and set pace for half an hour. Do your worst, and when you're all in I'll go ahead and give you half an hour of the real worst."

"Huh!" Shorty sneered genially. "An' him not dry be-hind the ears yet. Get outa the way an' let your father show you some goin'."

Half-hour by half-hour they alternated in setting pace. Nor did they talk much. Their exertions kept them warm, though their breath froze on their faces from lips to chin. So intense was the cold that they almost continually rubbed their noses and cheeks with their mittens.

Often they thought they had reached the lead, but always they overtook more stampeders who had started before them. Occasionally groups of men attempted to swing in behind to their pace, but invariably they were discouraged after a mile or two and disappeared in the darkness to the rear.

"We've been out on trail all winter," was Shorty's comment. "An' them geezers, soft from layin' around their cabins, has the nerve to think they can keep our stride. Now if they was real sourdoughs it'd be different. If they's one thing a sourdough can sure do it's walk."

Once, Smoke lit a match and glanced at his watch. He never repeated it, for so quick was the bite of the frost on his bared hands that half an hour passed before they were again comfortable.

"Four o'clock," he said, as he pulled on his mittens, "and we've already passed three hundred."

"Three hundred and thirty-eight," Shorty corrected. "I been keepin' count. Get outa the way, stranger. Let somebody stampede that knows how to stampede."

This latter was addressed to a man, evidently exhausted, who could no more than stumble along and who blocked the trail. This, and one other, were the only played-out men they encountered, for they were very near to the head of the stampede. Nor did they learn till afterward the horrors of that night. Exhausted men sat down to rest by the way and failed to get up again. Seven were frozen to death, while scores of amputations of toes, feet and fingers were performed in the Dawson hospital on the survivors. For the stampede to Squaw Creek occurred on the coldest night of the year. Before morning the spirit thermometers at Dawson registered seventy degrees below zero.

The other played-out man they found a few minutes later, sitting on a piece of ice beside the trail.

"Hop along, sister Mary," Shorty gaily greeted him. "Keep movin'. If you sit there you'll freeze stiff."

The man made no response, and they stopped to investigate.

"Stiff as a poker," was Shorty's verdict. "If you tumbled him over he'd break."

"See if he's breathing," Smoke said, as, with bared hand, he sought through furs and woolens for the man's heart.

Shorty lifted one ear flap and bent to the iced lips. "Nary breath," he reported.

"Nor heartbeat," said Smoke.

He mittened his hand and beat it violently for a minute before exposing it to the frost to strike a match. It was an old man, incontestably dead. In the moment of illumination they saw a long gray beard, massed with ice to the nose, cheeks that were white with frost, and closed eyes with frost-rimmed lashes frozen together. Then the match went out.

"Come on," Shorty said, rubbing his ear. "We can't do nothin' for the old geezer. An' I've sure frosted my ear. Now all the blamed skin'll peel off, and it'll be sore for a week."

A few minutes later, when a flaming ribbon spilled fire over the heavens, they saw on the ice a quarter of a mile ahead two forms. Beyond, for a mile, nothing moved.

"Those two're leading the procession," Smoke said, as darkness fell again. "Come on, let's get them."

At the end of half an hour, not yet having overtaken the two in front, Shorty broke into a run. "Even if we catch 'em we'll never pass 'em," he panted. "Lord, what a pace

they're hittin'. Dollars to doughnuts they're no cheechakos. They're the real sourdough variety, you can stack on
that."

Smoke was leading when they finally caught up, and he
was glad to ease to a walk at their heels. Almost immediately he got the impression that the one nearest him was
a woman. Hooded and furred, the dark form was as any
form; yet there was a haunting sense of familiarity about
it. He waited for the next flame of the aurora, and by its
light saw the smallness of the moccasined feet. But he
saw more—the walk, and knew it for the walk he had
once resolved never to forget.

"How do you do, Miss Gastell?" Smoke addressed her.

"How do you do?" she answered, with a turn of the
head and a quick glance. "It's too dark to see. Who are
you?"

"Smoke."

She laughed in the frost, and he was certain it was the
prettiest laughter he had ever heard. "How many cheechakos are there behind?"

"Several thousand, I imagine. We passed over three
hundred. And they weren't wasting any time."

"It's the old story," she said bitterly. "The newcomers
get in on the rich creeks, and the old-timers, who dared
and suffered and made this country, get nothing. Old-
timers made this discovery on Squaw Creek—how it
leaked out is a mystery—and they sent word up to all the
old-timers on Sea Lion Creek. But that's ten miles farther
down than Dawson, and when they arrive they'll find
the creek staked to the sky line by the Dawson cheechakos.
It isn't right, it isn't fair."

"It is too bad," Smoke sympathized. "But I'm hanged

if I know what you are going to do about it. First come, first served."

"I'd like to see them all freeze on the trail, or have everything terrible happen to them, so long as the Sea Lion stampede arrived first."

"You've certainly got it in for us hard," he laughed.

"It isn't that," she said quickly. "I know the crowd from Sea Lion, and they are men. They starved in this country in the old days, and they worked like giants to develop it. They deserve some reward, and yet here are thousands of green softlings, who haven't earned the right to stake anything, miles and miles ahead of them. And now I'll save my breath, for I don't know when you and all the rest may try to pass dad and me."

No further talk passed between Joy and Smoke for an hour or so, though he noticed that for a time she and her father talked in low tones.

"I know 'em too," Shorty told Smoke. "He's old Louis Gastell, the real goods. That must be his kid. He come into this country so long ago they ain't nobody can recollect, an' he brought the girl with him, she only a baby. Him an' Beetles was tradin' partners, an' they ran the first dinky little steamboat up the Koyukuk."

"I don't think we'll try to pass them," Smoke said. "We're at the head of the stampede, and there are only four of us."

Shorty agreed, and another hour of silence followed, during which they swung steadily along. At seven o'clock, the blackness was broken by a last display of the aurora borealis, which showed to the west a broad opening between snow-clad mountains.

"Squaw Creek!" Joy exclaimed.

"Goin' some," Shorty exulted. "We oughtn't to been

there for another half hour to the least, accordin' to my reckonin'. I must 'a' been spreadin' my legs."

It was at this point that the Dyea trail, baffled by ice jams, swerved abruptly across the Yukon to the east bank. And here they must leave the hard-packed, main-traveled trail, mount the jams, and follow a dim trail, but slightly packed, that hovered on the west bank.

Louis Gastell, leading, slipped in the darkness on the rough ice, and sat up, holding his ankle in both hands. He struggled to his feet and went on but at a slower pace and with a perceptible limp. After a few minutes he abruptly halted.

"It's no use," he said to his daughter. "I've sprained a tendon. You go ahead and stake for me as well as yourself."

"Can't we do something?" Smoke asked.

Louis Gastell shook his head. "She can stake two claims as well as one. I'll crawl over to the bank, start a fire, and bandage my ankle. I'll be all right. Go on, Joy. Stake ours above the *Discovery* claim; it's probably richer higher up."

"Here's some birchbark," Smoke said, dividing his supply equally. "We'll take care of your daughter."

Louis Gastell laughed harshly. "Thank you just the same," he said, "but she can take care of herself. Follow her and watch her."

"Do you mind if I lead?" she asked Smoke, as she headed on. "I know this country better than you."

"Lead on," Smoke answered gallantly.

After a quarter of a mile, she turned sharply to the west. Smoke noticed that they were going through unpacked snow, but neither he nor Shorty observed that the dim trail they had been on still led south. Had they been able to witness the subsequent actions of Louis Gastell, the history of the Klondike might have been written differently; for they would have seen that old-timer, his limp strangely disappeared, running with his nose to the trail like a hound, following them. Also, they would have seen him trample and widen the turn to the fresh trail they had made to the west. And, finally, they would have seen him slip onto the old dim trail that still led south.

A trail did run up the creek, but so slight that they continually lost it in the darkness. After a quarter of an hour, Joy Gastell was willing to drop to the rear and let the two men take turns in breaking a way through the snow. This slowness of the leaders enabled the whole stampede to catch up, and when daylight came, at nine o'clock, as far back as they could see was an unbroken line of men. Joy's dark eyes sparkled at the sight.

"How long since we started up the creek?" she asked.

"Fully two hours," Smoke answered.

"And two hours to get back make four," she laughed. "The stampede from Sea Lion is saved."

A faint suspicion crossed Smoke's mind and he stopped. "I don't understand," he said.

"You don't? Then I'll tell you. This is Norway Creek. Squaw Creek is the next to the south."

Smoke was speechless.

"You did it on purpose?" Shorty demanded.

"I did it to give the old-timers a chance." She laughed mockingly. The men grinned at each other and finally joined her. "I'd lay you across my knee an' give you a wallopin', if womenfolk wasn't so scarce in this country," Shorty assured her.

"Your father waited till we were out of sight and then went on?" Smoke asked.

She nodded.

"And you were the decoy?"

Again she nodded, and Smoke's laughter rang out; the laughter of a frankly beaten man.

"Well, we might as well be startin' back," Shorty urged. "My feet's gettin' cold standin' here."

Smoke shook his head. "That would mean four hours lost. We must be eight miles up this creek now, and from the look ahead Norway is making a long swing south. We'll follow it, then cross over the divide somehow, and tap Squaw Creek somewhere above *Discovery*." He looked at Joy. "Won't you come along with us? I told your father we'd look after you."

"I—" She hesitated. "I think I shall, if you don't mind." She was looking straight at him, and her face was no longer defiant and mocking. "Really, Mr. Smoke, you make me almost sorry for what I have done. But somebody had to save the old-timers."

"It strikes me that stampeding is at best a sporting proposition."

"And it strikes me you two are very game about it," she went on. "What a pity you are not old-timers!"

For two hours more they kept to the frozen creek bed of Norway, then turned into a narrow and rugged tributary that flowed from the south. By midday they began the ascent of the divide itself. Behind them, looking down and back, they could see the long line of stampeders breaking up. Here and there, in scores of places, thin smoke columns advertised the making of camps.

The going was hard. They wallowed through snow to their waists, and were compelled to stop every few yards to breathe. Shorty was the first to call a halt.

"We been hittin' the trail for over twelve hours," he

said. "Smoke, I'm plumb willin' to say I'm good an' tired.
An' so are you. I'm free to shout that I can sure hang on
to this here stampede like a starvin' Indian to a hunk of
bear-meat. But this poor girl here can't keep on her legs
if she don't get something in her stomach. Here's where
we build a fire. What d'ye say?"

So deftly and methodically did they go about making
a temporary camp that Joy admitted to herself that old-
timers could not do better. Spruce boughs, with a spread
blanket on top, gave a foundation for rest and cooking
operations. But they kept away from the heat of the fire
until noses and cheeks had been rubbed cruelly.

Smoke spat in the air, and the resultant crackle was so
immediate and loud that he shook his head. "I give up,"
he said. "I've never seen cold like this."

"One winter on the Koyukuk it went to eighty-six below," Joy answered. "It's at least seventy or seventy-five
right now, and I know I've frosted my cheeks. They're
burning like fire."

On the steep slope of the divide there was no ice, so
snow, fine and hard and crystalline as granulated sugar,
was poured into the gold-pan by the bushel until enough
had been melted for the coffee. Smoke fried bacon and
thawed biscuits. Shorty kept the fuel supplied and tended
the fire, and Joy set the simple table composed of two
plates, two cups, two spoons, a tin of mixed salt and pepper, and a tin of sugar. When it came to eating, she and
Smoke shared one set between them.

It was nearly two in the afternoon when they cleared
the crest of the divide and began dropping down a feeder
of Squaw Creek. Earlier in the winter some moose-hunter
had made a trail up the canyon; that is, in going up and
down he had stepped always in his previous tracks. As a

result, in the midst of soft snow and veiled under later
snowfalls, was a line of irregular hummocks. If one's foot
missed a hummock, he plunged down through unpacked
snow and usually to a fall. Also, the moose-hunter had
been an exceptionally long-legged individual. Joy, eager
now that the two men should stake, and fearing they were
slackening their pace on account of her evident weariness,
insisted on taking her turn in the lead. The speed and
manner in which she negotiated the precarious footing
called out Shorty's unqualified approval.

"Look at her!" he cried. "She's the real goods an' the
red meat. Look at them moccasins swing along. No high
heels there. She uses the legs God gave her. She's the right
squaw for any bear-hunter."

She flashed back a smile of acknowledgment that included Smoke. He caught a feeling of comradeship,
though at the same time he was aware that it was very
much of a woman who embraced him in that comradely
smile.

Looking back, as they came to the bank of Squaw Creek,
they could see the stampede, strung out irregularly behind
them, struggling down the descent of the divide.

They slipped down the bank to the creek bed. The
stream, frozen solidly to bottom, was from twenty to thirty
feet wide between six- and eight-foot banks. No recent
feet had disturbed the snow that lay upon its ice, and they
knew they were above the *Discovery* claim and the last
stakes of the Sea Lion stampeders.

"Look out for springs," Joy warned, as Smoke led the
way down the creek. "At seventy below you'll lose your
feet if you break through."

These springs, common to most Klondike streams, never
cease, even at the lowest temperatures. The water flows

out from the banks and lies in pools cuddled from the cold
by later surface-freezings and snowfalls. Thus, a man,
stepping on dry snow, might break through half an inch
of ice and find himself up to the knees in water. In five
minutes, unless able to remove the wet gear, the loss of
one's feet was the penalty.

At three in the afternoon, the long gray twilight of the
arctic had already settled down. They watched for a
blazed tree on either bank, which would show the center-
stake of the last claim located. Joy was the first to find it.
She darted ahead of Smoke, crying:

"Somebody's been here! See the snow! Look for the
blaze! There it is! On that spruce!" Then she suddenly
sank to her waist in the snow. "Now I've done it," she
said woefully. "Don't come near me! I'll wade out."

Step by step, each time breaking through the thin skin
of ice concealed under the dry snow, she forced her way
to solid footing. Smoke did not wait, but sprang to the
bank, where dry and seasoned twigs and sticks, lodged
among the brush by spring freshets, waited the match.
By the time she reached his side the first flames and flick-
ers of an assured fire were rising.

"Sit down!" he commanded.

She obediently sat down in the snow. He slipped his
pack from his back, and spread a blanket for her feet.

From above drifted the voices of the stampeders who
followed them.

"Let Shorty stake," she urged.

"Go on, Shorty," Smoke said, as he attacked her moccasins, already stiff with ice. "Pace off a thousand feet and
place the two center-stakes. We can fix the corner-stakes
afterward."

With his knife, Smoke cut away the lacings and leather

of the moccasins. So stiff were they with ice that they snapped under the sawing. The siwash socks and heavy woolen stockings were sheaths of ice. It was as if her feet and calves were encased in corrugated iron.

"How are your feet?" he asked as he worked.

"Pretty numb. I can't move or feel my toes. But it will be all right. The fire is burning beautifully. Watch out you don't freeze your hands. They must be numb now from the way you're fumbling."

He slipped his mittens on, and for nearly a minute smashed the open hands savagely against his sides. When he felt the blood prickle, he pulled off the mittens and ripped and tore and sawed and hacked at the frozen garments. The white skin of one foot appeared, then that of the other, to be exposed to the bite of seventy below zero, one hundred and two below freezing.

Then came the rubbing with snow, carried on with an intensity of cruel fierceness, till she squirmed and shrank and moved her toes, and joyously complained of the hurt. He half dragged her, and she half lifted herself, nearer to the fire. He placed her feet on the blanket close to the flesh-saving flames.

She could now safely remove her mittens and work and manipulate her own feet, watchful that the heat of the fire was absorbed slowly. While she did this, he attacked his hands. The snow did not melt or moisten. Its crystals were like so much sand. Slowly the stings and pangs of circulation came back into the chilled flesh. Then he tended the fire, unstrapped the pack from her back, and got out a complete change of footgear.

Shorty returned along the creek bed and climbed the bank to them. "I sure staked a full thousan' feet," he proclaimed. "Number twenty-seven an' twenty-eight, though

I'd only got the upper stake of twenty-seven when I met the first geezer of the bunch behind. He just straight declared I wasn't goin' to stake twenty-eight. An' I told him—"

"What did you tell him?" Joy cried.

"Well, I told him straight that if he didn't back up plumb five hundred feet I'd sure punch his frozen nose into raspberry ice cream. He backed up, an' I've got in the center-stakes of two full an' honest five-hundred-foot creek claims. He staked next, an' I guess by now the bunch has Squaw Creek located to headwaters an' down the other side. Ourn is safe. It's too dark to see now, but we can put out the corner-stakes in the mornin'."

When they awoke, they found a change had taken place during the night. So warm was it, that Shorty and Smoke, still in their mutual blankets, estimated the temperature at no more than twenty below. The cold snap had broken. On top of their blankets lay six inches of frost-crystals.

Joy Gastell, carefully shaking aside the snow, was already sitting up in her sleeping-furs.

Shorty built the fire and quarried ice from the creek, while Smoke cooked breakfast. Daylight came on as they finished the meal.

"You go an' fix them corner-stakes, Smoke," Shorty said. "There's gravel under where I chopped ice for the coffee, an' I'm goin' to melt snow and wash a pan of that same gravel for luck."

Smoke departed, ax in hand, to blaze the stakes. From the down-stream center-stake of twenty-seven, he headed at right angles across the narrow valley toward its rim. He proceeded methodically, almost automatically, for his mind was alive with recollections of the night before. In

dim and fiery ways a feeling of possession mastered him.
It seemed that all that was necessary was for him to walk
up to Joy Gastell, take her hand in his, and say, "Come."

Then he discovered something that made him forget
her. At the valley rim he blazed no corner-stake. He
did not even reach the valley rim, but instead, he found
himself confronted by *another stream*. He lined up with
his eye a blasted willow and a big and recognizable
spruce. Then he returned to the stream with the center-
stake. He followed the creek around a wide horseshoe bend
and found that the two creeks were *the same creek*. Next,
he floundered twice through the snow from valley rim to
valley rim, running the first line from the lower stake of
twenty-seven, the second from the upper stake of twenty-
eight; and he found that *the upper stake of the latter was
lower than the lower stake of the former*. In the gray twilight and half-darkness, Shorty had located their two
claims on the horseshoe.

Smoke plodded back to the little camp. Shorty, at the
end of washing a pan of gravel, exploded at the sight of
him.

"We got it!" Shorty cried, holding out the pan. "Look
at it! A nasty mess of gold. Two hundred right there if it's
a cent. She runs rich from the top of the wash gravel. I've
churned around placers some, but I never got butter like
what's in this pan."

Smoke cast an incurious glance at the coarse gold,
poured himself a cup of coffee at the fire, and sat down.
Joy sensed something wrong and looked at him with eager
eyes.

"Why don't you get excited?" Shorty demanded. "We
got our pile right here, unless you're stickin' up your nose
at two-hundred-dollar pans."

Smoke took a swallow of coffee before replying. "Shorty, why are our two claims here like the Panama Canal?"

"What's the answer?"

"Well, the eastern entrance of the Panama Canal is west of the western entrance, that's all."

"Go on," Shorty said. "I ain't seen the joke yet."

"In short, Shorty, you staked our two claims on a big horseshoe bend."

Shorty set the gold-pan down in the snow and stood up. "Go on."

"The upper stake of twenty-eight is ten feet below the lower stake of twenty-seven."

"You mean we ain't got nothin', Smoke?"

"Worse than that; we've got ten feet less than nothing."

Shorty departed down the bank on the run. Five minutes later he returned. In response to Joy's look he nodded. Without a word, he went over to a log and sat down to gaze steadily at the snow in front of his moccasins.

"We might as well break camp and start back for Dawson," Smoke said, beginning to fold the blankets.

"I'm sorry, Smoke," Joy said. "It's all my fault."

"It's all right. All in the day's work," he answered.

"But it's my fault," she persisted. "Dad's staked for me down near *Discovery*. I'll give you my claim."

He shook his head.

"Shorty," she pleaded.

Shorty shook his head and began to laugh. It was a colossal laugh. Chuckles and muffled explosions yielded to hearty roars.

"It ain't hysterics," he explained. "I sure get powerful amused at times, an' this is one of them."

His gaze chanced to fall on the gold-pan. He walked over and gravely kicked it, scattering gold all over the landscape. "It ain't ourn," he said. "It belongs to the geezer I backed up five hundred feet last night. An' what gets me is, four hundred and ninety of them feet was to the good—his good. Come on, Smoke. Let's start the hike to Dawson. If you're hankerin' to kill me I won't lift a finger to prevent."

CHAPTER 4

Shorty Dreams

UNNY YOU don't gamble none," Shorty said to Smoke one night in the Elkhorn Saloon. "Ain't it in your blood?"

All about them, in the huge barroom, arose the click and rattle and rumble of a dozen games, at which fur-clad, moccasined men tried their luck. Smoke waved his hand to include them all.

"Look at them," he said. "It's cold mathematics that they will lose more than they win tonight. The big proportion are losing right now."

"Don't you ever get one of them streaky hunches that all you got to do is put your money down an' pick a winner?" Shorty asked.

Smoke laughed. "I'm too scared of the percentage against me. I'll tell you what, Shorty, I'll throw a dollar on 'high card' right now, and see if it will buy us a drink." Smoke was edging his way in to the faro table when Shorty caught his arm.

"Hold on! I'm gettin' a hunch now. You put that dollar on roulette."

They went over to the roulette table near the bar.

"Wait till I give the word," Shorty counseled.

"What number?" Smoke asked.

"Pick it yourself. Now! Let her go!"

The gamekeeper had just sent the little ivory ball whirling around the smooth rim above the revolving, many-slotted wheel. Smoke, at the lower end of the table, reached over a player, and blindly tossed the dollar. It slid along the smooth, green cloth and stopped fairly in the center of "34."

The ball came to a rest, and the gamekeeper announced, "Thirty-four wins!" He swept the table, but alongside Smoke's dollar stacked thirty-five more. Smoke drew the money in, and Shorty slapped him on the shoulder.

"Now that was the real goods of a hunch, Smoke! I just knew you'd win. Why, if that dollar of yourn'd fell on any other number it'd won just the same. When the hunch is right, you just can't help winnin'. I got a hunch, after pickin' you for a winner, that I can pick some numbers myself."

"Are you playing a system?" Smoke asked, at the end of ten minutes, when his partner had dropped a hundred dollars.

Shorty shook his head indignantly, as he spread his chips out in the vicinities of "3," "11," and "17," and tossed a spare chip on the green. "Hell is sure cluttered with geezers that played systems," he exposited, as the keeper raked the table.

From idly watching, Smoke became fascinated, following closely every detail of the game from the whirling of the ball to the making and the paying of the bets. He made no plays, however, merely contenting himself with looking on. Yet so interested was he that Shorty, announcing that he had had enough, with difficulty drew Smoke away from the table.

The gamekeeper returned Shorty the gold-sack he had deposited as a credential for playing, and with it went a slip of paper on which was scribbled, "Out—$350.00." Shorty carried the sack and the paper across the room and handed them to the weigher, who sat behind a large pair of gold-scales. Out of Shorty's sack he weighed three hundred and fifty dollars, which he poured into the coffer of the house.

"Never mind, Shorty," Smoke laughed. "I've got a hunch right now—"

Shorty's eyes sparkled as he cried eagerly: "What is it? Kick in an' play it pronto."

"It's not that kind, Shorty. I've got a hunch I can actually work out a system that will beat the spots off that table."

"System!" Shorty groaned, then surveyed his partner with a vast pity. "Smoke, listen to your sidekick an' leave system alone. Systems is sure losers. They ain't no hunches in systems."

"That's why I like them," Smoke answered. "A system is statistical. When you get the right system you can't lose. That's the difference between it and a hunch. You never know when the right hunch is going wrong."

Shorty's response was another groan.

"I don't want you bucking any more games on your own," Smoke went on. "We're going to divide the winnings, and I'll need all our money to get started. The system's liable to trip me for a few falls before I get it lined up."

After long hours and days spent at watching the table, the night came when Smoke proclaimed that he was ready, and Shorty, glum and pessimistic, accompanied his

partner to the Elkhorn. Smoke bought a stack of chips and
stationed himself at the gamekeeper's end of the table.
Again and again the ball was whirled, and the other players won or lost, but Smoke did not venture a chip. Shorty
waxed impatient.

"Buck in, buck in," he urged. "Let's get this funeral
over. What's the matter? Cold feet?"

Smoke shook his head and waited. A dozen plays went
by, and then, suddenly he placed ten one-dollar chips
on "26." The number won, and the keeper paid Smoke
three hundred and fifty dollars. A dozen plays went by,
twenty plays, and thirty, when Smoke placed ten dollars
on "32." Again he received three hundred and fifty dollars.

"It's a hunch!" Shorty whispered vociferously in his
ear. "Ride it! Ride it!"

Half an hour went by, during which Smoke was inactive, then he placed ten dollars on "34" and won.

"A hunch!" Shorty whispered.

"Nothing of the sort," Smoke whispered back. "It's the
system. Isn't she something?"

"You can't tell me," Shorty contended. "Hunches comes
in mighty funny ways. You might think it's a system, but
it ain't. Systems is impossible. They can't happen. It's a
sure hunch you're playin'."

Smoke now altered his play. He bet more frequently,
with single chips, scattered here and there, and he lost
more often than he won.

"Quit it," Shorty advised. "Cash in. You've rung the
bull's-eye three times, an' you're ahead a thousand. You
can't keep it up."

At this moment the ball started whirling, and Smoke

dropped ten chips on "26." The ball fell into the slot of "26," and the keeper again paid him three hundred and fifty dollars.

"If you're plumb crazy an' got the immortal cinch, bet 'em the limit," Shorty said. "Put down twenty-five next time."

A quarter of an hour passed, during which Smoke won and lost on small scattering bets. Then, with the abruptness that characterized his big betting, he placed twenty-five dollars on "00," and the keeper paid him eight hundred and seventy-five dollars.

"Wake me up, Smoke, I'm dreamin'," Shorty moaned.

Smoke smiled, consulted his notebook, and became absorbed in calculation. He continually drew the notebook from his pocket, and from time to time jotted down figures.

A crowd had packed densely around the table, while the players themselves were attempting to cover the same numbers he covered. It was then that a change came over his play. Ten times in succession he placed ten dollars on "18" and lost. At this stage he was deserted by the hardiest. He changed his number and won another three hundred and fifty dollars. Immediately the players were back with him, deserting again after a series of losing bets.

"Quit it, Smoke, quit it," Shorty advised. "The longest string of hunches is only so long, an' your string's finished. You're something like thirty-six hundred to the good. No more bull's-eyes for you."

"I'm going to ring her once again before I cash in," Smoke answered.

For a few minutes, with varying luck, he played, scattering chips over the table, and then dropped twenty-five dollars on "00."

"I'll take my slip now," he said to the dealer, as he won.

"Don't crowd your luck," Shorty pleaded with Smoke, the next night, in the cabin, as he prepared to return to the Elkhorn. "You played a mighty long string of hunches, but you played it out. If you go back you'll sure drop all your winnings."

"But I tell you it isn't hunches, Shorty. It's a system. It can't lose."

"System the devil. They ain't no such a thing as system. I made seventeen straight passes at a crap table once. Was it system? Nope. It was fool luck, only I had cold feet an' didn't dast let it ride. If it'd rid, instead of me drawin' down after the third pass I'd 'a' won over thirty thousan' on the original two-bit piece."

"Just the same, Shorty, this is a real system."

"Huh! You got to show me."

"I did show you. Come on with me now, and I'll show you again."

When they entered the Elkhorn all eyes centered on Smoke, and those about the table made way for him as he took up his old place at the keeper's end. His play was quite unlike that of the previous night. In the course of an hour and a half he made only four bets, but each bet was for twenty-five dollars, and each bet won. He cashed in thirty-five hundred dollars, and Shorty carried the dust home to the cabin.

"Now's the time to jump the game," Shorty advised, as he sat on the edge of his bunk and took off his moccasins. "You're seven thousan' ahead. A man's a fool that'd crowd his luck harder."

"Shorty, a man would be a lunatic if he didn't keep on backing a winning system like mine."

"Smoke, in a dream all things is possible. In real life a system ain't possible. This gamblin' orgy of ourn is a sure-enough dream. I'm dreamin', Smoke, an' you're just snoopin' around in my dream an' tormentin' me with system. If you love me, if you sure do love me, you'll just yell: 'Shorty! Wake up!' An' I'll wake up an' start breakfast."

The third night of play, as Smoke laid his first bet, the gamekeeper shoved fifteen dollars back to him.

"Ten's all you can play," he said. "The limit's come down."

"Gettin' cheap," Shorty sneered.

"No one has to play at this table that don't want to," the keeper retorted. "And I'm willing to say we'd sooner your pardner didn't play at our table."

"Scared of his system, eh?" Shorty challenged, as the keeper soon paid over three hundred and fifty dollars.

"I ain't saying I believe in system, because I don't. There never was a system that'd beat roulette or any percentage game. But just the same I've seen some queer strings of luck, and I ain't going to let this bank go bust if I can help it."

"Cold feet."

"Gambling is just as much business, my friend, as any other business. We ain't philanthropists."

Night by night, Smoke continued to win. His method of play varied. Expert after expert, in the jam about the table, scribbled down his bets in vain attempts to work out his system. They complained of their inability to get a clue to start with, and swore that it was pure luck, the most colossal streak of it they had ever seen.

It was Smoke's varied play that confused them. Sometimes, consulting his notebook or engaging in long calculations, an hour elapsed without his staking a chip. At other times he would win three limit-bets and clean up more than a thousand dollars in five or ten minutes. At still other times, his tactic would be to scatter single chips prodigally and amazingly over the table. This would continue for ten to thirty minutes of play, when, abruptly, as the ball whirled through the last few of its circles, he would play the limit on column, color, and number, and win all three. Once, to complete the confusion in the minds of those that strove to divine his secret, he lost forty straight bets, each at the limit. But each night Shorty carried home thirty-five hundred dollars for him.

"It ain't no system," Shorty expounded at one of their bed-going discussions. "I follow you, an' follow you, but they ain't no figgerin' out. You never play twice the same. All you do is pick winners when you want to, an' when you don't want to you just on purpose don't."

"Maybe you're nearer right than you think, Shorty. I've got to pick losers sometimes. That's also part of the system."

"System the devil! I've talked with every gambler in town, an' the last one is agreed they ain't no such thing as system."

"Yet I'm showing them one all the time."

"Look here, Smoke." Shorty paused over the candle, in the act of blowing it out. "I'm real irritated. I'm gettin' mangy an' mad. If this here dream keeps up much more I'm goin' to bite my veins an' howl."

On the sixth night of play at the Elkhorn, the limit was reduced to five dollars.

"It's all right," Smoke assured the gamekeeper. "I want thirty-five hundred tonight, as usual, and you only compel me to play longer. I've got to pick twice as many winners, that's all."

"Why don't you buck somebody else's table?" the keeper demanded wrathfully.

"Because I like this one." Smoke glanced over at the roaring stove only a few feet away. "Besides, there are no drafts here, and it is warm and comfortable."

On the ninth night, when Shorty had carried the dust home, he had a fit. "I quit, Smoke, I quit," he began. "I know when I got enough. I ain't dreamin'. I'm wide awake. A system can't *be*, but you got one just the same. There's nothin' in the rule o' three. The almanac's clean out. The world's gone smash. There's nothin' regular an' uniform no more. The multiplication table's gone loco. Two is eight, nine is eleven, and two-times-two is eight hundred an' forty-six—an'—an' a half. Anything is everything, an' nothing's all, an' twice all is cold cream, milk shakes, an' calico horses. You've got a system. Figgers beat the figgerin'. What ain't is, an' what isn't has to be. The sun rises in the west, the moon's a pay streak, the stars is canned corn-beef, scurvy's the blessin' of God, him that dies kicks again, rocks floats, water's gas, I ain't me, you're somebody else, an' mebbe we're twins if we ain't hashed-brown potatoes fried in verdigris. Wake me up, somebody! Oh, wake me up!"

The next morning a visitor came to the cabin. Smoke knew him, Harvey Moran, the owner of all the games in the Tivoli Saloon. There was a note of appeal in his deep gruff voice as he plunged into his business.

"It's like this, Smoke," he began. "You've got us all guessing. I'm representing nine gameowners and myself

from all the saloons in town. We know that no system
ever worked against roulette. Roulette itself is the system,
the one and only system, and no system can beat it. That
would mean arithmetic has gone bughouse." Shorty nodded his head violently.

"Well, you've seen me play," Smoke answered defiantly; "if you think it's only a string of luck on my part,
why worry?"

"That's the trouble. We can't help worrying. It's a system you've got, and all the time we know it can't be. I've
watched you five nights now myself, and all I can make
out is that you favor certain numbers and keep on winning. Now ten of us gameowners have got together, and
we want to make a friendly proposition. We'll put a roulette table in a back room of the Elkhorn, pool the bank
against you, and have you buck us. It will be all quiet
and private. Just you and Shorty and us. What do you
say?"

"I'll be playing in the barroom of the Elkhorn tonight,"
Smoke answered. "You can watch me there just as well."

That night, when Smoke took up his customary place
at the table, the keeper shut down the game. "The game's
closed," he said. "Boss's orders."

But the other assembled gameowners were not balked.
In a few minutes they arranged a pool, each putting in a
thousand, and took over the Elkhorn table.

"Come on and buck us," Harvey Moran challenged, as
the keeper sent the ball on its first whirl around.

"At the twenty-five limit?" Smoke suggested.

"Sure; go to it."

Smoke immediately placed twenty-five chips on "00"
and won.

Moran wiped the sweat from his forehead. "Go on," he said. "We got ten thousand in this bank."

At the end of an hour and a half, the ten thousand was Smoke's.

"The bank's bust," the keeper announced.

"Had enough?" Smoke asked.

The gamekeepers looked at one another. They were awed. They, the high priests of the laws of chance, were undone. They were up against one who had more intimate access to those laws, or who had invoked higher and undreamed laws.

"We quit," Moran said. "Right, Burke?"

Big Burke, who owned the games in the M. and G. Saloon, nodded. "Smoke here has got a system all right. If we let him go on we'll all bust. All I can see, if we're goin' to keep our tables running, is to cut down the limit to a dollar, or to ten cents, or a cent. He won't win much in a night with those stakes."

All looked at Smoke.

He shrugged his shoulders. "In that case, gentlemen, I'll have to hire a gang of men to play at all your tables. I can pay them ten dollars for a four-hour shift and still make money."

"Then we'll shut down our tables," Big Burke replied. "Unless—" He hesitated and ran his eye over his fellows to see that they were with him. "Unless you're willing to talk business. What will you sell the system for?"

"Thirty thousand dollars," Smoke answered. "Three thousand apiece."

They debated and nodded. "And you'll tell us your system?"

"Yes."

"And you'll promise not to play roulette in Dawson ever again?"

"No, sir," Smoke said positively. "I'll just promise not to play *this* system again."

"My God!" Moran exploded. "You haven't got other systems, have you?"

"Hold on!" Shorty cried. "I want to talk to my pardner. Come over here, Smoke, on the side."

Smoke followed into a quiet corner of the room, while hundreds of curious eyes centered on him and Shorty.

"Look here, Smoke," Shorty whispered hoarsely. "Mebbe it ain't a dream. In which case you're sellin' out almighty cheap. You've sure got the world by the slack of its pants. They's millions in it. Shake it! Shake it hard!"

"But if it's a dream?" Smoke queried softly.

"Then, for the sake of the dream an' the love of Mike, stick them gamblers up good an' plenty. What's the good of dreamin' if you can't dream to the real right, dead sure, eternal finish?"

"Fortunately, this isn't a dream, Shorty."

"Then if you sell out for thirty thousan', I'll never forgive you."

"When I sell out for thirty thousand, you'll fall on my neck an' wake up to find out that you haven't been dreaming at all. This is no dream, Shorty. In about two minutes you'll see you have been wide awake all the time. When I sell out it's because I've got to sell out."

Back at the table, Smoke informed the gameowners that his offer still held. They proffered him their paper to the extent of three thousand each.

"Hold out for dust," Shorty cautioned.

The owner of the Elkhorn cashed their paper, and Shorty took possession of the gold dust.

"Now I don't want to wake up," he chortled, as he hefted the various sacks. "Toted up, it's a seventy-thousan' dream. It'd be too blamed expensive to open my eyes, roll out of the blanket, an' start breakfast."

"What's your system?" Big Burke demanded. "We've paid for it, and we want it."

Smoke led the way to the table. "Now, gentlemen, this isn't an ordinary system. It can scarcely be called legitimate, but its one great virtue is that it works. I've got my suspicions, but I'm not saying anything. You watch. Mr. Keeper, be ready with the ball. I am going to pick '26.' Consider I've bet on it. Ready, Mr. Keeper. Now!"

The ball whirled around.

"You observe," Smoke went on, "that '9' was directly opposite."

The ball finished in "26."

Big Burke swore deep in his chest, and all waited.

"For '00' to win, '11' must be opposite. Try it yourself and see."

"But the system?" Moran demanded impatiently. "We know you can pick winning numbers, and we know what those numbers are, but how do you do it?"

"By observed sequences. By accident I chanced twice to notice the ball whirled when '9' was opposite. Both times '26' won. After that I saw it happen again. Then I looked for other sequences, and found them. 'Double zero' opposite fetches '32,' and '11' fetches '00.' It doesn't always happen, but it *usually* happens. You notice, I say 'usually.' As I said before, I have my suspicions, but I'm not saying anything."

Big Burke, with a sudden flash of comprehension, reached over, stopped the wheel, and examined it carefully. The heads of the nine other gameowners bent over and joined in the examination. Then Big Burke straightened up and cast a glance at the near-by stove.

"Hell," he said. "It wasn't any system at all. The table stood close to the fire, and the blamed wheel's warped. And we've been worked to a frazzle. No wonder he liked this table. He couldn't have bucked for sour apples at any other table."

Harvey Moran gave a great sigh of relief and wiped his forehead. "Well, anyway," he said, "it's cheap at the price just to find out that it wasn't a system." His face began to work, and then he broke into laughter and slapped Smoke on the shoulder. "Smoke, you had us going for a while, and we patting ourselves on the back because you were letting our tables alone! Say, I've got some real champagne I'll open if you'll all come over to the Tivoli with me."

Later, back in the cabin, Shorty silently overhauled and hefted the various bulging gold-sacks. He finally piled them on the table, sat down on the edge of his bunk, and began taking off his moccasins.

"Seventy thousan'," he calculated. "It weighs three hundred and fifty pounds. And all out of a warped wheel an' a quick eye. Smoke, you eat'm raw, you eat'm alive, you work under water, you've given me the jimjams; but just the same I know it's a dream. It's only in dreams that the good things comes true. I'm almighty unanxious to wake up. I hope I never wake up."

CHAPTER 5

The Man on the Other Bank

SMOKE, WITH the dog team, went south from
the upper Klondike. His quest was Surprise
Lake and Two Cabins. His traverse was to cut
the headwaters of the Indian River and cross
the unknown region over the mountains to the Stewart
River. Here, somewhere, rumor persisted, was Surprise
Lake, surrounded by jagged mountains and glaciers, its
bottom paved with raw gold. Old-timers, it was said, whose
very names were forgotten in the frosts of earlier years, had
dived into the icy waters of Surprise Lake and fetched
lump-gold to the surface in both hands. But the water was
too cold. Some died in the water. Others died later of con-
sumption. All survivors had planned to return and drain
the lake, yet none had ever gone back. Disaster always
smote them. One man fell into an air-hole below Forty-
Mile; another was killed and eaten by his dogs; a third
was crushed by a falling tree. And so the tale ran. Surprise
Lake was a hoodoo; its location was unremembered; and
the gold still paved its undrained bottom.

Two Cabins was more definitely located. "Five sleeps"
up the McQuesten River from the Stewart stood two ancient cabins. So ancient were they that they must have

been built before the first gold-hunter had entered the
Yukon Basin.

"I wish you wasn't goin'." Shorty said wistfully, at parting. "Ain't no reason for to go pokin' into trouble. They's
no gettin' away from it, that's loco country you're bound
for. The hoodoo's sure on it, from the first flip to the last
call, judgin' from all you an' me has hearn tell about it."

"It's all right, Shorty," replied Smoke. "I'll make the
round trip and be back in Dawson in six weeks. The Yukon
trail is packed, and the first hundred miles or so of the
Stewart ought to be packed. Old-timers from Henderson
told me a number of outfits went up last fall after the
freeze-up. When I strike their trail I ought to hit her up
to forty or fifty miles a day. I'm likely to be back inside a
month, once I get across."

"Yep, once you get acrost. It's the gettin' acrost that
worries me. Well, so long, Smoke. Keep your eyes open for
that hoodoo, that's all. An' don't be ashamed to turn back
if you don't kill any meat."

A week later, Smoke found himself among the jumbled
ranges south of Indian River. On the divide from the Klondike he had abandoned the sled and loaded his wolf dogs.
The six big huskies each carried fifty pounds, and on his
own back was an equal burden. Through the soft snow he
led the way, packing it down under his snowshoes, and
behind, in single file, toiled the dogs.

He loved the life, the deep arctic winter, the silent wil-
derness, the unending snow surface unpressed by the foot
of man. About him towered icy peaks unnamed and un-
charted. No hunter's camp smoke, rising in the still air of
the valleys, ever caught his eye. He, alone, moved through
the brooding quiet of the untraveled wastes. He loved it
all, the day's toil, the bickering dogs, the making of the

camp in the long twilight, the leaping stars overhead, and the flaming pageant of the aurora borealis.

Especially he loved his camp at the end of day—a beaten place in the snow, where burned his fire; his bed a couple of rabbit-skin robes spread on fresh-chopped spruce boughs; his shelter a stretched strip of canvas that caught and threw back the heat of the fire; the blackened coffee-pot and pail resting on a length of log, the moccasins propped on sticks to dry, the snowshoes up-ended in the snow; and across the fire the dogs snuggling to it for warmth, wistful and eager, furry and frost-rimed, with bushy tails curled protectingly over their feet; and all about, the wall of encircling darkness.

Then for days Smoke wandered through a chaos of canyons and divides which did not yield themselves to any rational topographical plan. It was as if they had been flung there by some cosmic joker. In vain he sought for a creek or feeder that flowed truly south toward the McQuesten and the Stewart. Then came a mountain storm that blew a blizzard across the riffraff of high and shallow divides. Above timber line, fireless, for two days he struggled blindly to find lower levels. On the second day he came out upon the rim of an enormous palisade. So thickly drove the snow that he could not see the base of the wall, nor dared he attempt the descent. He rolled himself in his robes and huddled the dogs about him in the depths of a snowdrift.

In the morning, the storm spent, he crawled out to investigate. A quarter of a mile beneath him lay a frozen, snow-covered lake. About it, on every side, rose jagged peaks. It answered the description. Blindly, he had found Surprise Lake.

"Well named," he muttered.

An hour later, he came out upon its margin. A clump of aged spruce was the only woods. In his way to it, he stumbled upon three graves, snow-buried, but marked by hand-hewn head posts and undecipherable writing. At the edge of the woods was a small ramshackle cabin. He pulled the latch and entered. In a corner, on what had once been a bed of spruce boughs, wrapped in mangy furs that had rotted to fragments, lay a skeleton. The last visitor to Surprise Lake, was Smoke's conclusion, as he picked up a lump of gold as large as his doubled fist. Beside the lump was a pepper can filled with nuggets the size of walnuts, rough-surfaced, showing no signs of wash.

Smoke accepted without question that the source of the gold was the lake's bottom—now under many feet of ice and completely inaccessible. There was nothing to be done, and at midday, from the rim of the palisade, he took a farewell look back and down at his find.

"Mr. Lake," he said, "you just keep right on staying there. I'm coming back to drain you—if that hoodoo doesn't catch me. I don't know how I got here, but I'll certainly remember the way I go out."

Four days later, in a little valley, beside a frozen stream under some spruce trees, he built a fire. Somewhere in that white anarchy he had left behind him was Surprise Lake— somewhere, he knew not where; for a hundred hours of drifting and struggle through blinding, driving snow had concealed his course from him, and he knew not in what direction lay *behind*. It was as if he had just emerged from a nightmare. He was not even sure whether four days or a week had passed. He had slept with the dogs, fought across a forgotten number of shallow divides, followed the windings of weird canyons that ended in pockets, and twice had managed to make a fire and thaw out frozen moose-meat. And here he was, well fed and well camped. The storm had passed, and it had turned clear and cold. The lay of the land had again become rational. The creek he was on was natural in appearance, and trended, as it should, toward the southwest. But Surprise Lake was as lost to him as it had been to all its seekers in the past.

Half a day's journey down the creek brought him to the valley of a larger stream which he decided was the Mc-Questen. Here he shot a moose, and once again each wolf dog carried a full fifty-pound pack of meat. As he turned down the McQuesten, he came upon a sled trail. The late snows had drifted over, but underneath it was well packed by travel. His conclusion was that two camps had been established on the McQuesten, and that this was the connecting trail. Two Cabins was probably the lower camp, so he headed down the stream.

It was forty below zero when he camped that night, and he fell asleep wondering who were the men at Two Cabins and if he would reach it next day. At the first hint of dawn he was under way, easily following the half-obliterated trail and packing the recent snow with his webbed shoes so that the dogs would not wallow.

And then it came, the unexpected, leaping out upon him at a bend of the river. It seemed that he heard and felt simultaneously. The crack of the rifle came from the right, and the bullet, tearing through and across the shoulders of his parka and woolen coat, pivoted him half around with the shock of its impact. He staggered on his twisted snowshoes to recover balance, and heard a second crack of the rifle. This time it was a clean miss. He did not wait for more, but plunged across the snow for the sheltering trees of the bank a hundred feet away. Again and again the rifle cracked, and he was unpleasantly aware of a trickle of warm moisture down his back.

He climbed the bank, the dogs floundering behind, and dodged in among the trees and brush. Slipping out of his snowshoes and reaching for his own rifle, he wallowed forward at full length and peered cautiously out. Nothing was to be seen. Whoever had shot at him was lying quiet among the trees of the opposite bank.

"If something doesn't happen pretty soon," he muttered at the end of half an hour, "I'll have to sneak away and build a fire or freeze my feet."

He crawled back a few yards, packed down the snow, danced a jig that sent the blood back into his feet, and managed to endure another half-hour. Then, from down the river, he heard the unmistakable jingle of dogbells. Peering out, he saw a sled round the bend. Only one man was with it, straining at the gee pole and urging the dogs along. The effect on Smoke was one of shock, for it was the first human he had seen since he parted from Shorty three weeks before. His next thought was of the potential murderer concealed on the opposite bank.

Without exposing himself, Smoke whistled warningly. The man did not hear, and came on rapidly. Again, and more sharply, Smoke whistled. The man whoaed his dogs, stopped, and had turned and faced Smoke when the rifle cracked. The instant afterward, Smoke fired into the woods in the direction of the sound. The man on the river had been struck by the first shot. The shock of the high-velocity bullet staggered him. He stumbled awkwardly to the sled, half falling, and pulled a rifle out from under the lashings. As he strove to raise it to his shoulder, he crumpled at the waist and sank down slowly to a sitting posture on the sled. Then, abruptly as the gun went off aimlessly, he pitched backward and across a corner of the sled-load, so that Smoke could see only his legs and stomach.

From below came more jingling bells. The man did not move. Around the bend swung three sleds, accompanied by half a dozen men. Smoke cried warningly, but they had seen the condition of the first sled, and they dashed on to it. No shots came from the other bank, and Smoke, calling his dogs to follow, emerged into the open. There were exclamations from the men, and two of them, flinging off the mittens of their right hands, leveled their rifles at him.

"Come on, you red-handed murderer, you," one of them, a black-bearded man, commanded. "An' jest pitch that gun of yourn in the snow."

Smoke hesitated, then dropped his rifle and came up to them.

"Go through him, Louis," the black-bearded man ordered.

Louis was a French-Canadian voyageur, Smoke decided, as were four of the others. His search revealed only Smoke's hunting knife, which was appropriated.

"What have you got to say for yourself, stranger, before I shoot you dead?" the black-bearded man demanded.

"You're making a mistake if you think I killed that man," Smoke answered.

A cry came from one of the voyageurs. He had gone along the trail and found Smoke's tracks where he had left it to take refuge on the bank.

"What'd you kill Joe Kinade for?" Blackbeard asked.

"I tell you I didn't," Smoke began.

"What's the good of talkin'? We got you red-handed.
Right up there's where you left the trail when you heard
him comin'. You laid among the trees an' bushwhacked
him. A short shot. You couldn't 'a' missed. Pierre, give me
that gun he dropped."

"You might let me tell what happened," Smoke objected.

"Shut up," the man snarled at him. "I reckon your
gun'll tell the story."

All the men examined Smoke's rifle, ejecting and counting the cartridges, and examining the barrel at muzzle
and breech.

"One shot," Blackbeard concluded.

Pierre, with nostrils that quivered and distended like a
deer's, sniffed at the breech. "Fresh shot," he said.

"The bullet entered his back," Smoke said. "He was
facing me when he was shot. It came from the other bank."

Blackbeard considered this proposition for a second, and
shook his head. "Nope. It won't do. Turn him around
to face the other bank—that's how you whopped him
in the back. Some of you boys run up an' down the trail,
and see if you can see any tracks making for the other
bank."

Their report was that on that side the snow was unbroken. Blackbeard, bending over the dead man, straightened up with a wooly, furry wad in his hand. Shredding
this, he found imbedded in the center the bullet which
had perforated the body. Its nose was spread to the size
of a half-dollar, its butt end, steel jacketed, was undam-
aged. He compared it with a cartridge from Smoke's belt.

"That's plain enough evidence, stranger, to satisfy a
blind man. Soft nosed an' steel jacketed; yourn is soft

nosed and steel jacketed. Thirty-thirty; yourn is thirty-thirty. Manufactured by the J. & T. Arms Company; yourn is manufactured by the J. & T. Arms Company. Now you come along, an' we'll go over to the bank an' see jest how you done it."

"I was bushwhacked myself," Smoke said. "Look at the hole in my parka."

While Blackbeard examined it, one of the voyageurs threw open the breech of the dead man's gun. The empty cartridge was still in the chamber.

"A damn shame poor Joe didn't get you," Blackbeard said bitterly. "But he did pretty well with a hole like that in him. Come on, you."

"Search the other bank first," Smoke urged.

"Shut up an' come on; let the facts do the talkin'."

They left the trail at the same spot that he had, and followed it up along the bank and then in among the trees.

"Him dance that place keep him feet warm," Louis pointed out. "That place him crawl on belly. That place him put one elbow w'en him shoot."

"And there's the empty cartridge he done it with!" was Blackbeard's discovery. "Boys, there's only one thing to do."

"You might ask me why I came to fire that shot," Smoke interrupted.

"An' I might knock your teeth into your gullet if you butt in again. You can answer them questions later on. We're decent an' law-abidin', an' we got to handle this right an' regular. How far do you reckon we've come, Pierre?"

"Twenty mile, I t'ink, for sure."

"All right. We'll cache this outfit an' run him an' poor

Joe back to Two Cabins. I reckon we've seen an' can testify to what'll stretch his neck."

It was three hours after dark when the dead man, Smoke, and his captors arrived at Two Cabins. By the star-light Smoke could make out a dozen or more recently built cabins snuggling about a larger and older cabin on a flat by the river bank. Thrust inside this older cabin, he found it tenanted by a young giant of a man, his wife, and an old blind man. The old man, Smoke learned afterward, had been a trapper on the Stewart for years, and had finally gone blind the winter before. The new camp of Two Cabins, he was also to learn, had been made the previous fall by a dozen men who arrived in half as many poling-boats loaded with provisions. Here they had found the blind trapper, on the site of Two Cabins, and about his cabin they had built their own. Later arrivals, mushing up the ice with dog teams, had tripled the population. There was plenty of meat in camp, and good low-pay dirt had been discovered along the McQuesten and was being worked.

In five minutes, all the men of Two Cabins were jammed into the room. Smoke, shoved off into a corner, ignored and scowled at, his hands and feet tied with thongs of moosehide, looked on. Thirty-eight men he counted, a wild and husky crew, all frontiersmen of the States or voyageurs from upper Canada. His captors told the tale over and over, each the center of an excited and wrathful group. There were mutterings of: "Lynch him now! Why wait?" One big man was restrained only by force from rushing upon the helpless prisoner and giving him a beating.

It was while counting the men that Smoke caught sight

of a familiar face. It was Breck, the man whose boat Smoke had run through the rapids. He wondered why the other did not come and speak to him, but himself gave no sign of recognition. Later, when with shielded face Breck passed him a wink, Smoke understood.

Blackbeard, whom Smoke heard called Eli Harding, ended the discussion as to whether or not the prisoner should be immediately lynched. "Hold on!" he roared. "Keep your shirts on. That man belongs to me. I caught him an' I brought him here. D'ye think I brought him all the way here to be lynched? Not on your life. I could 'a' done that myself when I found him. I brought him here for a fair an' impartial trial, an' by God, a fair an' impartial trial he's goin' to get. He's tied up safe an' sound. Chuck him in a bunk till morning. We'll hold the trial right here."

Smoke woke up. A draft that possessed all the rigidity of an icicle was boring into the front of his shoulders as he lay on his side facing the wall. When he had been tied into the bunk there had been no such draft, and now the outside air, driving into the heated atmosphere of the cabin with the pressure of fifty below zero, was sufficient advertisement that some one outside had pulled away the moss-chinking between the logs. He squirmed as far as his bonds would permit, then craned his neck forward until his lips just managed to reach the crack.

"Who is it?" he whispered.

"Breck," came the almost inaudible answer. "Be careful you don't make a noise. I'm going to pass a knife in to you."

"No good," Smoke said. "I couldn't use it. My hands are tied behind me and made fast to the leg of the bunk. Besides, you couldn't get a knife through that crack. Something else must be done. Those fellows are of a temper to hang me, and I didn't kill that man."

"It wasn't necessary to mention it, Smoke. But I want to get you out of this. It's a tough bunch of men here. You've seen them. They're shut off from the world, and they make and enforce their own law—by miners' meeting, you know. They handled two men already—both grub-thieves. One they hiked from camp without an ounce of grub and no matches. He made about forty miles and lasted a couple of days before he froze stiff. Two weeks ago they hiked the second man. They gave him his choice: no grub, or ten lashes for each day's ration. He stood for forty lashes before he fainted. And now they've got you, and every last one is convinced you killed Kinade."

"The man who killed Kinade shot at me, too. His bullet broke the skin on my shoulder. Get them to delay the trial till some one goes up and searches the bank where the murderer hid."

"No use. They take the evidence of Harding and the five Frenchmen with him. Besides, they haven't had a hanging yet, and they're keen for it. Things have been pretty monotonous. They haven't located anything big, and they got tired of hunting for Surprise Lake. They did some stampeding the first part of the winter, but they've got over that now. They're just ripe for excitement."

"And it looks like I'll furnish it. Breck, how did *you* ever fall in with such a God-forsaken bunch?"

"I came up here by way of the Stewart, hunting for Two Cabins. They'd beaten me to it, so I've been higher up the Stewart. Just got back yesterday out of grub."

"Find anything?"

"Nothing much. But I think I've got a hydraulic proposition that'll work big when the country's opened up. It's that, or a gold-dredger."

"Hold on," Smoke interrupted. "Wait a minute. Let me think."

He pursued an idea that had flashed into his mind.

"Breck, have they opened up the meat-packs my dogs carried?" he asked.

"A couple. I was watching. They put them in Harding's cache."

"Did they find anything?"

"Meat."

"Good. You've got to get into the brown canvas pack that's patched with moosehide. You'll find a few pounds of lumpy gold. You've never seen gold like it in this country, nor has anybody else. Here's what you've got to do. Listen."

A quarter of an hour later, fully instructed, Breck went away. Smoke, his nose and one cheek frosted by proximity to the chink, rubbed them against the blankets for half an hour before the blaze and bite of the returning blood assured him of the safety of his flesh.

"My mind's made up right now. There ain't no doubt but what he killed Kinade. We heard the whole thing last night. What's the good of goin' over it again? I vote guilty."

In such fashion Smoke's trial began. The speaker, a loose-jointed, hard-rock miner from Colorado, manifested irritation and disgust when Harding set his suggestion aside, demanded the proceedings should be regular, and nominated one Shunk Wilson for judge and chairman of the meeting. The whole population of Two Cabins constituted the jury, though, after some discussion, the woman,

Lucy, was denied the right to vote on Smoke's guilt or innocence.

While this was going on, Smoke, jammed into a corner on a bunk, overheard a whispered conversation between Breck and a miner.

"You haven't fifty pounds of flour you'll sell?" Breck queried.

"You ain't got the dust to pay the price I'm askin'," was the reply.

"I'll give you two hundred."

The man shook his head.

"Three hundred. Three fifty."

At four hundred, the man nodded, and said, "Come on over to my cabin an' weigh out the dust."

The two squeezed their way to the door and slipped out. After a few minutes Breck returned alone.

Harding was testifying when Smoke saw the door shoved open slightly, and in the crack appear the face of the man who had sold the flour. He was grimacing and beckoning emphatically to some one inside, who arose from near the stove and started to work toward the door.

"Where are you goin', Sam?" Shunk Wilson demanded.

"I'll be back in a jiffy," Sam explained. "I jes' got to go."

Smoke was permitted to question the witnesses, and he was in the middle of the cross-examination of Harding when from without came the whining of dogs in harness and the grind and churn of sled-runners. Somebody near the door peeped out.

"It's Sam an' his pardner an' a dog team hell-bent down the trail for Stewart River," the man reported.

Nobody spoke for a long half-minute, but men glanced significantly at one another, and a general restlessness pervaded the packed room. Out of the corner of his eye, Smoke caught a glimpse of Breck, Lucy, and her husband whispering together.

"Come on, you," Shunk Wilson said gruffly to Smoke. "Cut this questionin' short. We knew what you're tryin' to prove—that the other bank wa'n't searched. The witness admits it. We admit it. It wa'n't necessary. No tracks led to that bank. The snow wa'n't broke."

"There was a man on the other bank just the same," Smoke insisted.

"That's too thin for skatin', young man. There ain't many of us on the McQuesten, an' we got every man accounted for."

"Who was the man you hiked out of camp two weeks ago?" Smoke asked.

"Alonzo Miramar. What's that grub-thief got to do with it?"

"Nothing, except that you haven't accounted for *him*, Mr. Judge."

"He went down river, not up."

"How do you know where he went?"

"Saw him start."

"And that's all you know of what became of him?"

"No, it ain't, young man. I know, we all know, he had four days' grub an' no gun to shoot meat with. If he didn't make Sixty-Mile on the Yukon he'd croaked long before this."

"I suppose you've got all the guns in this part of the country accounted for, too," Smoke observed pointedly.

Shunk Wilson was angry. "You'd think I was the prisoner the way you slam questions into me. Now then, come on with the next witness. Where's French Louis?"

While French Louis was shoving forward, Lucy opened the door.

"Where you goin'?" Shunk Wilson shouted.

"I reckon I don't have to stay," she answered defiantly. "I ain't got no vote, an' besides, this cabin of mine's so jammed up I can't breathe."

In a few minutes her husband followed. The closing of the door was the first warning the judge received of it.

"Who was that?" he interrupted Pierre's narrative to ask.

"Bill Peabody," somebody spoke up. "Said he wanted to ask his wife something and was coming right back."

Instead of Bill, it was Lucy who re-entered, took off her furs, and resumed her place by the stove.

"I reckon we don't need to hear the rest of the witnesses," was Shunk Wilson's decision, when Pierre had finished. "We know they can only testify to the same facts we've already heard. Say, Sorensen, you go an' bring Bill Peabody back. We'll be votin' a verdict pretty short. Now, stranger, you can get up an' say your say concernin' what happened. In the meantime, we'll just be savin' delay by passin' around the two rifles, the ammunition, an' the bullet that done the killin'."

Midway in his narrative, at the point where he described his own ambush and how he had fled to the bank, Smoke was interrupted by the indignant Shunk Wilson.

"Young man, what sense is there in you testifyin' that way? You're just takin' up valuable time. Of course you got the right to lie to save your neck, but we ain't goin' to stand for such foolishness. The rifle, the ammunition, an' the bullet that killed Joe Kinade is against you. What's that? Open the door, somebody!"

The frost rushed in, taking form and substance in the heat of the room, while through the open door came the whining of dogs that decreased rapidly with distance.

"It's Sorensen an' Peabody," some one cried, "a-throwin' the whip into the dawgs an' headin' down trail!"

"Now what the—?" Shunk Wilson paused with dropped jaw, and glared at Lucy. "I reckon you can explain, Mrs. Peabody."

She tossed her head and compressed her lips, and Shunk Wilson's wrathful and suspicious gaze passed and rested on Breck.

"An' I reckon that newcomer you've been chinning with could explain if *he* had a mind to."

Breck, now very uncomfortable, found all eyes centered on him.

"Sam was chewing the rag with him, too, before he lit out," some on said.

"Look here, Mr. Breck," Shunk Wilson continued. "You've been interruptin' proceedings, and you got to explain the meanin' of it. What was you chinnin' about?"

Breck cleared his throat timidly and replied, "I was just trying to buy some grub."

"What with?"

"Dust, of course."

"Where'd you get it?"

Breck did not answer.

"He's been snoopin' round up the Stewart," a man volunteered. "I run across his camp a week ago when I was huntin'. An' I want to tell you he was almighty secretious about it."

"The dust didn't come from there," Breck said. "That's only a low-grade hydraulic proposition."

"Bring your poke here an' let's see your dust," Wilson commanded.

"I tell you it didn't come from there."

"Let's see it, just the same."

Breck made as if to refuse, but all about him were menacing faces. Reluctantly, he fumbled in his coat pocket. In the act of drawing forth a pepper can, it rattled against what was evidently a hard object.

"Fetch it all out!" Shunk Wilson thundered.

And out came the big nugget, fist-size, yellow as no gold any onlooker had ever seen. Shunk Wilson gasped. Half a dozen, catching one glimpse, made a break for the door. They reached it at the same moment, and, with cursing and scuffling, jammed and pivoted through. The judge emptied the contents of the pepper can on the table, and the sight of the rough lump-gold sent half a dozen more toward the door.

"Where are you goin'?" Eli Harding asked, as Shunk started to follow.

"For my dogs, of course."

"Ain't you goin' to hang him?"

"It'd take too much time right now. He'll keep till we get back, so I reckon this court is adjourned. This ain't no place for lingerin'."

Harding hesitated. He glanced savagely at Smoke, saw Pierre beckoning to Louis from the doorway, took one last look at the lump-gold on the table, and decided.

"No use you tryin' to get away," he flung back over his shoulder. "Besides, I'm goin' to borrow your dogs."

"What is it?—another one of them blamed stampedes?"

the old blind trapper asked in a queer and petulant falsetto, as the cries of men and dogs and the grind of the sleds swept the silence of the room.

"It sure is," Lucy answered. "An' I never seen gold like it. Feel that, ole man."

She put the big nugget in his hand. He was but slightly interested.

"It was a good fur country," he complained, "before them danged miners come in an' scared back the game."

The door opened, and Breck entered. "Well," he said, "we four are all that are left in camp. It's forty miles to the Stewart by the cutoff I broke, and the fastest of them can't make the round trip in less than five or six days. But it's time you pulled out, Smoke, just the same."

Breck drew his hunting knife across the other's bonds, and glanced at the woman, "I hope you don't object?" he said, with significant politeness.

"Go on, don't mind me," Lucy answered. "If I ain't good enough to hang a man, I ain't good enough to hold him."

Smoke stood up, rubbing his wrists where the thongs had impeded the circulation.

"I've got a pack all ready for you," Breck said. "Ten days' grub, blankets, matches, tobacco, an ax, and a rifle."

"Go to it," Lucy encouraged. "Hit the high places, stranger. Beat it as fast as God'll let you."

"I'm going to have a square meal before I start," Smoke said. "And when I start it will be *up* the McQuesten, not down. I'm going to search that other bank for the man that really did the killing."

"If you'll listen to me, you'll head down for the Stewart

and the Yukon," Breck objected. "When this gang gets
back it'll be seeing red."

Smoke laughed and shook his head. "I can't jump this
country, Breck. I've got interests here. I've found Surprise
Lake. That's where that gold came from. Besides, they
took my dogs, and I've got to wait to get them back. Also,
I know what I'm about. There *was* a man hidden on that
bank."

Half an hour afterward, with a big plate of moose-steak
before him and a big mug of coffee at his lips, Smoke half
started up from his seat. He had heard the sounds first.
Lucy threw open the door.

"Hello, Spike; hello, Methody," she greeted the two
frost-rimed men who were bending over the burden on
their sled.

"We just come down from Upper Camp," one said, as
the pair staggered into the room with a fur-wrapped object which they handled with exceeding gentleness. "An'
this is what we found by the way. He's all in, I guess."

"Put him in the rear bunk there," Lucy said. She bent
over and pulled back the furs, disclosing a face composed
principally of large, staring, black eyes and of skin, dark
and scabbed by repeated frostbite, tightly stretched across
the bones.

"If it ain't Alonzo!" she cried. "You pore, starved
devil!"

"The man on the other bank," Smoke said in an undertone to Breck.

"We found him raidin' a cache that Harding must 'a' just
made," one of the men was explaining. "He was eatin'
raw flour an' frozen bacon, cryin' an' squealin' like a
hawg. Look at him! He's all starved, an' most of him
frozen. He'll cash in any moment."

Half an hour later, when the furs had finally been drawn over the face of the still form in the bunk, Smoke turned to Lucy. "If you don't mind, Mrs. Peabody, I'll have another whack at that steak. Make it thick and not so well done. I'm a real meat-eater."

CHAPTER 6

The Race for Number Three

HUH! Get onto the glad rags!"

Shorty surveyed his partner with simulated disapproval, and Smoke, vainly attempting to rub the wrinkles out of the pair of trousers he had just put on, was irritated.

"What's her name?"

"There isn't any her, my friend. I'm having dinner at Colonel Bowie's, if you want to know. You're envious because I'm going into high society and you're not invited."

"I reckon they won't be a man not in moccasins."

"But there are to be women, Shorty. I'm going to sit down and eat with real live women—Mrs. Bowie, and several others, so the colonel told me."

"Well, moccasins won't spoil their appetite none," was Shorty's comment. "Wonder what the colonel wants with you?"

"I don't know, unless he's heard about my finding Surprise Lake. It will take a fortune to drain it, and the Guggenheims are out for investment."

As became a high-salaried expert and the representative of the great investment house of M. Guggenheim and

Sons, Colonel Bowie lived in one of the most magnificent cabins in Dawson. And there Smoke finally met the social elect of Dawson—not the mere pick-handle millionaires, but the ultracream of a mining city whose population had been recruited from all the world—men like Warburton Jones, the explorer and writer; Captain Consadine, of the Northwest Mounted Police; Haskell, gold commissioner of the North-West Territory; and Baron Von Schroeder, an emperor's favorite with an international dueling reputation. And here, dazzling in evening gown, he met Joy Gastell, whom hitherto he had encountered only on trail, befurred and moccasined. At dinner he found himself beside her.

"I never dreamed such Oriental luxury existed in the Klondike," he confessed. "Look at Von Schroeder there. He's actually got a dinner jacket, and Consadine's got a starched shirt. I noticed he wore moccasins just the same. How do you like *my* outfit?" He moved his shoulders about, preening himself for Joy's approval.

"It looks as if you'd grown stout since you came over the Pass," she laughed.

"Wrong. Guess again."

"Somebody else's?"

"You win. I bought it from one of the clerks at the A. C. Company."

"It's a shame clerks are so narrow shouldered," she sympathized. "You haven't told me what you think of *my* outfit."

"I've been living on trail too long. I'd quite forgotten that women have arms and shoulders. Tomorrow morning, like my friend Shorty, I'll wake up and know it's all a dream. The last time I saw you on Squaw Creek—"

"I was just a squaw," she broke in.

"I hadn't intended to say that. I was remembering that it was on Squaw Creek that I discovered you had feet."

"And I can never forget that you saved them for me," she said. "I've been wanting to see you ever since, to thank you."

"You asked the colonel to invite me?"

"No; Mrs. Bowie. And here's my chance. Everybody's talking. Listen. You know Mono Creek?"

"Yes."

"It has turned out rich. They estimated the claims as worth a million and more apiece. It was located only the other day."

"I remember the stampede."

"Well, the whole creek was staked to the sky line, and all the feeders, too. And yet, right now, on the main creek, Number Three below *Discovery* is unrecorded. The creek was so far away from Dawson that the commissioner allowed sixty days for recording after location. Every claim was recorded except Number Three below. It was staked by Cyrus Johnson. And that was all. Johnson has disappeared, and in six days the time for recording will be up. Then the man who stakes it, and reaches Dawson first and records it, gets it."

"A million dollars," Smoke murmured.

"Gilchrist, who has the next claim below, has got six hundred dollars in a single pan of bedrock. He's burned one hole down. And the claim on the other side is even richer. I know."

"But why doesn't everybody know?" Smoke queried skeptically.

"They're beginning to know. It was kept secret a long time, and only now it's coming out. Good dog teams will be at a premium in another twenty-four hours. Now you've got to get away as decently as you can as soon as dinner is over."

"I—er—I fail to follow."

"You must get out tonight and hustle dog teams. I know of two. There's Hanson's team, seven big Hudson Bay dogs—he's holding them at four hundred each. That's top price tonight, but it won't be tomorrow. And Sitka Charley has eight Malemutes he's asking thirty-five hundred for. Tomorrow he'll laugh at an offer of five thousand. Then you've got your own team of dogs. And you'll have to buy several more teams. That's your work tonight. Get the best. Dogs as well as men will win this race. It's a hundred and ten miles, and you'll have to relay as frequently as you can."

"You want *me* to go for it?" Smoke drawled. "Aren't you afraid this is gambling?"

"It's a sporting proposition, if that's what you mean," she retorted. "A race for a million with some of the stiffest dog-mushers in the country entered against you. They haven't entered yet, but by this time tomorrow they will, and dogs will be worth whatever the richest man can afford to pay. Big Olaf is in town. He came up from Circle City last month. If he enters he will be your most dangerous competition. Arizona Bill is another. He's been a professional freighter and mail carrier for years."

"And you intend me to come along as a sort of dark horse?"

"Exactly. After all, you are still classed as a cheechako. You haven't seen the four seasons go around. Nobody will take notice of you until you come into the home stretch in the lead. Remember, I shall never forgive myself for the trick I played on you in the Squaw Creek stampede unless you win this Mono claim. And if any man can win this race against the old-timers, it's you."

"Who?" Captain Consadine broke in from across the table.

"Big Olaf," she answered. "I was just telling Mr. Bellew what a traveler he is."

"You're right," the captain's voice boomed. "Big Olaf is the greatest traveler in the Yukon. I'd back him against Old Nick himself for snow bucking and ice travel. He brought in the government despatches in 1895, and he did it after two couriers were frozen on Chilkoot and the third drowned in the open water of Thirty-Mile."

Smoke traveled in a leisurely fashion up to Mono Creek, fearing to tire his dogs before the big race. He had familiarized himself with every mile of the trail and located his delay camps. So many men had entered the race that the hundred and ten miles of its course were almost a continuous village. Relay camps were everywhere along the trail. Von Schroeder, who had gone in purely for sport, had no less than eleven dog teams—a fresh one every ten miles. Arizona Bill had been forced to content himself with eight teams. Big Olaf had seven, the same as Smoke. Over two score of men were in the running. Not every day, even in the golden north, was a million dollars the prize for a dog race. The country had been swept of dogs, and their prices had doubled and quadrupled in the course of the frantic speculation.

Number Three below *Discovery* was ten miles up Mono Creek from its mouth. The remaining hundred miles was to be run on the frozen breast of the Yukon. On Number Three itself were fifty tents and over three hundred dogs.

The old stakes, blazed and scrawled sixty days before by Cyrus Johnson, still stood, and every man had gone over the boundaries of the claim again and again, for the race with the dogs was to be preceded by a foot and obstacle race. Each man had to relocate the claim for himself, and this meant that he must place two center-stakes and four corner-stakes and cross the creek twice, before he could start for Dawson with his dogs.

Furthermore, there were to be no "sooners." Not until the stroke of midnight of Friday night was the claim open for relocation, and not until the stroke of midnight could a man plant a stake. This was the ruling of the Gold Commissioner at Dawson, and Captain Consadine sent up a squad of mounted police to enforce it. Discussion had arisen about the difference between sun time and police time, but Consadine had announced that police time went, and, further, that it was the watch of Lieutenant Pollock that went.

The Mono trail ran along the level creek bed, and, less than two feet in width, was like a groove, walled on either side by the snowfall of months. The problem was how forty-odd sleds and three hundred dogs were to start in so narrow a course.

"Huh!" said Shorty. "It's goin' to be the gosh-dangdest mix-up that ever was. I can't see no way out, Smoke, except main strength an' sweat an' to plow through. If the whole creek was glare-ice they ain't room for a dozen teams abreast. I got a hunch right now they's goin' to be a heap of scrappin' before they get strung out. An' if any of it comes our way, you got to let me do the punchin'."

Smoke squared his shoulders and laughed noncommittally.

"No, you don't!" his partner cried. "No matter what happens, you don't dast hit. You can't handle dogs a hundred miles with a busted knuckle."

Smoke slowly nodded his head. "You're right, Shorty. I couldn't risk it."

"An' just remember," Shorty went on, "that I got to do all the shovin' for them first ten miles, an' you got to take it easy as you can. I'll jerk you through to the Yukon. After that it's up to you an' the dogs. Schroeder's got his first team a quarter of a mile down the creek, an' he'll know it by a green lantern. We'll use a red flare."

The day had been clear and cold, but a blanket of cloud formed across the face of the sky, and the night came on warm and dark, with the hint of snow impending. The thermometer registered fifteen below zero, and in the Klondike winter fifteen below is esteemed very warm.

A few minutes before midnight, leaving Shorty with the dogs five hundred yards down the creek, Smoke joined the racers on Number Three. There were forty-five of them waiting the start for the million dollars Cyrus Johnson had left lying in the frozen gravel. Each man carried six stakes and a heavy wooden mallet.

Lieutenant Pollock, in a big bearskin coat, looked at his watch by the light of a fire. It lacked a minute of midnight. "Ready," he said, as he raised a revolver in his right hand and watched the second-hand tick around.

Forty-five hoods were thrown back from parkas, forty-five pairs of hands were unmittened, and forty-five pairs of moccasins pressed tensely into the packed snow. Also, forty-five stakes were thrust into the snow, and the same number of mallets lifted in the air.

The shot rang out. Cyrus Johnson's right to his million had expired, and the mallets fell.

Smoke drove in his stake and was away with the leading dozen. Fires had been lighted at the corners, and by each fire stood a policeman, list in hand, checking off the names of the runners. A man had to call out his name and show his face. There was to be no staking by proxy while the real racer was off and away down the creek.

At the first corner, beside Smoke's stake, Von Schroeder placed his. The mallets struck at the same instant. As they hammered, more arrived from behind, jostling and shoving. Squirming through the press and calling his name to the policeman, Smoke saw the Baron, struck by one of the rushers, hurled clean off his feet into the snow. But Smoke did not wait. Others were still ahead of him. By the light of the vanishing fire, he saw the huge, looming back of Big Olaf, and at the southwestern corner Big Olaf and he drove their stakes side by side.

It was no light work, this preliminary obstacle race. The boundaries of the claim totaled nearly a mile, and most of it was over the uneven surface of a snow-covered flat. All about Smoke men tripped and fell, and several times he pitched forward himself, jarringly, on hands and knees. Once, Big Olaf fell so immediately in front of him as to bring him down on top.

The upper center-stake was driven by the edge of the bank, and down the bank the racers plunged, across the frozen creek bed, and up the other side. Here, as Smoke clambered, a hand gripped his ankle and jerked him back. In the flickering light of a distant fire, it was impossible to see who had played the trick. But Arizona Bill, who had been treated similarly, rose to his feet and drove his fist with a crunch into the offender's face. Smoke saw and heard as he was scrambling to his feet, but before he could make another lunge for the bank a fist dropped him half stunned

into the snow. He staggered up, located the man, half
swung a hook to his jaw, then remembered Shorty's warning and refrained. The next moment, struck below the
knees by a hurtling body, he went down again.

It was a foretaste of what would happen when the men
reached their sleds. They swarmed up the bank in
bunches, and in bunches were dragged back by their impatient fellows. More blows were struck and curses rose
from the panting chests of those who still had wind to
spare. Overthrown, trod upon, groping in the snow for
his lost stakes, Smoke at last crawled out of the crush and
attacked the bank farther along. Others were doing this,
and it was his luck to have many men in advance of him
in the race for the northwestern corner.

Reaching the fourth corner, he tripped headlong, and
in the sprawling fall lost his remaining stake. For five
minutes he groped in the darkness before he found it. All
the time the panting runners were passing him, but from
the last corner to the creek he began overtaking men for
whom the mile run had been too much. In the creek itself bedlam had broken loose. A dozen sleds were piled up
and overturned, and nearly a hundred dogs were locked
in combat. Among them men struggled, tearing the tangled animals apart, or beating them apart with clubs.

Leaping down the bank beyond the glutted passage, he
gained the hard footing of the sled trail and made better
time. Here, in packed harbors beside the narrow trail,
sleds and men waited for runners that were still behind.
From the rear came the whine and rush of dogs, and
Smoke had barely time to leap aside into the deep snow.
A sled tore past, and he made out a man kneeling and
shouting madly. Scarcely was it by when it stopped with
a crash of battle. The excited dogs of a harbored sled, re-

senting the passing animals, had got out of hand and sprung upon them.

Smoke plunged around and by. He could see the green lantern of Von Schroeder and, just below it, the red flare that marked his own team. Two men with short clubs were guarding Von Schroeder's dogs, interposed between them and the trail.

"Come on, Smoke! Come on, Smoke!" he could hear Shorty calling anxiously.

"Coming!" he gasped.

By the red flare, he could see the snow torn up and trampled, and from the way his partner breathed he knew a battle had been fought. He staggered to the sled, and, in the moment he was falling on it, Shorty's whip snapped as he yelled:

"Mush! you devils! Mush!"

The dogs sprang into the breastbands, and the sled jerked abruptly ahead. They were big animals—Hanson's prize team of Hudson Bays—and Smoke had selected them for the first stage, which included the ten miles of Mono Creek, the heavy going of the cutoff across the flat at the mouth, and the first ten miles of the Yukon stretch.

"How many ahead?" he asked.

"Shut up an' save your wind," Shorty answered. "Hi! you brutes! Hit her up! Hit her up!"

He was running behind the sled, holding onto a short rope. Smoke could not see him; nor could he see the sled on which he lay full length. The fires had been left in the rear, and they were tearing through a wall of blackness as fast as the dogs could spring into it.

Smoke felt the sled heel up on one runner as it rounded an invisible curve, and from ahead came the snarls of beasts and the oaths of men. Into the jam, at full speed, piled Smoke's seven big fighters. Scarcely more than semi-domesticated wolves, the excitement of that night on Mono Creek had sent every dog fighting mad. The Klondike dogs, driven without reins, could not be stopped except by voice, so there was no stopping this glut of struggle that heaped itself between the narrow rims of the creek. From behind, sled after sled hurled into the turmoil. Men who had their teams nearly extricated were overwhelmed by fresh avalanches of dogs—each animal well fed, well rested, and ripe for battle.

"It's knock down an' drag out an' plow through!" Shorty yelled in his partner's ear. "Watch out for your knuckles! You drag dogs out an' let me do the punchin'!"

What happened in the next half-hour Smoke never distinctly remembered. At the end he emerged exhausted, sobbing for breath, his jaw sore from a fist blow, his shoulder aching from the bruise of a club, the blood running warmly down one leg from a rip of a dog's fangs, and both sleeves of his parka torn to shreds. As in a dream, while the battle still raged behind, he helped Shorty reharness the dogs. One, dying, they cut from the traces, and in the darkness felt their way to the repair of the disrupted harness.

"Now lie down an' get your wind back," Shorty commanded.

Through the darkness the dogs sped with unabated strength, down Mono Creek, across the long cutoff, and to the Yukon. Here, at the junction with the main river-trail, somebody had lit a fire, and here Shorty said good-by. By the light of the fire, as the sled leaped behind the flying dogs, Shorty, swaying and sinking down limply in the snow, yelled his parting encouragement, one eye blackened and closed, knuckles bruised and broken, and one arm, ripped and fang-torn, gushing forth a steady stream of blood.

"How many ahead?" Smoke asked, as he dropped his tired Hudson Bays and sprang upon the waiting sled at his first relay station.

"Counted eleven," the man called after him, for he was already away, behind the leaping dogs.

Fifteen miles on the next stage would carry him to the mouth of White River. The twenty-five miles between White River and Sixty-Mile he had broken into two stages because of ice jams, and here two of his heaviest, toughest teams were stationed.

Smoke lay on the sled at full length, face down, holding on with both hands. Whenever the dogs slacked from topmost speed he rose to his knees, and, yelling and urging, clinging precariously with one hand, threw his whip into them. Weakest team that it was, he passed two sleds before White River was reached. Here, at the freeze-up, a jam had piled a barrier, allowing the open water that formed for half a mile below to freeze smoothly. This smooth stretch enabled the racers to make flying exchanges of sleds.

Over the jam and out onto the smooth ice, Smoke tore along, calling loudly, "Billy! Billy!"

Billy heard and answered, and by the light of the many fires on the ice, Smoke saw a sled swing in from the side and come abreast. Its fresh dogs overhauled his. As the sleds swerved toward each other he leaped across, and Billy promptly rolled off.

"Where's Big Olaf?" Smoke cried.

"Leading!" Billy's voice answered; and again the fires were left behind, and Smoke was flying through the wall of blackness.

In the jams of that relay, where the way led across a chaos of up-ended ice cakes, and where Smoke slipped off the forward end of the sled and with a haul-rope toiled behind the wheel-dog, he passed three sleds. Accidents had happened, and he could hear the men cutting out dogs and mending harnesses.

Among the jams of the next short relay into Sixty-Mile, he passed two more teams. And that he might know what had happened to them, one of his own dogs wrenched a shoulder, was unable to keep up, and was dragged in the harness. Its teammates, angered, fell upon it with their fangs, and Smoke was forced to club them off with the heavy butt of his whip. As he cut the injured animal out, he heard the whinning cries of dogs behind him and a familiar voice. It was Von Schroeder. Smoke called a warning, and the baron, hawing his animals and swinging on the gee pole, went by a dozen feet to the side. Yet so impenetrable was the blackness that Smoke heard but did not see him pass.

On the smooth stretch of ice beside the trading post at Sixty-Mile, Smoke overtook two more sleds. All had just changed teams, and for five minutes they ran abreast, each man on his knees, pouring whip and voice into the maddened dogs. But Smoke had studied that portion of the trail, and now spotted the tall pine on the bank that showed faintly in the light of many fires. Below that pine was not merely darkness, but an abrupt cessation of the smooth stretch. There the trail, he had noted beforehand, narrowed to single sled-width. Leaning out, he caught the haul-rope and drew his leaping sled up to his wheel-dog. He caught the animal by the hind legs and threw it. With a snarl of rage it tried to slash him with its fangs, but was dragged on by the rest of the team. Its body proved an efficient brake, and the two other teams, still abreast, dashed ahead into the darkness.

Smoke heard the crash and uproar of their collision, released his wheeler, sprang to the gee pole, and urged his team to the right into the soft snow where the straining animals wallowed to their necks. It was exhausting work, but he passed the tangled teams and regained the hard-packed trail beyond.

On the relay out of Sixty-Mile, Smoke had next to his poorest team, and though the going was good, he had set it a short fifteen miles. Two more teams would bring him into Dawson and to the gold recorder's office, and Smoke had selected his best animals for the last two stretches. Sitka Charley himself waited with the eight Malemutes that would jerk Smoke along for twenty miles, and for the finish, with a fifteen-mile run, was his own team—the team he had had all winter and which had been with him in the search for Surprise Lake.

The two men he had left entangled at Sixty-Mile failed to pass him, but on the other hand, his own sled failed to overtake any of the three that still led. His animals were willing, though they lacked stamina and speed, and little urging was needed to keep them going at their best. There was nothing for Smoke to do but to lie face downward and hold on. Now and again he would plunge out of the darkness into the circle of light about a blazing fire, catch a glimpse of furred men standing by harnessed and waiting dogs, and plunge into the darkness again. Mile after mile, with only the grind and jar of the runners in his ears, he sped on. Almost automatically he kept his place as the sled bumped ahead or half lifted and heeled on the swings and swerves of the bends.

The gray twilight of the morning was breaking as he

exchanged his weary dogs for Sitka Charley's eight fresh
Malemutes. Lighter animals than the Hudson Bays, they
were capable of greater speed, and ran with the supple
tirelessness of true wolves. Sitka Charley called out the
order of the teams ahead. Big Olaf led, Arizona Bill was
second, and Von Schroeder third—the three best men in
the country.

As daylight strengthened, Smoke caught sight of a sled
ahead. In half an hour, his own lead-dog was leaping at
its tail. Not until the man turned his head did Smoke recognize Arizona Bill. Von Schroeder had evidently passed
him. The trail, hard-packed, ran too narrowly through
the soft snow, and for another half-hour Smoke was forced
to stay in the rear. Then they topped an ice jam and struck
a wide smooth stretch. On his knees, swinging his whip
and yelling, Smoke drew abreast of Arizona Bill; then
pulled ahead.

Bill dropped behind very slowly, but when the last relay
station was in sight he was fully half a mile in the rear.
Ahead, bunched together, Smoke could now see Big Olaf
and Von Schroeder. Smoke rose to his knees and lifted his
jaded dogs into a burst of speed. He drew up close to the
tail of Von Schroeder's sled, and the three sleds dashed out
on the smooth going below a jam, where many men and
dogs waited. Dawson was fifteen miles away.

Von Schroeder, with his ten-mile relays, had changed
five miles back and would change five miles ahead. So he
held on, keeping his dogs at full leap. Big Olaf and Smoke
made flying changes, and their fresh teams immediately
regained what had been lost to the Baron. Big Olaf led
the way past him, and Smoke followed into the narrow
trail beyond.

Of Von Schroeder, now behind, he had no fear; but

ahead was the greatest dog-driver in the country. To pass
him seemed impossible. Again and again, Smoke forced
his leader to the other's sled-tail, and each time Big Olaf
drew away. Smoke contented himself with taking the
pace, and hung on grimly. The race was not lost until one
or the other won, and in fifteen miles many things could
happen.

Three miles from Dawson something *did* happen. To
Smoke's surprise, Big Olaf rose up and with oaths and
leather proceeded to fetch out the last ounce of effort in
his animals It was a spurt that should have been reserved
for the last hundred yards instead of three miles from the
finish. Sheer dog-killing that it was, Smoke followed. His
own team was superb. No dogs on the Yukon had had
harder work or were in better condition.

They topped a small jam and struck the smooth going
below. Big Olaf was barely fifty feet ahead. Then a sled
shot out from the side and drew in toward him, and Smoke
understood Big Olaf's terrific spurt. He had tried to gain
a lead for the change. This fresh team that waited to jerk
him down the homestretch had been a private surprise.

Smoke strove desperately to pass during the exchange
of sleds. Lifting his dogs to the effort, he ate up the intervening fifty feet. With urging and pouring of leather, he
went to the side and on until his head-dog was jumping
abreast of Big Olaf's wheeler. On the other side, abreast,
was the relay sled. At the speed they were going, Big Olaf
did not dare try the flying leap. If he missed and fell off,
Smoke would be in the lead, and the race would be lost.

Big Olaf tried to spurt ahead, and lifted his dogs magnificently, but Smoke's leader still continued to jump beside Big Olaf's wheeler. For half a mile the three sleds tore
and bounced along side by side. The smooth stretch was

nearing its end when Big Olaf took the chance. As the flying sleds swerved toward each other, he leaped, and the instant he struck, was on his knees, with whip and voice spurting the fresh team. The smooth stretch pinched out into the narrow trail, and he jumped his dogs ahead and into it with a lead of barely a yard.

A man was not beaten until he was beaten, and Big Olaf failed to shake Smoke off. No team Smoke had driven that night could have stood such a killing pace and kept up with fresh dogs—no team save this one. Nevertheless, the pace *was* killing it, and as they began to round the bluff at Klondike City, he could feel the pitch of strength going out of his animals. Almost imperceptibly they lagged behind, and foot by foot Big Olaf drew away until he led by a score of yards.

A great cheer went up from the population of Klondike City assembled on the ice. Here the Klondike entered the Yukon, and half a mile away, across the Klondike, stood Dawson. An outburst of madder cheering arose, and Smoke suddenly caught a glimpse of a sled shooting out to him. He recognized the splendid animals that drew it. They were Joy Gastell's, and Joy drove them. The hood of her squirrel-skin parka was tossed back. Mittens discarded, with bare hands she clung to whip and sled.

"Jump!" she cried, as her leader snarled at Smoke's.

Smoke struck the sled behind her. It rocked violently from the impact of his body, but she was full up on her knees and swinging the whip.

"Hi! You! Mush on! Chook! Chook!" and the dogs whined and yelped in eagerness to overtake Big Olaf.

And then, as the lead-dog caught the tail of Big Olaf's sled, and yard by yard drew up abreast, the great crowd on the Dawson bank went mad. It *was* a great crowd, for the men had dropped their tools on all the creeks and come down to see the outcome of the race, and a dead heat at the end of a hundred and ten miles justified any madness.

"I'm going to drop off!" Joy cried out over her shoulder. Smoke tried to protest.

"Watch out for the dip curve halfway up the bank," she warned.

Dog by dog, separated by half a dozen feet, the two teams were running abreast. Big Olaf, with whip and voice, held his own for a minute. Then, slowly, an inch at a time, Joy's leader began to forge past.

"Get ready!" she cried to Smoke. "I'm going to leave you in a minute. Get the whip."

And as he shifted his hand to clutch the whip, they heard Big Olaf roar a warning, but too late. His lead dog, incensed at being passed, swerved in to the attack. His fangs struck Joy's leader on the flank. The rival teams flew at one another's throats. The sleds overran the fighting brutes and capsized. Smoke struggled to his feet and tried to lift Joy up. But she thrust him from her, crying,

"Go!"

On foot, already fifty feet in advance, was Big Olaf, still intent on finishing the race. Smoke obeyed, and when the two men reached the foot of the Dawson bank, he was at the other's heels.

Five blocks down the main street was the gold recorder's office. The street was packed as for a parade. Not easily did Smoke gain to his giant rival, and when he did he was unable to pass. Side by side they ran along the narrow aisle between the solid walls of cheering men. Now one, now the other, with great convulsive jerks, gained an inch or so, only to lose it immediately after.

If the pace had been a killing one for their dogs, the

one they now set themselves was no less so. But they were racing for a million dollars. The only impression that came to Smoke on that last mad stretch was one of astonishment that there should be so many people in the Klondike. He had never seen them all at once before.

He felt himself involuntarily lag, and Big Olaf sprang a full stride in the lead. To Smoke it seemed that his heart would burst, while he had lost all consciousness of his legs. He knew they were flying under him, but he did not know how he continued to make them fly, nor how he put even greater pressure upon them and compelled them again to carry him to his giant competitor's side.

The open door of the recorder's office appeared ahead of them. Both men made a final, futile spurt. Neither could draw away from the other, and side by side they hit the doorway, collided violently, and fell in headlong on the office floor.

They sat up, too exhausted to rise. Big Olaf, sweat pouring from him, breathing with tremendous, painful gasps, pawed the air and vainly tried to speak. Then he reached out his hand with unmistakable meaning; Smoke extended his, and they shook.

"It's a dead heat," Smoke could hear the recorder saying, but it was in a dream, and the voice was very thin and very far away. "All I can say is that you both win. You'll have to divide the claim between you. You're partners."

Their two arms pumped up and down as they ratified the decision. Big Olaf nodded his head with great emphasis, and spluttered. At last he got it out.

"You damn cheechako," was what he said, but in the saying of it was admiration. "I don't know how you done it, but you did."

Outside, the great crowd was noisily massed, while the office was jamming. Smoke and Big Olaf essayed to rise, and each helped the other to his feet. Smoke found his legs weak under him, and staggered drunkenly. Big Olaf tottered toward him.

"Say. That girl—one damn fine girl, eh?"

"One damn fine girl," Smoke agreed.

CHAPTER 7

The Little Man

I WISHT you wasn't so set," Shorty protested. "I'm sure scairt of that big glacier. No man ought to tackle it by his lonely."

Smoke laughed cheerfully, and ran his eye up the head of the valley. "Here it is August already, and the days have been getting shorter for two months. You know quartz, and I don't. But I can bring up the grub, while you keep after that mother lode. So long. I'll be back by tomorrow evening."

He turned and started.

"I got a hunch something's goin' to happen," Shorty pleaded after him.

But Smoke's reply was another laugh. He held on down the little valley, occasionally wiping the sweat from his forehead, while his feet crushed through ripe mountain raspberries and delicate ferns that grew beside patches of sun-sheltered ice.

In the early spring he and Shorty had again come up the Stewart River and launched out into the amazing chaos of the region where Surprise Lake lay. All spring and half the summer had been consumed in futile wanderings, when, on the verge of turning back, they finally caught a glimpse of the baffling, gold-bottomed sheet of water which had lured and fooled a generation of miners. Making camp in the old cabin Smoke had discovered on his previous visit, they learned three things: first, heavy nugget gold was carpeted thickly on the lake bottom; next, the gold could be dived for in the shallower portions, but the temperature of the water was man-killing; and, finally, the draining of the lake was too stupendous a task for two men in the shorter half of a short summer. Undeterred, reasoning from the coarseness of the gold that it had not traveled far, they set out in search of the mother lode. They had crossed the big glacier that frowned on the southern rim and devoted themselves to the puzzling maze of small valleys and canyons beyond, which drained, or had at one time drained, into the lake.

The valley Smoke was now descending gradually widened after the fashion of any normal valley; but, at the lower end, it pinched narrowly between high precipitous walls and abruptly stopped in a cross wall. At the base of this, in a welter of broken rock, the streamlet disappeared, evidently finding its way out underground. Climbing the cross wall, Smoke saw the lake beneath him. Unlike any mountain lake he had ever seen, it was not blue. Instead, its intense peacock-green tokened its shallowness. It was this shallowness that made its draining feasible. All about rose jumbled mountains, with ice-scarred peaks and crags, grotesquely shaped and grouped. All was topsy-turvy and unsystematic—a geologic nightmare. It was more like a cosmic landscape-joke than a rational portion of earth's surface. There were many glaciers in the canyons, most of them tiny, and, as he looked, one of the larger ones, on the north shore, caved amid thunders and splashings. Across the lake, seemingly not more than half a mile, but, as he well knew, five miles away, he could see the bunch

of spruce trees and the cabin. He looked again to make
sure, and saw smoke clearly rising from the chimney.
Somebody else had surprised themselves into finding Surprise Lake.

From the top of the southern wall, Smoke came down
into a little valley, flower-floored and lazy with the hum
of bees, that behaved quite as a reasonable valley should,
in so far as it made legitimate entry on the lake. What
was wrong with it was its length—scarcely a hundred
yards; its head a straight up-and-down cliff of a thousand
feet, over which a stream pitched itself in descending veils
of mist.

And here he encountered still more smoke, floating
lazily upward in the warm sunshine beyond an outjut of
rock. As he came around the corner he heard a light, metallic tap-tapping and a merry whistling that kept the
beat. Then he saw the little man, an upturned shoe between his knees, into the sole of which he was driving
hob-spikes.

"Hello!" was the stranger's greeting. "Just in time for
a snack. There's coffee in the pot, a couple of cold flapjacks, and some jerky."

"It's a deal," said Smoke, and sat down. "I've been
rather skimped on the last several meals, but there's lots
of grub over in the cabin."

"Across the lake? That's where I was heading."

"Seems Surprise Lake is becoming populous," Smoke
complained, emptying the coffeepot.

"Surprise Lake! You're joking, aren't you?" Astonishment was painted on the man's face.

Smoke laughed. "That's the way it takes everybody.
You see those high ledges across there to the northwest?

There's where I first saw it. No warning. Just suddenly caught the view of the whole lake. I'd given up looking, too."

"Same here," the other agreed. "I'd headed back and was expecting to reach the Stewart last night, when out I popped in sight of the lake. If this is Surprise Lake, where's the Stewart? And where have I been all the time? And how did you come here? And what's your name?"

"Bellew. Kit Bellew."

"Oh! I know you." The man's eyes and face were bright, and his hand flashed eagerly out to Smoke's. "I might have recognized you if you'd been shaved. I watched you bucking roulette in the Elkhorn. My name's Carson—Andy Carson; I'm glad to meet up with you."

He was a slender man, wiry with health, with quick black eyes.

"So this is Surprise Lake?" he murmured incredulously.

"It certainly is."

"And the bottom's buttered with gold?"

"Sure. There's some of the churning." Smoke dipped in his pockets and brought forth half a dozen nuggets. "That's the stuff. All you have to do is go down to bottom, blindfolded if you want to, and pick up a handful. Then run half a mile to get up your circulation."

"Well, you've beaten me to it," Carson swore whimsically, but his disappointment was obvious. "Anyway, I've had the fun of getting here."

"Fun!" Smoke cried. "Why, if we can ever get our hands on that bottom, we'll make Rockefeller look like thirty cents."

"But it's yours," was Carson's objection.

"Nothing to it, my friend. You've got to realize that no

gold deposit like it has been discovered in all the history of mining. It will take you and me and my partner and all the friends we've got to lay our hands on it. All of Bonanza and Eldorado Creeks dumped together wouldn't be richer than half an acre down here. The only problem is to drain the lake. It will take a year or two, with all the money we can raise, but it can be done. Are you in?"

"Am I in? I feel so much like a millionaire that I'm real timid about crossing that big glacier. Couldn't afford to break my neck now. Wish I had some more of those hobspikes. I was just hammering the last in when you came along. How's yours? Let's see."

Smoke held up his foot.

"Worn smooth as a skating rink!" Carson cried. "You've certainly been hiking some. Wait a minute, and I'll pull some of mine out for you."

Smoke refused to listen. "I've got about forty feet of rope cached where we take the ice. My partner and I used it coming over. It will be a cinch."

It was a hard, hot climb. The sun blazed dazzlingly on the ice surface, and with streaming pores they panted from the exertion. There were places, crisscrossed by countless fissures and crevasses, where an hour of dangerous toil advanced them no more than a hundred yards. At two in the afternoon, beside a pool of water bedded in the ice, Smoke called a halt.

"Let's tackle some of that jerky," he said. "I've been on short feed, and my knees are shaking. Besides, we're across the worst. Three hundred yards will bring us to the rocks, and then it's easy going, except for a couple of nasty fissures and one bad one that heads us down toward the bulge. There's a weak ice-bridge there, but Shorty and I managed it."

"I'm lighter than you by forty pounds," Carson said half an hour later, after they had eaten. "Let me go first."

They stood on the edge of the crevasse. It was enormous and ancient, fully a hundred feet across, with sloping, age-eaten sides instead of sharp-angled rims. At this one place it was bridged by a huge mass of pressure-hardened snow, itself half ice. Even the bottom of this mass they could not see, much less the bottom of the crevasse. Crumbling and melting, the bridge threatened imminent collapse. There were signs where recent portions had broken away, and even as they studied it a mass of half a ton dislodged and fell.

"Looks pretty bad," Carson admitted with an ominous head-shake. "And it looks much worse than if I wasn't a millionaire."

"We've got to tackle it," Smoke said. "We're almost across. We can't camp here on the ice all night. And there's no other way. Shorty and I explored for a mile up. It was in better shape, though, when we crossed."

"It's one at a time, and me first." Carson took the coil of rope from Smoke's hand. "You'll have to cast off. I'll take the rope and the pick. Gimme your hand so I can slip down easy."

Slowly and carefully he lowered himself the several feet to the bridge, where he stood, making final adjustments for the perilous traverse. On his back was his pack outfit. Around his neck, resting on his shoulders, he coiled the rope, one end of which was still fast to his waist.

"I'd give a mighty good part of my millions right now for a bridge construction gang," he said, but his cheery, whimsical smile belied the words. "It's all right; I'm a cat."

The pick, and the long stick he used as an alpenstock,

he balanced horizontally like a ropewalker. He thrust one foot forward tentatively, drew it back, and steeled himself with visible physical effort.

"I wish I was flat broke," he smiled up. "If ever I get out of being a millionaire this time, I'll never be one again. It's too uncomfortable."

"It's all right," Smoke encouraged. "I've been over it before. Better let me try it first."

"And you forty pounds to the worse," the little man flashed back. "I'm all right. Well, here goes," and his foot went out, this time to rest carefully and lightly while the other foot was brought up and past. Very gently and circumspectly he continued on his way until two-thirds of the distance was covered. Here he stopped to examine a depression he must cross, at the bottom of which was a fresh crack. Smoke, watching, saw him glance to the side and down into the crevasse itself, and then begin a slight swaying.

"Keep your eyes up!" Smoke commanded sharply. "Now! Go on!"

The little man obeyed, nor faltered on the rest of the journey. The sun-eroded slope of the farther edge of the crevasse was slippery, but not steep, and he worked his way up to a narrow ledge, faced about, and sat down.

"Your turn," he called across. "Just keep a-coming and don't look down. That's what got me. Just keep a-coming, that's all. And get a move on. It's mighty rotten."

Balancing his own stick horizontally, Smoke began his passage. The bridge was on its last legs. He felt a jar under foot, a slight movement of the mass, and then a heavier jar, followed by a single sharp crackle. Behind him something was happening. If for no other reason, he knew it by the strained, tense face of Carson. From beneath, thin

and faint, came the murmur of running water, and
Smoke's eyes involuntarily wavered to a glimpse of the
shimmering depths. He jerked them right back. Two-
thirds over, he came to the depression. The sharp edges
of the crack, slightly touched by the sun, showed how recent it was. His foot was lifted to make the step across,
when the crack began slowly widening, at the same time
emitting numerous sharp snaps. He made the step quickly,
increasing his stride, but the worn nails of his shoe skated
on the farther slope of the depression. He fell on his face,
and without pause slipped down and into the crack, his
legs hanging clear, his chest supported by the stick which
he had managed to twist crosswise as he fell.

His first sensation was nausea caused by the sickening
up-leap of his pulse; his first idea was of surprise that he
had fallen no farther. Behind him was crackling and jar
and movement to which the stick vibrated. From beneath,
in the heart of the glacier, came the soft and hollow thunder of dislodged masses striking bottom. And still the
bridge, broken from its farthest support and ruptured in
the middle, held, though the portion he had crossed tilted
downward at a pitch of twenty degrees. He could see
Carson, perched on his ledge, his feet braced against the
melting surface, swiftly recoiling the rope from his shoulders to his hand.

"Wait!" he cried. "Don't move, or the whole shooting-
match will come down."

He calculated the distance with a quick glance, took
the bandana from his neck and tied it to the rope, and increased the length by a second bandana from his pocket.
The rope, manufactured from sled-lashings and short
lengths of plaited rawhide knotted together, was both light
and strong. The first cast was lucky as well as deft, and

Smoke's fingers clutched it. He evidenced a hand-over-hand intention of crawling out of the crack. Carson, who had refastened the rope around his own waist, stopped him.

"Make it fast around yourself as well," he ordered.

"If I go I'll take you with me," Smoke objected.

The little man became very peremptory.

"Shut up," he ordered. "The sound of your voice is enough to start the whole thing going."

"If I ever start going——" Smoke began.

"Shut up! You ain't going to ever start going. Do what I say. That's right—under the shoulders. Make it fast. Now! Start! Get a move on, but easy as you go. I'll take in the slack. Just keep a-coming. That's it. Easy. Easy."

Smoke was still a dozen feet away when the final collapse of the bridge began. Without noise, but in a jerky way, it crumbled to an increasing tilt.

"Quick!" Carson called, coiling in hand-over-hand on the slack of the rope which Smoke's rush gave him.

When the crash came, Smoke's fingers were clawing into the hard face of the wall of the crevasse, while his body dragged back with the falling bridge. Carson, sitting up, feet wide apart and braced, was heaving on the rope. This effort swung Smoke in to the side wall, but it jerked Carson out of his niche. Like a cat, he faced about, clawing wildly for a hold on the ice and slipping down. Beneath him, with forty feet of taut rope between them, Smoke was clawing just as wildly; and as the thunder from below announced the arrival of the bridge, both men had come to rest. Carson had achieved this first, and the several pounds of pull he was able to put on the rope helped bring Smoke to a stop.

Each lay in a shallow niche, but Smoke's was so shallow that, tense with the strain of flattening and sticking, he would have slid on had it not been for the slight assistance he took from the rope. He was on a bulge and could not see beneath him. Several minutes passed, in which they took stock of the situation and made rapid strides in learning the art of sticking to wet and slippery ice. The little man was the first to speak.

"Gee!" he said; and, a minute later, "If you can dig in for a moment and slack on the rope, I can turn over. Try it."

Smoke made the effort, then rested on the rope again. "I can do it," he said. "Tell me when you're ready. And be quick."

"About three feet down is holding for my heels," Carson said. "It won't take a moment. Are you ready?"

"Go on."

It was hard work to slide down a yard, turn over and sit up; but it was even harder for Smoke to remain flattened and maintain a position that from instant to instant made greater call upon his muscles. As it was, he could feel the almost perceptible beginning of another slip when the rope tightened and he looked up into his companion's face. Smoke noted the yellow pallor of sun tan forsaken by the blood, and wondered what his own complexion was like. But when he saw Carson, with shaking fingers, fumble for his sheath knife, he decided the end had come. The man was going to cut the rope.

"Don't m-mind m-m-me," the little man chattered. "I ain't scared. It's only my nerves, gosh-dang them. I'll b-b-be all right in a minute."

And Smoke watched him, doubled over, his shoulders

between his knees, shivering and awkward, holding a slight tension on the rope with one hand while with the other he hacked and gouged holes for his heels in the ice.

"Carson," he breathed up to him, "you're some guy."

The answering grin was ghastly and pathetic. "I never could stand height," Carson confessed. "It always did get me. Do you mind if I stop a minute and clear my head? Then I'll make those heel holds deeper so I can heave you up."

Smoke's heart warmed. "Look, Carson. The thing to do is to cut the rope. You can never get me up, and there's no use both of us being lost. You can make it out with your knife."

"Shut up!" was the hurt retort. "Who's running this?"

And Smoke could not help but see that anger was a good restorative for the other's nerves. As for himself, it was the more nerve-racking strain, lying plastered against the ice with nothing to do but strive to stick on.

A groan and a quick cry of "Hold on!" warned him. With face pressed against the ice, he made a supreme sticking effort, felt the rope slacken, and knew Carson was slipping toward him. He did not dare look up until he felt the rope tighten and knew the other had again come to rest.

"Gee, that was close," Carson chattered. "I came down over a yard. Now you wait. I've got to dig new holds. If this danged ice wasn't so melty we'd be O.K."

Holding the few pounds of strain necessary for Smoke with his left hand, the little man jabbed and chopped at the ice with his right. Ten minutes of this passed.

"I'll tell you what I've done," Carson called down. "I've made heel holds and hand holds for you alongside of me. I'm going to pull the rope in slow and easy, and you just come along sticking an' not too fast. I'll tell you what, first of all. I'll take you on the rope and you worry out of that pack. Get me?"

Smoke nodded, and with infinite care unbuckled his packstraps. With a wriggle of the shoulders he dislodged the pack, and Carson saw it slide over the bulge and out of sight.

"Now, I'm going to ditch mine," he called down. "You just take it easy and wait."

Five minutes later the upward struggle began. Smoke, drying his hands on the insides of his sleeves, clawed into the climb—bellied, and clung, and stuck, and plastered—sustained and helped by the pull of the rope. Alone, he could not have advanced. A third of the way up, where the pitch was steeper and the ice less eroded, he felt the strain on the rope decreasing. He moved slower and slower. Here was no place to stop and remain. His most desperate effort could not prevent the stop, and he could feel the down-slip beginning.

"I'm going," he called up.

"So am I," was the reply, gritted through Carson's teeth.

"Then cast loose."

Smoke felt the rope tauten in a futile effort, then the pace quickened, and as he went past his previous lodgment and over the bulge the last glimpse he caught of Carson he was turned over, with madly moving hands and feet striving to overcome the downward draw. To Smoke's surprise, as he went over the bulge, there was no sheer fall. The rope restrained him as he slid down a steeper pitch, which quickly eased until he came to a halt in another niche on the verge of another bulge. Carson was now out of sight, ensconced in the place previously occupied by Smoke.

"Gee!" he could hear Carson shiver. "Gee!"

An interval of quiet followed, and then Smoke could feel the rope agitated.

"What are you doing?" he called up.

"Making more hand- and foot-holds," came the trembling answer. "Just wait. I'll have you up here in a jiffy. Don't mind the way I talk. I'm just excited. But I'm all right. You wait and see."

"Soon or late, with the ice melting, you'll slip down after me. The thing for you to do is to cut loose. There's no use both of us going. Get that? You're the biggest little man in creation, but you've done your best. You cut loose."

"Shut up. I'm going to make holes this time deep enough to haul up a span of horses."

"You've held me up long enough," Smoke urged. "You've been coming down all the time."

"And I've been learning the game all the time. I'm going on holding you up until we get out of here. Savvy? When God made me a lightweight I guess he knew what he was about. Now, shut up. I'm busy."

Several silent minutes passed. Smoke could hear the metallic hack of the knife, and occasional driblets of ice slid over the bulge and came down to him. Thirsty, clinging with hand and foot, he caught fragments in his mouth and melted them to water.

He heard a gasp that slid into a groan of despair, and felt a slackening of the rope that made him claw. Immediately the rope tightened again. Straining his eyes in an upward look along the steep slope, he stared a moment, then saw the knife, point first, slide slowly over the bulge and down upon him. He tucked his cheek to it, shrank from the pang of cut flesh, tucked more tightly, and felt the knife come to rest.

"I'm a slob," came the wail down the crevasse.

"Cheer up, I've got it," Smoke answered.

"Hooray! Wait! I've a lot of string in my pocket. I'll drop it down to you, and you send the knife up."

Smoke made no reply. He was battling with a sudden rush of thought.

"Here comes the string! Tell me when you've got it."

A small pocketknife, weighting the end of the string, slid down the ice. Smoke got it, opened the larger blade by a quick effort of his teeth and one hand, and made sure that the blade was sharp. Then he tied the sheath knife to the end of the string.

"Haul away!" he called.

With strained eyes he saw the upward progress of the knife. But he saw more—a little man, afraid and indomitable, who shivered and chattered, whose head swam with giddiness, and who mastered his qualms and distresses and played a hero's part. Not since his meeting with Shorty had Smoke so quickly liked a man. Here was a proper meat-eater, eager with friendliness, generous to destruction, with a grit that shaking fear could not shake. He considered the situation cold-bloodedly. There was no chance for two. Steadily, they were sliding into the heart of the glacier, and it was his greater weight that was dragging the little man down. The little man could stick like a fly. Alone, he could save himself.

"Now we'll get out of here in two shakes," came the voice from above, down and across the bulge of ice.

The awful struggle for good cheer and hope in Carson's voice, decided Smoke.

"Listen to me," he said steadily. "I sent that knife up for you to get out with. Get that? I'm going to cut loose with the jackknife. It's one or both of us."

"Two or nothing," came the grim but shaky response. "If you'll hold on a minute—"

"I've held on for too long now!"

"Wait!" Carson screamed down. "You can't do that! Give me a chance to get you out. We'll make it. You'll see. I'm going to dig holds that'll lift a house and barn."

Smoke made no reply. Slowly and gently, fascinated by the sight, he cut with the knife until one of the three strands popped and parted.

"What are you doing?" Carson cried desperately. "I tell you it's two or nothing We're going to get out. Wait! For God's sake!"

And Smoke, staring at the parted strand, five inches before his eyes, knew fear. He did not want to die; he recoiled from the shimmering abyss beneath him, and his panicky brain urged all the preposterous optimism of delay. It was fear that prompted him to compromise.

"All right," he called up. "I'll wait. Do your best. But Carson, if we both start slipping again I'm going to cut."

"Forget it. When we start, we start up. I'm like adhesive tape. I could stick here if it was twice as steep. I'm getting a sizable hole for one heel already. Now, let me work."

The slow minutes passed. Smoke centered his soul on the dull hurt of a hangnail on one of his fingers. He should have clipped it away that morning—it was hurting then —he decided; and he resolved, once clear of the crevasse, that it should immediately be clipped. Then, with short focus, he stared at the hangnail and the finger with a new comprehension. In a minute, or a few minutes at best, that hangnail, that finger, cunningly jointed and efficient, might be part of a mangled carcass at the bottom of the crevasse. He tried to attribute the cause of his shivering to the fact that he was soaking wet from contact with the thawing ice; but he knew, in his heart, that this was untrue.

A gasp and a groan and an abrupt slackening of the rope warned him. He began to slip. The movement was very slow. The rope tightened loyally, but he continued to slip. Carson could not hold him, and was slipping with him. The toe of his foot encountered vacancy, and he knew that it was over the straightaway fall. And he knew, too, that in another moment his falling body would jerk Carson's after it.

Blindly, desperately, he brought the knife-edge across the rope, saw the strands part, felt himself slide more rapidly, and then fall.

What happened then, he did not know. He was not unconscious, but it happened too quickly, and it was unexpected. Instead of falling to his death, his feet almost immediately struck in water, and he sat violently down with it splashing coolingly on his face. His first impression was that the crevasse was shallower than he had imagined and that he had safely reached bottom. But of this he was quickly disabused. The opposite wall was still a dozen feet away. He lay in a basin formed in an out-jut of the ice wall by melting water that dribbled and trickled over the bulge above and fell straight down a distance of a dozen feet. This had hollowed out the basin. Where he sat the water was two feet deep and flush with the rim. He peered over the rim and looked down the narrow chasm hundreds of feet to the torrent that foamed along the bottom.

"Oh, why did you?" he heard a wail from above.

"Listen," he called up. "I'm perfectly safe, sitting in a pool of water up to my neck. And here's both our packs.

I'm going to sit on them. There's room for a half-dozen
here. If you slip, stick close and you'll land. In the meantime try to hike up and get out. Go to the cabin. Somebody's there. I saw smoke before. Get a rope, or anything
that will make rope, and come back and fish for me."

"Honest!" came Carson's incredulous voice.

"Cross my heart. Now, get a hustle on, or I'll catch my
death of cold."

Smoke kept himself warm by kicking a channel through
the rim with the heel of his shoe. By the time he had
drained off the last of the water, a faint call from Carson
announced that he had reached the top.

After that Smoke occupied himself with drying his
clothes. The late afternoon sun beat down warmly upon
him, and he wrung out his garments and spread them
about him. His matchcase was waterproof, and he manipu-
lated and dried sufficient tobacco and paper to make
cigarettes.

Two hours later, perched naked on the two packs and
smoking, he heard a voice above that he could not fail to
identify.

"Oh, Smoke! Smoke!"

"Joy Gastell!" he called back. "Where'd you drop
from?"

"Your cabin. Are you hurt?"

"Not even any skin off!"

"Father's paying the rope down now. Do you see it?"

"Yes, and I've got it," he answered. "Now, wait a couple
of minutes, please."

"What's the matter?"

"I'm dressing."

"Dressing?"

"Yes. I've been in swimming. Now! Ready? Hoist away!"

He sent up the two packs on the first trip, was consequently rebuked by Joy, and on the second trip came up himself.

Joy looked at him with glowing eyes, while her father and Carson were busy coiling the rope. "How could you cut loose that way? Carson told me. You sacrificed yourself to save him."

"Nothing of the sort," Smoke lied. "I could see that swimming pool right under me all the time."

CHAPTER 8

A Flutter in Eggs

IT WAS in the A. C. Company's big store at Dawson the following winter, on a morning of crisp frost, that Lucille Arral beckoned Smoke Bellew over to the dry goods counter. The clerk had gone on an expedition into the storerooms, and Smoke obeyed her call with alacrity.

The man did not exist in Dawson who would not have been flattered by the notice of Lucille Arral, the singing soubrette of the tiny stock company that performed nightly at the Palace Opera House.

"Things are dead," she complained, with pretty petulance. "There hasn't been a stampede for a week. That masked ball Skiff Mitchell was going to give has been postponed. There's no dust in circulation. And there hasn't been a mail from the Outside for two whole weeks. This burg has crawled into its cave and gone to sleep. We've got to do something. It needs livening—and you and I can do it. Just the two of us. I've broken with Wild Water Charley, you know."

Smoke caught a vision of himself in the midst of a bleak snow-stretch, under a cold arctic moon, being pot-shotted

with accurateness and dispatch by the aforesaid Wild
Water.

"I'm not thinking what you are thinking at all, thank
you," she chided, with a laugh. "Take it from me, Mr.
Smoke Bellew, I'm not going to make love to you, and if
you dare to make love to me, Wild Water will take care
of you. You know *him*. Besides, I—I'll give it to you
straight. Wild Water *thinks* I've broken with him."

"Well, have you, or haven't you?"

"Between you and me in confidence, I haven't! I just
made a noise like breaking with him. He deserved it, too."

"Where do I come in, stalking-horse or fall guy?"

"Neither. You put the laugh on Wild Water, cheer
Dawson up, and, best of all, he gets disciplined. He needs
it. He's too turbulent. Just because he owns more rich
claims than he can keep count of—"

"And because he's engaged to the prettiest little woman
in Alaska," Smoke interpolated.

"Yes, and because of that, too, thank you, is no reason
for him to get riotous. Last night I finally broke our en-
gagement, and he's going around making a noise like a
broken heart. Now we come to it. I like eggs."

"What have eggs got to do with it?" Smoke demanded.

"Everything, if you'll only listen. I like eggs. There's
only a limited supply of eggs in Dawson."

"Sure. I know that, too. Slavovitch's Restaurant has
most of them. Ham and one egg, three dollars. Ham and
two eggs, five dollars. That's two dollars an egg, retail.
Only the swells and the Arrals and the Wild Waters can
afford them."

"He likes eggs, too," she continued. "But that's not the
point. I like them. I have breakfast every morning at

eleven o'clock at Slavovitch's. I invariably eat two eggs."
She paused impressively. "Suppose, just suppose, somebody corners eggs."

She waited, and Smoke regarded her blankly.

"You're not following," she said.

"Go on," he replied. "I give up. What's the answer?"

"Stupid! You know Wild Water. When he sees I'm lan-
guishing for eggs, and I know how to *languish*, what will
he do?"

"Go on."

"Why, he'll just start stampeding for the man that's
got the corner in eggs. He'll buy the corner, no matter
what it costs. Picture: I come into Slavovitch's at eleven
o'clock. Wild Water at the next table. He'll make it his
business to be there. 'Two eggs, shirred,' I'll say to the
waiter. 'Sorry, Miss Arral,' the waiter will say; 'they ain't
no more eggs.' Then up speaks Wild Water, in that big
bear voice of his, 'Waiter, six eggs, soft boiled.' And the
waiter says, 'Yes, sir,' and the eggs are brought. Picture:
Wild Water looks sideways at me, and I look like a particularly indignant icicle and summon the waiter. 'Sorry,
Miss Arral,' he says, 'but them eggs is Mr. Wild Water's.
You see, Miss, he owns 'em.' Picture: Wild Water, tri-
umphant, doing his best to look unconscious while he eats
his six eggs.

"Another picture: Slavovitch himself bringing two
shirred eggs to me and saying, 'Compliments of Mr. Wild
Water, Miss.' What can I do? What can I possibly do but
smile at Wild Water, and then we make up, of course,
and he'll consider it cheap, even if he has been compelled
to pay ten dollars for each and every egg in the corner."

"Go on, go on," Smoke urged. "At what station do I

climb on the choo-choo, and at what water tank do I get thrown off?"

"You don't get thrown off. You ride the egg-train straight into the Union Depot. *You* can make that corner in eggs. Start in immediately, today. You can buy every egg in Dawson for three dollars and sell out to Wild Water at almost any advance. Then, afterward, the laugh will be on Wild Water. Some of his turbulence will be subdued. You make a pile of money. And Dawson wakes up with a grand ha! ha!"

"Hey! Shorty!" Smoke called across the main street to his partner, trudging along in his swift, slack-jointed way, a naked bottle with frozen contents conspicuously tucked under his arm. Smoke crossed over.

"Where have you been all morning? Been looking for you everywhere."

"Up to Doc's," Shorty answered, holding out the bottle. "Something's wrong with Sally. I seen last night, at feedin' time, the hair on her tail an' flanks was fallin' out. Doc says—"

"Never mind that," Smoke broke in impatiently.

"What's eatin' you?" Shorty demanded in indignant astonishment. "An' Sally gettin' naked bald in this crimpy weather! I tell you that dog's sick. Doc says—"

"Let Sally wait. Listen to me—"

"I tell you she can't wait. It's cruelty to animals. She'll be frostbit. What are you in such a fever about anyway?"

"I want you to buy eggs for me—"

"Sure, an' Floridy water an' talcum powder, if you say the word. An' poor Sally sheddin' something scand'lous! Look here, Smoke, if you want to go in for high livin', go

an' buy your own eggs. Beans an' bacon's good enough
for me."

"I *am* going to buy, but I want you to help me buy.
Now shut up, Shorty. I've got the floor. You go straight to
Slavovitch's. Pay as high as three dollars, but buy all the
eggs he's got."

"Three dollars!" Shorty groaned. "I heard tell only yesterday that he's got all of seven hundred in stock! Twenty-
one hundred dollars for hen-fruit! Say, Smoke, you run
right up and see Doc. He'll tend to your case. An' he'll
only charge you an ounce for the first prescription. So
long. I gotta be pullin' my freight."

He started off, but Smoke caught his partner by the
shoulder, whirling him around.

"Smoke, I'd sure do anything for you," Shorty protested earnestly. "If you had a cold in the head an' was
layin' with both arms broke, I'd set by your bedside, day
an' night, an' wipe your nose for you. But I'll be everlastin'ly damned if I'll squander twenty-one hundred
good iron dollars on hen-fruit for you or any other two-
legged man."

"Shorty, it's a deal I have on. What I'm after is to corner
every blessed egg in Dawson, in the Klondike, on the
Yukon. You've got to help me out. I haven't the time now
to tell you the inside story. I will afterward, but the thing
right now is to get the eggs. Now hustle up to Slavovitch's
and buy all he's got."

"But what'll I tell 'm? He'll sure know I ain't goin' to
eat 'em."

"Tell him nothing. Money talks. He sells them cooked
for two dollars. Offer him up to three uncooked, but only
if he promises not to admit he sold them to you. If he gets
curious, tell him you're starting a chicken ranch. What I

want is the eggs. Then keep on; nose out every egg in Dawson and buy it. Understand? Buy it! That little joint across the street from Slavovitch's has a few. Buy them. I'm going over to Klondike City. There's an old man there, with a bad leg, who's broke and who has six dozen. He's held them all winter for a rise, intending to get enough out of them to pay his passage back to Seattle. Now hustle. And they say that little woman down beyond the sawmill who makes moccasins has a couple of dozen."

"All right, if you say so, Smoke. But Slavovitch seems the main squeeze. I'll just get an ironbound option, black an' white, an' gather in the scatterin' first."

"All right. Hustle. I'll tell you all about the scheme tonight."

But Shorty flourished the bottle. "I'm goin' to doctor up Sally first. The eggs can wait that long. If they ain't all eaten already, they won't be eaten while I'm takin' care of a poor sick dog that's saved your life an' mine more'n once."

Never was a market cornered more quickly. In three days every known egg in Dawson, with the exception of several dozen, was in the hands of Smoke and Shorty. Smoke had been the more liberal in purchasing. He un-blushingly pleaded guilty to having given the old man in Klondike City five dollars apiece for his seventy-two eggs. Shorty had bought most of the eggs, and he had driven bargains. He had given only two dollars an egg to the woman who made moccasins, and he prided himself that he had come off fairly well with Slavovitch, whose seven hundred and fifteen eggs he had bought at a flat rate of two dollars and a half. On the other hand, he grumbled because the little restaurant across the street had held him up for two dollars and seventy-five cents for a paltry hundred and thirty-four eggs.

The several dozen not yet gathered in were in the hands of two persons. One, with whom Shorty was dealing, was an Indian woman who lived in a cabin on the hill back of the hospital.

"I'll get her today," Shorty announced next morning. "You wash the dishes, Smoke. I'll be back in a jiffy, if I don't bust myself a-shovin' dust at her. Gimme a man to deal with every time. These blamed women—it's something sad the way they can hold out on a buyer. The only way to get 'em is sellin'. Why, you'd think them eggs of hern was solid nuggets."

In the afternoon, when Smoke returned to the cabin, he found Shorty squatted on the floor, rubbing ointment into Sally's tail, his countenance so expressionless that it was suspicious.

"What luck?" Shorty asked carelessly, after several minutes had passed.

"Nothing doing," Smoke answered. "How did you get on with the squaw?"

Shorty only cocked his head triumphantly toward a tin pail of eggs on the table.

"I offered ten dollars finally," Smoke admitted, "and then the fellow told me he'd already sold his eggs. Now that looks bad, Shorty. Somebody else is in the market. Those twenty-eight eggs are liable to cause us trouble. You see, the success of a corner consists in holding every last—"

He broke off to stare at his partner. A pronounced change was coming over Shorty—one of agitation masked by extreme deliberation. He closed the salve-box, wiped his hands slowly and thoroughly on Sally's furry coat, stood up, went over to the corner, looked at the thermometer, and came back again. He spoke in a low, toneless, and superpolite voice.

"Do you mind kindly just repeating over how many eggs you said the man didn't sell to you?" he asked.

"Twenty-eight."

"Hum," Shorty communed to himself, with a slight duck of the head of careless acknowledgment. "Well, kindly please direct them handsome eyes of yourn at that there pail settin' on the table. See it?"

Smoke nodded.

"I want to tell you one thing, just one thing. They's just exactly, preecisely, nor nothin' more or anythin' less'n twenty-eight eggs in the pail, an' they cost, every danged last one of 'em, just exactly seven great big round iron dollars a throw. That geezer you was dickerin' with is a big Indian. Am I right?"

Smoke nodded.

"He's got one cheek half gone where a bald-face grizzly swatted him. Am I right? He's a dog trader—right, eh? His name is Scar-Face Jim. That's so, ain't it? D'ye get my drift?"

"You mean we've been bidding—"

"Against each other. Sure thing. That squaw's his wife, an' they keep house on the hill back of the hospital. I could 'a' got them eggs for two a throw if you hadn't butted in."

"And so could I," Smoke laughed, "if you'd kept out, blame you! But it doesn't amount to anything. We've got the corner, now. That's the big thing."

Shorty spent the next hour wrestling with a stub of pencil on the margin of a three-year-old newspaper, and

the more interminable and hieroglyphic grew his figures
the more cheerful he became.

"There she stands," he said at last. "Pretty? I guess yes.
Lemme give you the totals. You an' me has right now in
our possession exactly nine hundred an' seventy-three eggs.
They cost us exactly two thousand, seven hundred an' sixty
dollars, reckonin' dust at sixteen an ounce an' not countin'
time. An' now listen to me. If we stick up Wild Water for
ten dollars a egg we stand to win, clean net an' all to the
good, just exactly six thousand nine hundred and seventy
dollars. Now that's bookmakin' what is, if anybody should
ride up on a dog sled an' ask you. Put her there, Smoke.
I'm that thankful I'm sure droolin' gratitude. Bookmakin'!
Say, I'd sooner run with the chicks than the ponies any
day."

At eleven that night Smoke was routed from sound sleep
by Shorty, whose fur parka exhaled an atmosphere of keen
frost.

"I just had to tell you the good news. I seen Slavovitch.
Or Slavovitch seen me, I guess, because he started the
séance. He says to me: 'Shorty, I want to speak to you
about them eggs. I've kept it quiet, like I promised. Nobody knows I sold 'em to you. But if you're speculatin', I
can put you wise to a good thing.' An' he did, too, Smoke.
Now what'd you guess that good thing is?"

"Go on. Name it."

"Well, it sounds uncredible, but that good thing was
Wild Water Charley. *He's* lookin' to buy eggs. He goes
around to Slavovitch an' offers him five dollars an egg,
an' before he quits he's offerin' eight. An' Slavovitch ain't
got no eggs. Last thing Wild Water says to Slavovitch is
that he'll beat the head offen him if he ever finds out
Slavovitch has eggs cached away somewheres. Slavovitch

had to tell'm he'd sold the eggs, but that the buyer was secret.

"Slavovitch says to let him say the word to Wild Water who's got the eggs. 'Shorty,' he says to me, 'Wild Water'll come a-runnin'. You can hold him up for eight dollars.' 'Eight dollars, your grandmother,' I says. 'He'll fall for ten before I'm done with him.' Anyway, I told Slavovitch I'd think it over and let him know in the mornin'. Of course we'll let 'm pass the word on to Wild Water. Right?"

"Certainly. First thing in the morning tip off Slavovitch. And have him tell Wild Water that you and I are partners in the deal."

Five minutes later Smoke was again aroused by Shorty.

"Say! Smoke! Oh, Smoke!"

"Yes?"

"Not a cent less than ten a throw. Get that?"

"Sure thing—all right," Smoke returned sleepily.

The next noon, up in their cabin, Shorty placed on the table a pot of beans, a pot of coffee, a pan of sourdough biscuits, a tin of butter and a tin of condensed cream, a smoking platter of moose-meat and bacon, a plate of stewed dried peaches, and called: "Grub's ready. Take a slant at Sally first."

Smoke put aside the harness he was sewing, opened the door, and saw Sally spiritedly driving away a bunch of foraging sled-dogs that belonged to the next cabin. Also he saw something else that made him close the door hurriedly and dash to the stove. The frying pan, still hot from moose-meat and bacon, he put back on the front lid. Into the frying pan he put a generous dab of butter, then reached for an egg, which he broke and dropped spluttering into the pan. As he reached for a second egg, Shorty gained his side and clutched his arm in an excited grip.

"Hey! What you doin'?" he demanded.

"Frying eggs," Smoke informed him, breaking the second one and throwing off Shorty's detaining hand.

"Don't you feel well?" Shorty queried anxiously, as Smoke broke a third egg and dexterously thrust him back with a stiff-arm jolt on the breast. "Or are you just plain loco? That's thirty dollars' worth of eggs already."

"And I'm going to make it sixty dollars' worth," was the answer, as Smoke broke the fourth. "Get out of the way, Shorty. Wild Water's coming up the hill, and he'll be here in five minutes."

Shorty sighed vastly with comprehension and relief, and sat down at the table. By the time the expected knock came at the door, Smoke was facing him across the table, and, before each, was a plate containing three hot, fried eggs.

"Come in!" Smoke called.

Wild Water Charley, a strapping young giant just a fraction of an inch under six feet in height and carrying a clean weight of one hundred and ninety pounds, entered and shook hands.

"Set down an' have a bite, Wild Water," Shorty invited. "Smoke, fry him some eggs. I'll bet he ain't scoffed an egg in a coon's age."

Smoke broke three more eggs into the hot pan, and in several minutes placed them before his guest, who looked at them with so strange and strained an expression that Shorty confessed afterward his fear that Wild Water would slip them into his pocket and carry them away.

"Say, them swells down in the States ain't got nothin' over us in the matter of eats," Shorty gloated. "Here's you an' me an' Smoke gettin' outside ninety dollars' worth of eggs an' not battin' an eye."

Wild Water stared at the rapidly disappearing eggs and seemed petrified.

"Pitch in an' eat," Smoke encouraged.

"They—they ain't worth no ten dollars," Wild Water said slowly.

Shorty accepted the challenge. "A thing's worth what you can get for it, ain't it?" he demanded.

"Yes, but—"

"But nothin'. I'm tellin' you what we can get for 'em. Ten a throw, just like that. We're the egg trust, Smoke an' me, an' don't you forget it. When we say ten a throw, ten a throw goes." He mopped his plate with a biscuit. "I could almost eat a couple more," he sighed, then helped himself to the beans.

"You can't eat eggs like that," Wild Water objected. "It—it ain't right."

"We just dote on eggs, Smoke an' me," was Shorty's excuse.

Wild Water finished his own plate in a halfhearted way and gazed dubiously at the two comrades. "Say, you fellows can do me a great favor," he began tentatively. "Sell me, or lend me, or give me, about a dozen of them eggs."

"Sure," Smoke answered. "I know what a yearning for eggs is myself. But we're not so poor that we have to sell our hospitality. They'll cost you nothing—" Here a sharp kick under the table admonished him that Shorty was getting nervous. "A dozen, did you say, Wild Water?"

Wild Water nodded.

"Go ahead, Shorty," Smoke went on. "*Cook* them up for him. I can sympathize. I've seen the time myself when I could eat a dozen, straight off the bat."

But Wild Water laid a restraining hand on the eager Shorty as he explained. "I don't mean cooked. I want them with the shells on."

"So that you can carry 'em away?"

"That's the idea."

"But that ain't hospitality," Shorty objected. "It's—it's tradin'."

Smoke nodded concurrence. "That's different, Wild Water. I thought you just wanted to eat them. You see, we went into this for speculation."

The dangerous blue of Wild Water's eyes began to grow more dangerous. "I'll pay you for them," he said sharply. "How much?"

"Oh, not a dozen," Smoke replied. "We couldn't sell a dozen. We're not retailers; we're speculators. We can't break our own market. We've got a hard and fast corner, and when we sell out it's the whole corner or nothing."

"How many have you got, and how much do you want for them?"

"How many have we, Shorty?" Smoke inquired.

Shorty cleared his throat and performed mental arithmetic aloud. "Lemme see. Nine hundred an' seventy-three minus nine, that leaves nine hundred an' sixty-two. An' the whole shootin' match, at ten a throw, will tote up just about nine thousand six hundred an' twenty iron dollars. Of course, Wild Water, we're playin' fair, an' it's money back for bad ones—though they ain't none. That's one thing I never seen in the Klondike—a bad egg. No man's fool enough to bring in a bad egg."

"That's fair," Smoke added. "Money back for the bad ones, Wild Water. There's our proposition—nine thousand six hundred and twenty dollars for every egg in the Klondike."

"You might play them up to twenty a throw an' double your money," Shorty suggested.

Wild Water shook his head sadly and helped himself to the beans. "Too expensive, Shorty. I only want a few. I'll give you ten dollars for a couple of dozen. I'll give you twenty—but I can't buy 'em all."

"All or none," was Smoke's ultimatum.

"Look here, you two," Wild Water said in a burst of confidence. "I'll be perfectly honest with you, an' don't let it go any further. You know Miss Arral an' I was engaged. Well, she's broken everything off. You know it. Everybody knows it. It's for her I want them eggs."

"Huh!" Shorty jeered. "It's clear an' plain why you want 'em with the shells on. But I never thought it of you."

"Thought what?"

"It's low-down mean, that's what it is," Shorty rushed on, now virtuously indignant. "I wouldn't wonder somebody filled you full of lead for it, an' you'd deserve it, too. Wild Water, you're makin' a mistake. They ain't no crowd ever sat at the Opery House that'll stand for it. Just because she's a actress is no reason you can publicly lambaste her with hen-fruit."

For the moment it seemed that Wild Water was going to burst or have apoplexy. He gulped down a mouthful of scalding coffee and slowly recovered himself.

"You're wrong, Shorty," he said with cold deliberation. "I'm not going to throw eggs at her. Why, man," he cried, with growing excitement, "I want to give them eggs to her, on a platter, shirred—that's the way she likes 'em."

"I knowed you couldn't do a low-down trick like that," Shorty cried generously.

"That's all right, Shorty," Wild Water forgave him.

"But let's get down to business. You see why I want them eggs. I want 'em bad."

"Do you want 'em ninety-six hundred an' twenty dollars' worth?" Shorty queried.

"It's a holdup, that's what it is," Wild Water declared irately.

"It's business," Smoke retorted. "You don't think we're peddling eggs for our health, do you?"

"Listen to reason," Wild Water pleaded. "I only want a couple of dozen. I'll give you twenty apiece for 'em. What do I want with all the rest of them eggs? I've went years in this country without eggs, an' I guess I can keep on managin' without 'em somehow."

"Don't get het up about it," Shorty counseled. "If you don't want 'em, that settles it. We ain't a-forcin' 'em on you."

"But I do want 'em," Wild Water complained.

"Then you know what they'll cost you—ninety-six hundred an' twenty dollars. If my figurin's wrong, I'll treat."

"I should say Miss Arral's worth the price of the eggs," Smoke put in quietly.

"Worth it!" Wild Water stood up in the heat of his eloquence. "She's worth all the dust in Klondike." He sat down, and went on in a calmer voice. "But that ain't no call for me to gamble ten thousand dollars on a breakfast for her. I've got a proposition. Lend me a couple of dozen of them eggs. I'll turn 'em over to Slavovitch. He'll feed 'em to her with my compliments. She ain't smiled to me for a hundred years. If them eggs gets a smile for me, I'll take the whole boiling off your hands."

"Will you sign a contract to that effect?" Smoke said quickly.

Wild Water gasped. "You're almighty swift with business up here on the hill," he said, with a hint of a snarl.

"We're only accepting your own proposition," Smoke answered.

"All right—bring on the paper—make it out, hard and fast," Wild Water cried in the anger of surrender.

Smoke wrote out the document, wherein Wild Water agreed to take every egg delivered to him at ten dollars per egg, provided that the two dozen advanced to him brought about a reconciliation with Lucille Arral.

Wild Water paused, with uplifted pen, as he was about to sign. "Hold on," he said significantly. "When I buy eggs I buy *good* eggs."

"They ain't a bad egg in the Klondike," Shorty snorted.

"Just the same, if I find one bad egg you've got to come back with the money I paid for it."

"All right," Smoke placated. "That's only fair."

"Every bad egg you come back with *I'll* eat," Shorty declared.

Smoke inserted the word *good* in the contract, Wild Water signed, received the trial two dozen in a tin pail, pulled on his mittens, and opened the door.

"Good-by, robbers," he growled at them, and slammed the door.

Smoke was a witness to the play next morning in Slavovitch's. He sat, as Wild Water's guest, at the table adjoining Lucille Arral's. Almost to the letter, as she had forecast it, the scene came off.

"Haven't you found any eggs yet?" she murmured plaintively to the waiter.

"No, ma'am," came the answer. "They say somebody's cornered every egg in Dawson. Mr. Slavovitch is trying to buy a few just especially for you. But the fellow that's got the corner won't let loose."

At this juncture, Wild Water beckoned the proprietor to him, and, with one hand on his shoulder, drew his head down. "Look here, Slavovitch," Wild Water whispered hoarsely, "I turned over a couple of dozen eggs to you last night. Where are they?"

"In the safe. All but six I thawed and have ready for you any time you sing out."

"I don't want 'em for myself," Wild Water breathed in a still lower voice. "Shirr two of 'em up and present 'em to Miss Arral there."

"I'll attend to it personally myself," Slavovitch assured him.

"An' don't forget—compliments of me," Wild Water concluded, relaxing his detaining clutch on the proprietor's shoulder.

Pretty Lucille Arral was gazing forlornly at the strip of breakfast bacon and the tinned mashed potatoes on her plate when Slavovitch placed before her two shirred eggs.

"Compliments of Mr. Wild Water," they heard him say.

Smoke acknowledged to himself that it was a fine bit of acting—the quick, joyous flash in the face, her impulsive turn of the head, the spontaneous forerunner of a smile that was only checked by superb self-control which resolutely drew her face back so that she could say something to the restaurant proprietor.

Smoke felt the kick of Wild Water's moccasined foot under the table.

"Will she eat 'em?—that's the question—will she eat 'em?" the latter whispered agonizingly.

And with sidelong glances they saw Lucille Arral hesitate, almost push the dish from her, then surrender to its lure.

"I'll take them eggs," Wild Water said to Smoke. "The contract holds. Did you see her? Did you see her! She almost smiled. I know her. It's all fixed. Two more eggs tomorrow an' she'll forgive an' make up. If she wasn't here I'd shake hands, Smoke, I'm that grateful. You ain't a robber; you're a philanthropist."

Smoke returned jubilantly up the hill to the cabin, only to find Shorty playing solitaire in black despair. Smoke had long since learned that whenever his partner got out the cards for solitaire it was a warning signal that the bottom had dropped out of the world.

"Go 'way, don't talk to me," was the first rebuff Smoke received.

But Shorty soon thawed into a freshet of speech.

"It's all off with Wild Water," he groaned. "The corner's busted. They'll be sellin' sherry an' egg in all the saloons tomorrow at a dollar a flip. They ain't no starvin' orphan child in Dawson that won't be wrappin' its tummy around eggs. What d'ye think I run into?—a geezer with *three thousan' eggs*—d'ye get me? Three thousan', an' just freighted in from Forty-Mile."

"Fairy stories," Smoke doubted.

"Fairy hell! I seen them eggs. Gautereaux's his name— a whackin' big, blue-eyed French-Canadian husky. He asked for you first, then took me to the side and jabbed me straight to the heart. It was our cornerin' eggs that got him started. He knowed about them three thousan' at Forty-Mile an' just went an' got 'em. 'Show 'em to me,' I says. An' he did. There was his dog teams, an' a couple of In-

dian drivers, restin' down the bank where they'd just
pulled in from Forty-Mile. An' on the sleds was soap
boxes—teeny wooden soap boxes.

"We took one out behind a ice jam in the middle of the
river an' busted it open. Eggs!—full of 'em, all packed in
sawdust. Smoke, you an' me lose. We've been gamblin'.
D' ye know what he had the gall to say to me?—that they
was all ourn at ten dollars a egg. D'ye know what he was
doin' when I left his cabin?—drawin' a sign of *eggs for
sale*. Said he'd give us first choice, at ten a throw, till
2 P.M. After that, if we didn't come across, he'd bust the
market higher 'n a kite. Said he wasn't no business man,
but that he knowed a good thing when he seen it—meanin' you an' me, as I took it."

"It's all right," Smoke said cheerfully. "Keep your
shirt on. I'll get Wild Water here at two o'clock to take
delivery of the eggs. Buy that Gautereaux's eggs. Try and
make a bargain, but even if you pay ten dollars apiece for
them, Wild Water will take them off our hands at the
same price. If you can get them cheaper, why, we make a
profit as well. Now go to it. Have them here not later than
two o'clock. Borrow Colonel Bowie's dogs and take our
team."

"Say, Smoke," Shorty called, as his partner started
down the hill. "Better take an umbrella. I wouldn't be
none surprised to see the weather rainin' eggs before you
get back."

Smoke found Wild Water at the M. and G., and a
stormy half-hour ensued.

"We've picked up some more eggs," Smoke said casually, after Wild Water had agreed to bring his dust to the
cabin at two o'clock and pay on delivery.

"You're luckier at finding eggs than me," Wild Water

admitted. "How many eggs have you got now?—an' how much dust do I tote up the hill?"

Smoke consulted his notebook. "As it stands now, according to Shorty's figures, we've three thousand nine hundred and sixty-two eggs. Multiply by ten—"

"Forty thousand dollars!" Wild Water bellowed. "You said there was only something like nine hundred eggs. It's a stickup! I won't stand for it!"

Smoke drew the contract from his pocket and pointed to the *pay on delivery*. "No mention is made of the number of eggs to be delivered. You agreed to pay ten dollars for every egg we delivered to you. Well, we've got the eggs, and a signed contract is a signed contract. Honestly, though, Wild Water, we didn't know about those other eggs until afterward. Then we had to buy them in order to make our corner good."

For five long minutes, in choking silence, Wild Water fought a battle with himself, then reluctantly gave in.

"I'm in bad," he said brokenly. "The landscape's fair sproutin' eggs. The quicker I get out the better. There might come a landslide of 'em. I'll be there at two o'clock. But forty thousand dollars!"

"It's only thirty-nine thousand six hundred an' twenty," Smoke corrected.

"The dust'll weigh two hundred pounds," Wild Water raved on. "I'll have to freight it up with a dog team."

"We'll lend you our teams to carry the eggs away," Smoke volunteered.

"But where'll I cache 'em? Never mind. I'll be there. But as long as I live I'll never eat another egg. I'm sick of 'em."

At half-past one, doubling the dog teams for the steep pitch of the hill, Shorty arrived with Gautereaux's eggs.

"We dang near double our winnings," Shorty told Smoke, as they piled the soap boxes inside the cabin. "I holds 'm down to eight dollars, an' after he cussed loco in French he falls for it. Now that's two dollars clear profit to us for each egg, an' there're three thousan' of 'em. I paid 'm in full. Here's the receipt."

While Smoke got out the gold-scales and prepared for business, Shorty devoted himself to calculation.

"There's the figgers," he announced triumphantly. "We win twelve thousan' nine hundred an' seventy dollars. An' we don't do Wild Water no harm. He wins Miss Arral. Besides, he gets all them eggs. It's sure a bargain counter all around. Nobody loses."

"Even Gautereaux's twenty-four thousand to the good," Smoke laughed, "minus, of course, what the eggs and the freighting cost him. And if Wild Water plays the corner, he may make a profit out of the eggs himself."

Promptly at two o'clock, Shorty, peeping, saw Wild Water coming up the hill. When he entered he was brisk and businesslike. He took off his big bearskin coat, hung it on a nail, and sat down at the table.

"Bring on them eggs, you pirates," he commenced. "An' after this day, if you know what's good for you, never mention eggs to me again."

They began on the miscellaneous assortment of the original corner, all three men counting. When two hundred had been reached, Wild Water suddenly cracked an egg on the edge of the table and opened it deftly with his thumbs.

"Hey! Hold on!" Shorty objected.

"It's my egg, ain't it?" Wild Water said. "I'm paying ten dollars for it, ain't I? But I ain't buying no pig in a poke. When I cough up ten bucks an egg I want to know what I'm gettin'."

"If you don't like it, I'll eat it," Shorty volunteered maliciously.

Wild Water looked and smelled and shook his head. "No, you don't, Shorty. That's a good egg. Gimme a pail. I'm goin' to eat it myself for supper."

Thrice again Wild Water cracked good eggs experimentally and then carefully put them in the pail beside him.

"Two more than you figgered, Shorty," he said at the end of the count. "Nine hundred an' sixty-four, not sixty-two."

"My mistake," Shorty acknowledged handsomely. "We'll throw 'em in for good measure."

"Guess you can afford to," Wild Water accepted grimly. "Nine thousan' six hundred an' twenty dollars. I'll pay it now. Write a receipt, Smoke."

"Why not count the rest," Smoke suggested, "and pay all at once?"

Wild Water shook his head. "I'm no good at figgers. One batch at a time an' no mistakes."

Going to his fur coat, from each of the side pockets he drew forth two sacks of dust, so rotund and long that they resembled bologna sausages. To Smoke's concern, when the first batch had been paid for, there remained in the gold-sacks not more than several hundred dollars.

A soap box was carried to the table, and the count of the three thousand began. At the end of one hundred, Wild Water struck an egg sharply against the edge of the table. There was no crack. The sound was like that of solid marble.

"Frozen solid," he remarked, striking more sharply.

He held the egg up, and they could see the shell powdered to minute fragments along the line of impact.

"Huh!" said Shorty. "It ought to be solid, seein' it's just been freighted up from Forty-Mile. It'll take an ax to bust it."

"Me for the ax," said Wild Water.

Smoke brought the ax, and Wild Water, with the clever hand and eye of the woodsman, split the egg cleanly in half. The appearance of the egg's interior was anything but satisfactory. Smoke felt a premonitory chill. Shorty was more valiant. He held one of the halves to his nose.

"Smells all right," he said.

"But it looks all wrong," Wild Water contended. "An' how can it smell when the smell's frozen along with the rest of it? Wait a minute."

He put the two halves into a frying pan and placed the latter on the front lid of the hot stove. Then the three men, with distended, questing nostrils, waited in silence. Slowly, an unmistakable odor began to drift through the room. Wild Water forbore to speak, and Shorty remained dumb despite conviction.

"Throw it out," Smoke cried, gasping.

"What's the good?" asked Wild Water. "We've got to sample the rest."

"Not in this cabin." Smoke coughed and conquered a qualm. "Chop them open, and we can test by looking at them. Throw it out, Shorty—throw it out! Phew! And leave the door open!"

Box after box was opened; egg after egg, chosen at random, was chopped in two; and every egg carried the same message of hopeless, irremediable decay.

"I really won't ask you to eat 'em, Shorty," Wild Water

jeered, "an', if you don't mind, I can't get outa here too quick. My contract called for *good* eggs. If you'll loan me a sled an' team I'll haul them good ones away before they get contaminated."

Smoke helped in loading the sled. Shorty sat at the table, the cards laid before him for solitaire.

"Say, how long you been holdin' that corner?" was Wild Water's parting gibe.

Smoke made no reply, and, with one glance at his absorbed partner, proceeded to fling soap boxes out into the snow.

"Shorty, how much did you say you paid for those three thousand?" Smoke queried gently.

"Eight dollars. Go 'way. Don't talk to me. I can figger as well as you. We lose seventeen thousan' on the flutter. I figgered that out long ago, waitin' for that first egg to smell."

Smoke pondered a few minutes, then again broke silence. "Say, Shorty. Forty thousand dollars gold weighs two hundred pounds. Wild Water came up the hill without a sled, and those two sacks of dust in his coat pockets weighed only about twenty pounds each. Our understanding was cash on delivery. He brought only enough dust to pay for the good eggs. *He never expected to pay for those three thousand.* He knew they were bad. Now how did he know they were bad?"

Shorty gathered the cards, started to shuffle a new deal, then paused. "Huh! A child could answer it. We lose seventeen thousan'. Wild Water wins seventeen thousan'. Them eggs of Gautereaux's was Wild Water's all the time. Anything else you're curious to know?"

"Yes. Why in the name of common sense didn't you

180 *JACK LONDON*

find out whether those eggs were good before you paid for them?"

"As easy as the first question. Wild Water swung the bunco game timed to seconds. I hadn't no time to examine them eggs. I had to hustle just to get 'em here for delivery."

Shorty had lost the sixteenth consecutive game of solitaire, and Smoke was casting about to begin the preparation of supper, when Colonel Bowie knocked at the door, handed Smoke a letter, and went on to his own cabin.

"Did you see his face?" Shorty raved. "He was almost bustin' to keep it straight. It's the big ha! ha! for you an' me, Smoke. We won't never dast show our faces again in Dawson."

The letter was from Wild Water. Smoke read it aloud:

DEAR SMOKE AND SHORTY:
I write to ask, with compliments of the season, your presence at a supper tonight at Slavovitch's joint. Miss Arral will be there and so will Gautereaux. Him and me was pardners down at Circle five years ago. He is all right and is going to be best man. About them eggs. They come into the country four years back. They was bad when they come in. They was bad when they left California. They always was bad. They stopped at Carluk one winter, and one winter at Nutlik, and last winter at Forty-Mile, where they was sold for storage. And this winter I guess they stop at Dawson. Don't keep them in a hot room. Lucille says to say she guesses you and her and me has sure made some excitement for Dawson—

> *seventeen thousand worth. And I say the drinks*
> *is on you, and that goes.*
> > *Respectfully your friend,*
> > > *W. W.*

"Well? What have you got to say?" Smoke queried.
"We accept the invitation, of course?"

"I got one thing to say," Shorty answered. "Wild Water
won't never suffer if he goes broke. He's a good actor—
a gosh-blamed good actor. An' I got another thing to say:
her figgers is all wrong. Wild Water wins seventeen thousan' all right, but he wins more'n that. You an' me has
made him a present of every good egg in the Klondike—
nine hundred an' sixty-four of 'em, two thrown in for
good measure. An' he was that ornery mean cussed that
he packed off the four opened ones in a pail. An' I got a
last thing to say. You an' me is legitimate prospectors an'
practical gold miners. But when it comes to fi-nance we're
sure the fattest suckers that ever fell for the get-rich-quick
bunco. After this it's you an' me for the high rocks an'
tall timber. If you ever mention eggs to me we dissolve
pardnership there an' then. Get me?"

CHAPTER 9

The Hanging of Cultus George

THE WAY led steeply up through deep, powdery snow unmarred by sled track or moccasin impression. Smoke, in the lead, pressed the fragile crystals down under his fat, short snowshoes. The task required lungs and muscle, and he flung himself into it with all his strength. Behind, on the surface he packed, strained the string of six dogs, the steam-jets of their breathing attesting their labor and the lowness of the temperature. Between the wheel-dog and the sled toiled Shorty, his weight divided between the guiding gee pole and the haul, for he was pulling with the dogs. Every half-hour he and Smoke exchanged places, for the snowshoe work was even more arduous than the gee pole.

The whole outfit was fresh and strong. It was merely hard work being efficiently done—breaking a midwinter trail across a divide. On this severe stretch, ten miles a day was a decent stint. They kept in condition, but each night crawled tired into their sleeping-furs. This was their sixth day out from the lively camp of Mucluc on the Yukon. In two days, with loaded sled, they had covered the fifty

182

miles of packed trail up Moose Creek. Then had come the struggle with the four feet of untouched snow that was really not snow but frost-crystals, so lacking in cohesion that when kicked it flew with the thin hissing of granulated sugar. In three days they had wallowed thirty miles up Minnow Creek and across the series of low divides that separate the several creeks flowing south into Siwash River; and now they were breasting the big divide, past the Bald Buttes, where the way would lead them down Porcupine Creek to the middle reaches of Milk River. Higher up Milk River, it was rumored, were deposits of copper. And this was their goal—a hill of pure copper, half a mile to the right and up the first creek after Milk River, issued from a deep gorge to flow across a heavily timbered stretch of bottom. They would know it when they saw it. One-Eyed McCarthy had described it with sharp definiteness. It was impossible to miss—unless McCarthy had lied.

In the afternoon they cleared the divide, dipped down past Bald Buttes through a sharp elbow-canyon, and took the steep open slope that dropped into Porcupine Creek. Shorty, in the lead, stopped abruptly, and Smoke whoaed the dogs. Beneath them, coming up, was a procession of humans, scattered over a quarter of a mile.

"Siwash Indians. They move like a funeral," Shorty noted.

"They've no dogs," said Smoke.

"Yep; there's a couple of men pullin' on a sled."

"See that fellow fall down? There must be two hundred of them and there's something the matter, Shorty."

"Look at 'em stagger as if they was soused. There goes another."

"It's a whole tribe. There are children there."

The mass of Indians, at sight of the two men, raised a weird cry of joy and accelerated its pace.

"They're sure tolerable woozy," commented Shorty. "See 'em fallin' down in lumps and bunches."

"Look at the face of that first one," Smoke said. "It's starvation—that's what's the matter with them. They've eaten their dogs."

"What'll we do? Run for it?"

"And leave the sled and dogs?" Smoke demanded reproachfully.

"They'll sure eat *us* if we don't. They look hungry enough. Hello, old-timer. What's wrong with you? Don't look at that dog that way. No cookin'-pot for him—savvy?"

The forerunners were arriving and crowding about them, moaning in an unfamiliar jargon. The picture was grotesque and horrible. It was famine unmistakable. Their faces, hollow-cheeked and skin-stretched, were so many death's-heads. More and more arrived and crowded about, until Smoke and Shorty were hemmed in by the wild crew. Their ragged garments of skin and fur were cut and slashed away, and Smoke knew the reason for it when he saw a wizened child on a squaw's back that sucked and chewed a strip of filthy fur. Another child was steadily masticating a leather thong.

"Keep off there! Keep back!" Shorty yelled, falling back on English after futile attempts with the little Indian he did know.

Bucks and squaws and children tottered and swayed on shaking legs and continued to urge in, their mad eyes swimming with weakness and burning with ravenous desire. A woman, moaning, staggered past Shorty and fell with spread and grasping arms on the sled. An old man followed her, panting and gasping, with trembling hands striving to cast off the sled lashings, and get at the grub sacks beneath. A young man, with a naked knife, tried to rush in, but was flung back by Smoke. The whole mass pressed in upon them, and the fight was on.

At first Smoke and Shorty shoved and thrust and threw back. Then they used the butt of the dog whip and their fists on the food-mad crowd. And all this against a background of moaning and wailing women and children. Here and there, in a dozen places, the sled lashings were cut. Men crawled in on their bellies, regardless of a rain of kicks and blows, and tried to drag out the grub. These had to be picked up bodily and flung back. And such was their weakness that they fell continually, under the slightest shove. Yet they made no attempt to injure the two men who defended the sled.

It was the utter weakness of the Indians that saved Smoke and Shorty from being overborne. In five minutes the wall of up-standing, on-struggling Indians had been changed to heaps of fallen ones that moaned and gibbered in the snow, and cried and sniveled as their staring, swimming eyes focused on the food that meant life to them and that brought slaver to their lips. And behind it all arose the wailing of the women and children.

"Shut up! Oh, shut up!" Shorty yelled, thrusting his fingers into his ears and breathing heavily from his exertions. "Ah, you would, would you!" was his cry, as he plunged forward and kicked a knife from the hand of a man who, bellying through the snow, was trying to stab the lead-dog in the throat.

"This is terrible," Smoke muttered.

"I'm all het up," Shorty replied. "What 'r' we goin' to do with this ambulance outfit?"

An Indian crawled forward, his one eye fixed on Smoke instead of on the sled, and in it Smoke could see the struggle of sanity to assert itself. Shorty remembered having punched the other eye shut. The Indian raised himself on his elbow and spoke.

"Me Carluk. Me good Siwash. Me savvy Boston man plenty. Me plenty hungry. All people plenty hungry. All people no savvy Boston man. Me savvy. Me eat grub now. All people eat grub now. We buy 'm grub. Got 'm plenty gold. No got 'm grub. Summer, salmon no come Milk River. Winter, caribou no come. No grub. Me make 'm talk all people. Me tell 'em plenty Boston man come Yukon. Boston man have plenty grub. Boston man like 'm gold. We take 'm gold, go Yukon, Boston man give 'm grub. Plenty gold. Me savvy Boston man like 'm gold."

He began fumbling with wasted fingers at the drawstring of a pouch he took from his belt.

"Too much make 'm noise," Shorty broke in distractedly. "You tell 'm squaw, you tell 'm papoose, shut 'm up mouth."

Carluk turned and addressed the wailing women. Other bucks, listening, raised their voices authoritatively, and slowly the squaws stilled, and quieted the children near to them. Carluk paused from fumbling the drawstring and held up his fingers many times.

"Him people make 'm die," he said.

And Smoke, following the count, knew that seventy-five of the tribe had starved to death.

"Me buy 'm grub," Carluk said, as he got the pouch open and drew out a large chunk of heavy metal. Others were following his example, and on every side appeared similar chunks. Shorty stared.

"Great Jeminey!" he cried. "Copper! Raw, red copper! An' they think it's gold!"

"Him gold," Carluk assured them confidently.

"And they banked everything on it," Smoke muttered. "Look at it. That chunk there weighs forty pounds. They've got hundreds of pounds of it, and they've carried it when they didn't have strength enough to drag themselves. Look, Shorty. We've *got* to feed them."

"Huh! Sounds easy. You an' me has a month's grub, six meals times thirty, which is one hundred an' eighty meals. Here's two hundred Indians, with real, full-grown appetites. How the blazes can we give 'm one meal even?"

"There's the dog grub," Smoke answered. "A couple of hundred pounds of dried salmon ought to help out. We've got to do it."

"We got two nasty jobs cut out for us," Shorty said, "each just about twice as nasty as the other. One of us has got to make a run of it to Mucluc an' raise a relief. The other has to stay here an' run the hospital an' most likely be eaten. Don't let it slip your noodle that we've been six days gettin' here; an' travelin' light, all played out, it can't be made back in less 'n three days."

For a minute Smoke pondered the miles of the way they had come. "I can get there tomorrow night," he announced.

"All right," Shorty acquiesced cheerfully. "I'll stay an' be eaten."

"I'm going to take one fish each for the dogs," Smoke explained, "and one meal for myself."

"You'll sure need it if you try to make Mucluc tomorrow night."

Smoke, through the medium of Carluk, stated the program. "Make fires, long fires, plenty fires," he concluded. "Plenty Boston man stop Mucluc. Boston man much good. Boston man plenty grub. Five sleeps I come back plenty grub. This man, his name Shorty. He stop here. All grub stop here. Shorty, he give 'm grub. He boss—savvy?"

Carluk interpreted, and nods and guttural cries of agreement proceeded from the men.

Those who were able, crawled or staggered collecting firewood. Long Indian fires were built that accommodated all. Shorty, aided by a dozen assistants, with a short club handy for the rapping of hungry knuckles, plunged into the cooking. The women devoted themselves to thawing snow in every utensil that could be mustered. First, a tiny piece of bacon was distributed all around, and, next, a spoonful of sugar to cloy the edge of their razor appetites. Soon, on a circle of fires drawn about Shorty, many pots of beans were boiling, and he, with a wrathful eye for what he called poachers, was frying and apportioning the thinnest of flapjacks.

"Me for the big cookin'," was his farewell to Smoke. "You just keep a-hikin'. Trot all the way there an' run all the way back. It'll take you today an' tomorrow to get there, and you can't be back inside of three days more. Tomorrow they'll eat the last of the fish, an' then there'll be nary a scrap for three days. You gotta keep a-comin', Smoke. You gotta keep a-comin'."

Though the sled was light, loaded only with six dried salmon, a couple of pounds of frozen beans and bacon, and a sleeping-robe, Smoke could not make speed. Instead of riding the sled and running the dogs, he was compelled to plod at the gee pole. Also, a day of work had already been done, and the freshness and spring had gone out of the dogs and himself. The long arctic twilight was on when he cleared the divide and left Bald Buttes behind.

Down the slope better time was accomplished, and often he was able to spring on the sled for short intervals and get an exhausting six-mile clip out of the animals. Darkness caught him and fooled him in a wide-valleyed, nameless creek. Here the creek wandered in broad horseshoe curves through the flats, and here, to save time, he began short-cutting the flats instead of keeping to the creek bed. And black dark found him back on the creek bed feeling for the trail. After an hour of futile searching, too wise to go farther astray, he built a fire, fed each dog half a fish, and divided his own ration in half. Rolled in his robe, before quick sleep came he had solved the problem. The last big flat he had short-cut was the one at the forks of the creek. He had missed the trail by a mile. He was now on the main stream, below where his and Shorty's trail crossed the valley and climbed through a small feeder to the low divide on the other side.

At the first tint of daylight he was under way, breakfastless, and wallowed a mile upstream to pick up the trail. And breakfastless, man and dogs, without a halt, for eight hours held back transversely across the series of small creeks and low divides and down Minnow Creek. By four in the afternoon, with darkness fast-set about him, he emerged on the hard-packed, running trail of Moose Creek. Fifty miles of it would end the journey. He called a rest, built a fire, threw each dog its half-salmon, and thawed and ate his pound of beans. Then he sprang on the sled, yelled, "Mush!" and the dogs went out strongly against their breastbands.

"Hit her up, you huskies!" he cried. "No grub short of Mucluc! Dig in, you wolves! Dig in!"

Midnight had come and gone in the Annie Mine Saloon,
and the main room was still comfortably crowded. Roaring
stoves, combined with lack of ventilation, kept the big
room unsanitarily warm. The click of chips and boisterous
play at the crap table furnished a monotonous background
of sound to the equally monotonous rumble of men's voices
where they sat and stood about and talked in groups and
twos and threes. The gold weighers were busy at their
scales. Dust was the circulating medium, and even a dollar
drink of whiskey at the bar had to be paid for to the
weighers.

The walls of the room were of tiered logs, bark still on,
and the chinking between the logs, plainly visible, was
arctic moss. Through the open door that led to the dance
room came the rollicking strains of a Virginia reel, played
by a piano and a fiddle. The drawing of Chinese lottery
had just taken place, and the luckiest player, having
cashed at the scales, was drinking up his winnings with
half a dozen cronies. The faro and roulette tables were
busy and quiet. The draw poker and stud poker tables,
each with its circle of onlookers, were equally quiet. At
another table, a serious, concentrated game of Black Jack
was on. Only from the crap table came noise, as a man
rolled the dice, full sweep, down the green amphitheater in
pursuit of his elusive and long-delayed point. "Oh! you
Joe! Come a four! Come a Joe! Little Joe from Kokomo!
Bring home the bacon, Joe! Joe, you Joe, you!"

Cultus George, a big strapping Circle City Indian,
leaned distantly against the log wall. He was a civilized
Indian, if living like a white man connotes civilization;
and he was sorely offended, though the offense was of
long standing. For years he had done a white man's work,
alongside of white men, and often had done it better than

they. He wore the same pants they wore, the same hearty
woolens and heavy shirts. He sported as good a watch as
they, parted his short hair on the side, and ate the same
food—bacon, beans, and flour; and yet the Canadian Government denied him their greatest diversion; whiskey.
Cultus George was a money-earner. He had staked claims,
and bought and sold claims. He had been grubstaked, and
he had accorded grubstakes. Just now he was a dog-musher
and freighter, charging twenty-eight cents a pound for
the winter haul from Sixty-Mile to Mucluc—and for
bacon thirty-three cents, as was the custom. His poke was
fat with dust. He had the price of many drinks. Yet no
barkeeper could or would serve him. Only by subterranean
and cowardly and expensive ways could he get a drink.
And he was especially thirsty and resentful this night.
The white men would graciously permit him to lose his
gold across their gaming tables, but for neither love nor
money could he obtain a drink across their bars.

The Virginia reel in the dance room wound to a wild
close that interfered not with the three camp drunkards
who snored under the piano. "All couples promenade to
the bar!" was the caller's last cry as the music stopped.
And the couples were promenading through the wide doorway into the main room—the men in furs and moccasins,
the women in soft fluffy dresses, silk stockings, and dancing slippers—when the double storm doors were thrust
open, and Smoke Bellew staggered wearily in.

Eyes centered on him, and silence began to fall. He tried
to speak, pulled off his mittens, and clawed at the frozen
moisture of his breath which had formed in fifty miles of
running. He halted irresolutely, then went over and
leaned his elbow on the end of the bar.

Only the man at the crap table, without turning his

head, continued to roll the dice and to cry: "Oh! you Joe! Come on, you Joe!" The gamekeeper's gaze, fixed on Smoke, caught the player's attention, and he, too, with suspended dice, turned and looked.

"What's up, Smoke?" Matson, the owner of the Annie Mine, demanded.

With a last effort, Smoke clawed his mouth free. "I got some dogs out there—dead beat," he said huskily. "Somebody go and take care of them, and I'll tell you."

In a dozen brief sentences, he outlined the situation. The crap player, his money still on the table and his slippery point still uncaptured, came over to Smoke, and was the first to speak.

"We gotta do something. What's your plan? Spit it out."

"Here's what I've been thinking. We've got to hustle light sleds on the jump. Say a hundred pounds of grub on each sled. The driver's outfit and dog grub will fetch it up fifty more. But they can make time. Say we start five of these sleds pronto—best running teams, best mushers and trail-eaters. On the soft trail the sleds can take the lead turn about. They've got to start at once. At best, by the time they can get there, all those Indians won't have had a scrap to eat for three days. Then, as soon as we've got those sleds off, we'll follow with heavy sleds. Figure it out yourself. Two pounds a day is the very least we can keep those Indians traveling on. That's four hundred pounds a day, and, with the old people and the children, five days is the quickest we can bring them into Mucluc. Now what are you going to do?"

"Take up a collection to buy the grub," said the crap player.

"I'll stand for the grub," Smoke began impatiently.

"Nope," the other interrupted. "This ain't your treat.

We're all in. Fetch a washbasin somebody. Won't take a minute. Here's a starter."

He pulled a heavy gold-sack from his pocket, untied the mouth, and poured a stream of coarse dust and nuggets into the basin. A man beside him caught his hand up with a jerk and an oath, elevating the mouth of the sack so as to stop the run of the dust. Six or eight ounces had already run into the basin.

"Don't be a hawg," cried the second man. "You ain't the only one with a poke. Gimme a chance at it."

"Huh!" sneered the crap player. "You'd think it was a stampede, you're so goshdanged eager."

Men crowded and jostled for the opportunity to contribute, and when they were satisfied, Smoke hefted the heavy basin with both hands and grinned.

"It will keep the whole tribe in grub for the rest of the winter," he said. "Now for the dogs. Five light teams that have some run in them."

A dozen teams were volunteered, and the camp, as a committee of the whole, bickered and debated, accepted and rejected.

"Huh! Your dray horses!" Long Bill Haskell was told.

"They can pull," he bristled with hurt pride.

"They sure can," he was assured. "But they can't make time for sour apples. They've got theirs cut out for them bringing up the heavy loads."

As fast as a team was selected, its owner, with half a dozen aids, departed to harness up and get ready.

One team was rejected because it had come in tired that afternoon. One owner contributed his team, but apologetically exposed a bandaged ankle that prevented him from driving it. This team Smoke took, overriding the objection that he was played out.

Long Bill Haskell pointed out that while Fat Olsen's
team was a crackerjack, Fat Olsen himself was an ele-
phant. Fat Olsen's two hundred and forty pounds of heart-
iness was indignant. Tears of anger came into his eyes,
and his explosions could not be stopped until he was given
a place in the heavy division, the crap player jumping at
the chance to take out Olsen's light team.

Five teams were accepted and were being harnessed and
loaded, but only four drivers had satisfied the committee
of the whole.

"There's Cultus George," someone cried. "He's a trail-
eater, and he's fresh and rested."

All eyes turned upon the Indian, but his face was expressionless, and he said nothing.

"You'll take a team," Smoke said to him.

The big Indian made no answer. A restless shifting of
the group took place, forming a circle in which Smoke and
Cultus George faced each other. Smoke realized that he
had been made the representative of his fellows in what
was to take place. He was angered. It was beyond him that
any human creature, witness to this scramble of volun-
teers, should hang back. Smoke did not dream that the
Indian held back for any reason save the selfish, mer-
cenary one.

"You will take a team," Smoke said.

"How much?" Cultus George asked.

A spontaneous snarl grated in the throats and twisted
the mouths of the miners. With clenched fists they pressed
in on the offender.

"Wait a bit," Smoke cried. "Look, George. Nobody is
charging anything. They're giving everything to save two
hundred Indians from starving to death." He paused.

"How much?" said Cultus George.

"Wait, you fellows! Now listen, George. Don't make any mistake. You've seen what these men are doing—coughing up dust, giving dogs and sleds, falling over one another to hit the trail. Only the best men can go with the first sleds. You ought to be proud. We think you are a number-one musher. It isn't a case of how much, but how quick."

"How much?" said Cultus George.

"Kill him!" "Bust his head!" "Tar and feathers!" were several of the cries in the wild medley that went up.

In the storm center Cultus George stood imperturbable, while Smoke thrust back the fiercest and shouted:

"Wait! Who's running this?" The clamor died away. "Fetch a rope," he added quietly.

Cultus George shrugged his shoulders, his face twisting tensely in an incredulous grin. He knew this white-man breed. He had toiled on trail with it too long not to know it. It always punished the man who broke the law. But he had broken no law. He had neither murdered, stolen, nor lied. There was nothing in the white man's law against charging a price and driving a bargain. They all charged a price and drove bargains. He was doing nothing more than that, and it was the thing they had taught him. Besides, if he wasn't good enough to drink with them, then he was not good enough to be charitable with them.

Neither Smoke nor any man there glimpsed what lay in Cultus George's brain. To them, he was a selfish brute; to him, they were selfish brutes.

When the rope was brought, Long Bill Haskell, Fat Olsen, and the crap player, with awkwardness and angry haste, got the slip noose around the Indian's neck and threw the rope over a rafter. At the other end of the dangling thing a dozen men tailed on, ready to hoist away.

Nor had Cultus George resisted. He knew it for what it was—bluff. The whites were strong on bluff. Did they not buy and sell and make all bargains with bluff?

"Wait," Smoke commanded. "Tie his hands. We don't want him climbing."

More bluff, Cultus George decided, and passively permitted his hands to be tied behind his back.

"It's your last chance, George," said Smoke. "Will you take out the team?"

"How much?" said Cultus George.

Astounded at himself that he should be able to do such a thing, and at the same time angered by the apparent selfishness of the Indian, Smoke gave the signal. Nor was Cultus George any less astounded when he felt the noose tighten with a jerk and swing him off the floor. His stolidity broke on the instant. On his face, in quick succession, appeared surprise, dismay, and pain.

Smoke watched anxiously. Having never been hanged himself, he felt a tyro at the business. The body struggled convulsively, the tied hands strove to burst the bonds, and from the throat came unpleasant noises of strangulation. Suddenly Smoke held up his hand.

"Slack away!" he ordered.

Grumbling at the shortness of the punishment, the men on the rope lowered Cultus George to the floor. His eyes were bulging, and he was tottery on his feet, swaying from side to side and still making a fight with his hands. Smoke thrust violent fingers between the rope and the neck, and brought the noose back with a jerk. With a great heave of the chest, Cultus George got his first breath.

"Will you take that team out?" Smoke demanded.

Cultus George debated with himself. He was no coward. Perhaps this was the extent of their bluff, and if he gave in now he was a fool. And while he debated, Smoke suffered from secret worry lest he would persist in being hanged.

"How much?" said Cultus George.

Smoke started to raise his hand for the signal.

"Me go," Cultus George said very quickly, before the rope could tighten.

"An' when that rescue expedition found me," Shorty told it in the Annie Mine," that ornery Cultus George was the first in, beatin' Smoke's sled by three hours; an' don't you forget it, Smoke comes in second at that. Just the same, it was about time, when I heard Cultus George a-yellin' at his dogs from the top of the divide, for those blamed Siwashes had ate my moccasins, my mitts, the leather lacin's, my knife sheath, an' some of 'em was beginnin' to look mighty hungry at me—me bein' better nourished, you see."

CHAPTER 10

The Townsite of Tra-Lee

SMOKE and Shorty encountered each other, going in opposite directions, at the corner near the Elkhorn saloon. The former's face wore a pleased expression, and he was walking briskly. Shorty, on the other hand, was slouching along in depressed fashion.

"Whither away?" Smoke challenged.

"Danged if I know," came the disconsolate answer. "Wisht I did. They ain't nothin' to take me anywheres. I've set two hours in the deadest game of draw—nothing excitin', no hands, an' broke even. Played a rubber of cribbage with Skiff Mitchell for the drinks, an' now I'm that languid for somethin' doin' that I'm perambulatin' the streets on the chance of seein' a dogfight, or a argument, or somethin'."

"I've got something better on hand," Smoke answered. "Come on along."

"Now?"

"Sure."

"Where to?"

"Across the river to call on old Dwight Sanderson."

"Never heard of him," Shorty said dejectedly. "Never

heard of no one living *across* the river anyway. What's he
want to live there for? Ain't he got no sense?"

"He's got something to sell," Smoke laughed.

"Dogs? A gold mine? Tobacco? Rubber boots?"

Smoke shook his head to each question. "Come along
and find out. I'm going to buy it from him on spec, and
if you want you can come in half."

"Don't tell me it's eggs!" Shorty cried, his face twisted
into an expression of alarm.

"Come on along," Smoke told him. "I'll give you ten
more guesses while we're crossing the ice."

They dipped down the high bank at the foot of the
street and came out upon the ice-covered Yukon. Three-
quarters of a mile away, directly opposite, the other bank
of the stream rose in precipitous bluffs hundreds of feet
high. Toward these bluffs, winding and twisting in and
out among broken and upthrown blocks of ice, ran a
slightly traveled trail. Shorty trudged at Smoke's heels,
guessing what Dwight Sanderson had to sell.

"Reindeer? Copper mine or brick yard?—that's one
guess. Bearskins, or any kind of skins? Lottery tickets? A
potato ranch?"

"Getting near it," Smoke encouraged. "And better than
that."

"Two potato ranches? A cheese factory? A moss farm?"

"Not so bad, Shorty. It's not a thousand miles away."

"A quarry?"

"That's as near as the moss farm and potato ranch."

"Hold on. Let me think. I got one guess comin'." Minutes passed. "Say, Smoke, I ain't goin' to use that last
guess. When this thing you're buyin' sounds like a potato
ranch, a moss farm, an' a stone quarry, I quit. An' I don't
go in on the deal till I see it an' size it up. What is it?"

"You'll see the cards on the table soon enough. See the smoke from that cabin up there? That's where Dwight Sanderson lives. He's holding down a whole townsite location."

"What else is he holdin' down?"

"That's all," Smoke laughed. "Except rheumatism."

"Say!" Shorty's hand flashed out and brought his comrade to a halt. "You ain't telling me you're buyin' a townsite at this fallin'-off place?"

"That's your tenth guess, and you win. Come on."

"Wait a moment," Shorty pleaded. "Look at it—nothin' but bluffs an' slides, all up-and-down. Where could the town stand?"

"Search me."

"Then you ain't buyin' it for a town?"

"Dwight Sanderson's selling it for a town. Come on. We've got to climb this slide."

The slide was steep, and a narrow trail zigzagged up it on a formidable Jacob's ladder. Shorty moaned and groaned over the sharp corners and the steep pitches.

"Think of a townsite here. They ain't a flat space big enough for a postage stamp. Sanderson picked the wrong side of the river. All the freightin' goes the other way. Look at Dawson there. Room to spread for forty thousand more people. Smoke, I know you ain't buyin' it for a town. What in Heaven's name are you buyin' it for?"

"To sell, of course."

"But other folks ain't as crazy as old man Sanderson an' you."

"Maybe not in the same way, Shorty. But I'm going to take this townsite, break it up in parcels, and sell it to a lot of sane people who live over in Dawson."

"Huh! All Dawson's still laughing at you an' me an' them eggs. You want to make 'em laugh some more?"

"I certainly do."

"But it's too danged expensive, Smoke. I helped make 'em laugh with the eggs, but my share of the laugh cost nearly nine thousan' dollars."

"All right. You help me with this, and I promise you'll get back every penny you dropped on the eggs."

"Oh, I'll help all right. Then they can laugh at me some more. What's old Sanderson holdin' it at? A couple of hundred?"

"Ten thousand. I ought to get it for five."

"Wisht I was a minister," Shorty breathed fervently.

"What for?"

"So I could preach the gosh-dangdest, eloquentest sermon on a text you may have hearn—to wit: a fool an' his money."

"Come in," Dwight Sanderson yelled irritably when they knocked at his door. They entered to find him squatting by a stone fireplace, pounding coffee in a piece of flour-sacking.

"What d'ye want?" he demanded harshly, emptying the coffee into the pot that stood on the coals.

"To talk business," Smoke answered. "You've a townsite located here, I understand. What do you want for it?"

"Ten thousand dollars," came the answer. "And now that I've told you, laugh, and get out. There's the door. Good-by."

"But I don't want to laugh. I know plenty of funnier things to do than to climb up this cliff of yours. I want to buy your townsite."

"You do, eh? Well, I'm glad to hear sense." Sanderson

came over and sat down facing his visitors, his hands resting on the table and his eyes cocking apprehensively toward the coffeepot. "I've told you my price, and I ain't
ashamed to tell you again—ten thousand. You can laugh
or buy, it's all one to me."

To show his indifference he drummed with knobby
knuckles on the table, stared at the coffeepot, and began to
hum a monotonous *"Tra-la-loo, tra-la-lee, tra-la-lee, tra-
la-loo."*

"Look here, Mr. Sanderson," said Smoke. "This townsite isn't worth ten thousand. If it was worth that much it
would be worth a hundred thousand just as easily. If it
isn't worth a hundred thousand—and you know it isn't—
then it isn't worth *ten cents.*"

Sanderson drummed with his knuckles and hummed
"Tra-la-loo, tra-la-lee," until the coffee boiled over. Set-
tling it with some cold water, and placing it to one side of
the warm hearth, he resumed his seat. "How much do you
offer?" he asked Smoke.

"Five thousand."

Shorty groaned.

Again came an interval of drumming and *tra-loo-ing*
and *tra-lee-ing.*

"You ain't no fool," Sanderson suddenly announced to
Smoke. "You said if it wasn't worth a hundred thousand,
it wasn't worth ten cents. Yet you offer five thousand for
it. Then it *is* worth a hundred thousand."

"You can't make twenty cents out of it," Smoke replied
heatedly. "Not if you stayed here till you rot."

"I'll make it out of *you.*"

"No, you won't."

"Then I reckon I'll stay an' rot," Sanderson answered
with an air of finality.

He took no further notice of his guests, and went about his tasks as if he were alone. When he had warmed over a pot of beans and a slab of sourdough bread, he set the table for one and proceeded to eat.

"No, thank you," Shorty murmured. "We ain't a bit hungry. We et just before we come."

"Let's see your papers," Smoke said at last. Sanderson fumbled under the head of his bunk and tossed out a package of documents. "It's all tight and right," he said. "That long one there, with the big seals, come all the way from Ottawa. Nothing territorial about that. The Canadian government cinches me in the possession of this townsite."

"How many lots you sold in the two years you've had it?" Shorty queried.

"None of your business," Sanderson answered sourly. "There ain't no law against a man living alone on his townsite if he wants to."

"I'll give you five thousand," Smoke said. Sanderson shook his head.

"I don't know which is the craziest," Shorty lamented. "Come outside a minute, Smoke. I want to whisper to you."

Smoke yielded to his partner's persuasions.

"Ain't it never entered your head," Shorty said, as they stood in the snow outside the door, "that they's miles an' miles of cliffs on both sides this fool townsite that don't belong to nobody an' that you can have for the locatin' and stakin'?"

"They won't do," Smoke answered.

"Why won't they?"

"It makes you wonder, with all those miles and miles, why I'm buying this particular spot, doesn't it?"

"It sure does," Shorty agreed.

"That's the very point," Smoke went on triumphantly. "If it makes *you* wonder, it will make others wonder. And when they wonder they'll come a-running. By your own wondering you prove it's sound psychology. I'm going to hand Dawson a package that will knock the spots out of the egg-laugh. Come on inside."

"Hello," said Sanderson, as they re-entered. "I thought I'd seen the last of you."

"*Now* what is your lowest figure?" Smoke asked.

"Twenty thousand."

"I'll give you ten."

"All right, I'll sell. It's all I wanted in the first place. When will you pay the dust over?"

"Tomorrow, at the Northwest Bank. But there are two other things I want for that ten thousand. In the first place, when you receive your money you pull down the river to Forty-Mile and stay there the rest of the winter."

"That's easy. What else?"

"I'm actually going to pay you twenty-five thousand, but you rebate me fifteen of it."

"I'm agreeable." Sanderson turned to Shorty. "Folks said I was a fool when I come over here an' townsited," he jeered. "Well, I'm a ten thousand dollar fool, ain't I?"

"The Klondike's so full of fools," was all Shorty could retort, "some of 'em has to be lucky, don't they?"

Next morning the legal transfer of Dwight Sanderson's townsite—"henceforth to be known as the townsite of Tra-Lee," Smoke stated in the deed—was made. Also, at the Northwest Bank, twenty-five thousand of Smoke's gold was weighed out by the cashier, while half a dozen casual onlookers noted the weighing, the amount, and the recipient.

In a mining camp, any untoward act of any man is likely to be the cue to a secret gold strike, whether the act is no more than a hunting trip for moose or a stroll after dark to observe the aurora borealis. When it became known that so prominent a figure as Smoke Bellew had paid twenty-five thousand dollars to old Dwight Sanderson, Dawson wanted to know what he had paid it for. What had Dwight Sanderson, starving on his abandoned townsite, ever owned that was worth twenty-five thousand? Dawson contemplated this problem feverishly.

By midafternoon it was common knowledge that several score of men had made up light stampeding-packs and cached them in convenient saloons along Main Street. Wherever Smoke moved, he was observed by many eyes. And as proof that he was taken seriously, not one man of his acquaintance had the effrontery to ask him about his deal with Dwight Sanderson. Shorty was under similar surveillance and delicacy of friendliness.

"Makes me feel like I'd killed somebody, or had small-pox, the way they watch me an' seem afraid to speak," Shorty confessed, when he chanced to meet Smoke in front of the Elkhorn. "Look at Bill Saltman there acrost the way—just dyin' to look, an' keepin' his eyes down the street all the time. Wouldn't think he'd knowed you an' me existed, to look at him. But I bet you the drinks, Smoke, if you an' me flop around the corner quick, like we was goin' somewheres, an' then turn back from around the next corner, that we run into him a-hikin' hell-bent."

They tried the trick, and, doubling back around the second corner, encountered Saltman swinging a long trail-stride in pursuit.

"Hello, Bill," Smoke greeted. "Which way?"

"Hello. Just a-strollin'," Saltman answered, "just a-strollin'. Weather's fine, ain't it?"

When Shorty fed the dogs that evening, he was keenly conscious that from the encircling darkness a dozen pairs of eyes were boring in upon him. And when he stick-tied the dogs, instead of letting them forage free through the night, he knew that he had administered another jolt to the nervousness of Dawson.

According to program, Smoke ate supper downtown and then proceeded to enjoy himself. Wherever he appeared, he was the center of interest, and he purposely made the rounds. Saloons filled up after his entrance and emptied following his departure. If he bought a stack of chips at a sleepy roulette table, inside five minutes a dozen players were around him. He avenged himself, in a small way, on Lucille Arral, by getting up and sauntering out of the Opera House just as she came on to sing her most popular song. In three minutes two-thirds of her audience had vanished after him.

At one in the morning he walked along an unusually populous Main Street and took the turning that led up the hill to his cabin. And when he paused on the ascent, he could hear behind him the crunch of moccasins in the snow.

For an hour the cabin was in darkness, then he lit a candle, and, after a delay sufficient for a man to dress in, he and Shorty opened the door and began harnessing the dogs. As the light from the cabin flared out upon them and their work, a soft whistle went up from not far away. This whistle was repeated down the hill.

"Listen to it," Smoke chuckled. "They've relayed on us and are passing the word down to town. I'll bet you there are forty men right now rolling out of their blankets and climbing into their pants."

"Ain't folks fools," Shorty giggled back. "Say, Smoke, they ain't nothin' in hard graft. A geezer that'd work his hands these days is a—well, a geezer. The world's sure bustin' full an' dribblin' over the edges with fools a-honin' to be separated from their dust. An' before we start down the hill I want to make sure, if you're still agreeable, that I come in half on this deal."

The sled was lightly loaded with a sleeping and grub outfit. A small coil of steel cable protruded inconspicuously from underneath a grub-sack, while a crowbar lay half hidden along the bottom of the sled next to the lashings. Shorty fondled the cable with a swift-passing mitten, and gave a last affectionate touch to the crowbar.

They drove the dogs down the hill with cautious silence, emerged on the flat, and turned north along Main Street toward the sawmill, directly away from the business part of town. They had seen no one, yet when this change of direction was initiated, out of the dim starlit darkness behind arose a whistle. Past the sawmill and the hospital, at lively speed, they went for a quarter of a mile. Then they turned about and headed back over the ground they had just covered. At the end of the first hundred yards they barely missed colliding with five men racing along at a quick dogtrot. All were slightly stooped with the weight of stampeding-packs. One of them stopped Smoke's lead-dog, and the rest clustered around.

"Seen a sled goin' the other way?"

"Nope," Smoke answered. "That you, Bill?"

"Well, I'll be danged!" Bill Saltman ejaculated in honest surprise. "Smoke!"

"What are you doing out this time of night?" Smoke inquired. "Strolling?"

Before Bill Saltman could make reply, two running men joined the group. These were followed by several more, while the crunch of feet on the snow heralded the imminent arrival of many others.

"Who are your friends?" Smoke asked. "Where's the stampede?"

Saltman, lighting his pipe, did not reply. The ruse of his match was too obviously for the purpose of seeing the sled to be misunderstood. Smoke noted every pair of eyes focus on the coil of cable and the crowbar. Then the match went out.

"Just heard a rumor, that's all, just a rumor," Saltman mumbled with ponderous secretiveness.

"You might let Shorty and me in on it," Smoke urged.

Somebody snickered sarcastically in the background.

"Where are *you* bound?" Saltman demanded.

"Who are you?" Smoke countered. "Committee of Safety?"

"Just interested, just interested," Saltman said.

"You bet your sweet life we're interested," another voice spoke up out of the darkness.

"Say," Shorty put in, "I wonder who's feelin' the foolishest?"

Everybody laughed nervously.

"Come on, Shorty; we'll be getting along," Smoke said, mushing the dogs.

The crowd formed in behind and followed.

"Say, ain't you-all made a mistake?" Shorty gibed. "When we met you you was goin', an' now you're comin' without bein' anywheres. Have you lost your map?"

"Go to the devil," was Saltman's courtesy. "We go and

come just as we danged feel like. We don't travel with maps."

And the sled, with Smoke in the lead and Shorty at the pole, went on down Main Street escorted by three score men, each of whom, on his back, bore a stampeding-pack. It was three in the morning.

Half an hour later, the hill was climbed and the dogs unharnessed at the cabin door, the sixty stampeders grimly attendant.

"Good night, fellows," Smoke called, as he closed the door.

In five minutes the candle was put out, but before half an hour had passed Smoke and Shorty emerged softly, and without lights began harnessing the dogs.

"Hello, Smoke!" Saltman said, stepping near enough for them to see the loom of his form.

"Can't shake you, Bill, I see," Smoke replied cheerfully. "Where're your friends?"

"Gone to have a drink. They left me to keep an eye on you, and keep it I will. What's in the wind anyway, Smoke? You can't shake us, so you might as well let us in. We're all your friends. You know that."

"There are times when you can let your friends in," Smoke evaded, "and times when you can't. Bill, this is one of the times when we can't. You'd better go to bed. Good night."

"Ain't goin' to be no good night, Smoke. You don't know us. We're woodticks."

Smoke sighed. "Well, Bill, if you *will* have your way, I guess you'll have to have it. Come on, Shorty, we can't hang around here any longer."

Saltman emitted a shrill whistle as the sled started, and swung in behind. From down the hill and across the flat came the answering whistles of the relays. Shorty was at the gee pole, and Smoke and Saltman walked side by side.

"Look here, Bill," Smoke said. "I'll make you a proposition. Do you want to come in alone on this?"

Saltman did not hesitate. "An' throw the gang down? No, sir. We'll all come in."

"You first, then," Smoke exclaimed, lurching into a clinch and tipping the other into deep snow beside the trail.

Shorty hawed the dogs and swung the team to the south on the trail that led among the scattered cabins on the rolling slopes to the rear of Dawson. Smoke and Saltman, locked together, rolled in the snow. Smoke considered himself in gilt-edged condition, but Saltman outweighed him by fifty pounds of trail-hardened muscle and repeatedly mastered him. Time and time again he got Smoke on his back, and Smoke lay complacently and rested. But each time Saltman attempted to get off him and away, Smoke reached out a detaining, tripping hand that brought about a new clinch and wrestle.

"You can go some," Saltman acknowledged, panting at the end of ten minutes, as he sat astride Smoke's chest. "But I down you every time."

"That's just what I'm here for," Smoke panted back. "Where do you think Shorty's getting to all this time?"

Saltman made a wild effort to go clear, and all but succeeded. Smoke gripped his ankle and threw him in a headlong tumble. From down the hill came anxious questioning whistles. Saltman sat up and whistled a shrill answer, and was grappled by Smoke, who rolled him face upward and sat astride his chest, his knees resting on Saltman's biceps, his hands on Saltman's shoulders and holding him down. And in this position the stampeders found them. Smoke laughed and got up.

"Well, good night, fellows," he said, and started down the hill, sixty exasperated and grimly determined stampeders at his heels.

He turned north past the sawmill and the hospital and took the river trail along the precipitous bluffs at the base of Moosehide Hill. Circling the Indian village, he held on to the mouth of Moosehide Creek, then turned and faced his pursuers.

"You make me tired," he said, with a good imitation of a snarl.

"Hope we ain't a-forcin' you," Saltman murmured politely.

"Oh, no, not at all," Smoke snarled with an even better imitation, as he passed among them on the back-trail to Dawson. Twice he attempted to cross the trailless ice jams of the river, still resolutely followed, and both times he gave up and returned to the Dawson shore. Straight down Main Street he trudged, crossing the ice of Klondike River to Klondike City and again retracing to Dawson. At eight o'clock, as gray dawn began to show, he led his weary gang to Slavovitch's Restaurant, where tables were at a premium for breafast.

"Good night fellows," he said, as he paid his bill and took his climb up the hill. In the clear light of day they did not follow him, contenting themselves with watching him up the hill to his cabin.

For two days Smoke lingered about town, continually under vigilant espionage. Shorty, with the sled and dogs, had disappeared. Neither travelers up and down the Yukon, nor from Bonanza, Eldorado, nor the Klondike, had seen him. Remained only Smoke, who, sooner or later, was certain to try to connect with his missing partner; and upon Smoke everybody's attention was centered. On the second night he did not leave his cabin, putting out the lamp at nine in the evening and setting the alarm for two next morning. The watch outside heard the alarm go off, so that when, half an hour later, he emerged from the cabin, he found waiting him a band, not of sixty men, but at least three hundred. A flaming aurora borealis lighted the scene, and, thus hugely escorted, he walked down to town and entered the Elkhorn. The place was immediately packed and jammed by an anxious and irritated multitude that bought drinks, and for four weary hours watched Smoke play cribbage with his old friend Breck. Shortly after six in the morning, with an expression on his face of commingled hatred and gloom, seeing no one, recognizing no one, Smoke left the Elkhorn and went up Main Street. Behind him the three hundred formed in disorderly ranks, chanting: "Hayfoot! Strawfoot! Hep! Hep! Hep!"

"Good night, fellows," he said bitterly, at the edge of the Yukon bank where the winter trail dipped down. "I'm going to get breakfast and then go to bed."

The three hundred shouted that they were still with him, and followed him out upon the frozen river on the direct path he took for Tra-Lee. At seven in the morning he led his stampeding cohort up the zigzag trail and across the face of the slide that led to Dwight Sanderson's cabin. The light of a candle showed through the parchment-paper window, and smoke curled from the chimney. Shorty threw open the door.

"Come on in, Smoke," he greeted. "Breakfast's ready. Who-all are your friends?"

Smoke turned about on the threshold. "Well, good night, fellows. Hope you enjoyed your trip!"

"Hold on a moment, Smoke," Bill Saltman cried, his voice keen with disappointment. "Want to talk with you."

"Fire away," Smoke answered genially.

"What'd you pay old Sanderson twenty-five thousan' for. Will you answer that?"

"Bill, you give me a pain," was Smoke's reply. "I came over here for a country residence, so to speak, and here are you and a gang trying to cross-examine me when I'm looking for peace an' quietness an' breakfast. What's a country residence good for, except for peace and quietness?"

"You ain't answered the question," Bill Saltman came back.

"And I'm not going to, Bill. That affair is peculiarly a personal affair between Dwight Sanderson and me. Any other question?"

"How about that crowbar an' steel cable then, what you had on your sled the other night?"

"None of your blessed and ruddy business, Bill."

The door closed and the three hundred sagged into forlorn and grumbling groups.

"Say, Saltman," one man said, "I thought you was goin' to lead us to it."

"Not on your life," Saltman answered crustily. "I said Smoke would lead us to it."

"An' this is it?"

"You know as much about it as me, an' we all know Smoke's got something salted down somewheres. For what else did he pay Sanderson twenty-five thousand? Not for this mangy townsite, that's sure an' certain."

"Well, what are we goin' to do now?" some one queried dolefully.

"Me for one for breakfast," Wild Water Charley said cheerfully. "You led us up a blind alley this time, Bill."

"I tell you I didn't," Saltman objected. "Smoke led us. An' just the same, what about them twenty-five thousand?"

At half-past eight, when daylight had grown strong, Shorty carefully opened the door and peered out. "Shucks," he exclaimed. "They-all's hiked back to Dawson. I thought they was goin' to camp here."

"Don't worry; they'll come sneaking back," Smoke reassured him. "If I don't miss my guess you'll see half Dawson over here before we're done. Now lend me a hand. We've got work to do."

At the end of an hour, they surveyed the result of their toil—a windlass in the corner of the cabin, with an endless rope that ran around double log rollers.

Smoke turned it with a minimum of effort, and the rope slipped and creaked. "Now, Shorty, go outside and tell me what it sounds like."

Shorty, listening at the closed door, heard all the sound effects of a windlass hoisting a load, and caught himself unconsciously attempting to estimate the depth of shaft out of which this load was being hoisted. Next came a pause, and in his mind's eye he saw the bucket swinging short to the windlass. Then he heard the quick lower-away and the dull sound as of the bucket coming to abrupt rest on the edge of the shaft. He threw open the door, beaming.

"I almost fell for it myself," he cried. "What next?"

The next was the dragging into the cabin of a dozen

sled-loads of rock. And through an exceedingly busy day there were many other nexts.

"Run the dogs over to Dawson this evening," Smoke instructed, when supper was finished. "Leave them with Breck. He'll take care of them. They'll be watching what you do, so get Breck to go to the A. C. Company and buy up the rest of the blasting powder—there's only several hundred pounds in stock. Have Breck order half a dozen hard-rock drills from the blacksmith. And give Breck these location descriptions, so that he can record them at the Gold Commissioner's tomorrow. And finally, at ten o'clock, you be on Main Street listening."

At ten that night Shorty, strolling down Main Street, aware of many curious eyes, his ears keyed tensely, heard a faint and distant explosion. Thirty seconds later there was a second, sufficiently loud to attract the attention of others on the street. Then came a third, so violent that it rattled the windows and brought the inhabitants into the street.

"Shook 'em up beautiful," Shorty proclaimed breathlessly, an hour afterward, when he arrived at the cabin on Tra-Lee. He gripped Smoke's hand. "You should a-saw 'em. Ever kick over a anthill? Dawson's just like that. Main Street was crawlin' an' hummin' when I pulled my freight. You won't see Tra-Lee tomorrow for folks. If they ain't some a-sneakin' across right now I don't know minin' nature, that's all."

Shorty pulled out the moss chinking from between the logs so as to make peepholes on every side of the cabin. Then he blew out the candle.

"Now," he whispered at the end of half an hour.

Smoke turned the windlass slowly, paused after several minutes, caught up a galvanized bucket filled with earth and struck it with slide, scrape, and grind against the heap of rocks they had hauled in. Then he lit a cigarette, shielding the flame of the match in his hands.

"They's three of 'em," Shorty whispered. "You oughta saw 'em. Say, when you made that bucket-dump noise they was fair quiverin'. They's one at the window now tryin' to peek in."

"We've got to do this thing regularly," Smoke breathed. "We'll haul up a bucket every fifteen minutes. And in the meantime—"

Through triple thicknesses of sacking, he struck a cold chisel on the face of a rock.

"Beautiful, beautiful," Shorty moaned with delight. He crept over noiselessly from the peephole. "They've got their heads together. I can almost see 'em talkin'."

And from then until four in the morning, at fifteen-minute intervals, the bucket was seemingly hoisted on the windlass that creaked and ran around on itself and hoisted nothing. Then their visitors departed, and Smoke and Shorty went to bed.

After daylight, Shorty examined the moccasin prints. "Big Bill Saltman was one of them," he concluded. "Look at the size of it!"

Smoke looked out over the river. "Get ready for visitors. There are two crossing the ice now."

"Huh! Wait till Breck files that string of claims at nine o'clock. There'll be two thousand crossing over."

"And every mother's son of them yammering 'mother lode,' " Smoke laughed. " 'The source of Klondike placers found at last.' "

Shorty, who had clambered to the top of a steep shoulder

of rock, gazed with the eye of a connoiseur at the strip they had staked.

"It sure looks like a true fissure vein," he said. "A expert could almost trace the lines of it under the snow. It'd fool anybody. The slide fills the front of it, an' see them outcrops? Look like the real thing, only they ain't."

When the two men, crossing the river, climbed the zigzag trail up the slide, they found a closed cabin. Bill Saltman, who led the way, went softly to the door, listened, then beckoned Wild Water Charley up to him. From inside came the creak and whine of a windlass bearing a heavy load. They waited at the final pause, then heard the lower-away and the impact of a bucket on rock. Four times, in the next hour, they heard the thing repeated. Then Wild Water knocked on the door. From inside came low furtive noises, then silences, and more furtive noises, and at the end of five minutes Smoke, breathing heavily, opened the door an inch and peered out. They saw on his face and shirt powdered rock fragments. His greeting was suspiciously genial.

"Wait a minute," he added, "and I'll be with you."

Pulling on mittens, he slipped through the door and confronted the visitors outside in the snow. Their quick eyes noted his shirt, discolored and powdery across the shoulders, and the knees of his overalls that showed signs of dirt brushed hastily but not quite thoroughly away.

"Rather early for a call," he observed. "What brings you across the river? Going hunting?"

"We're on, Smoke," Wild Water said confidentially. "You'd just as well come through. You've got something here."

"If you're looking for more eggs—" Smoke began.

"Aw, cut it out. We mean business."

"You mean you want to buy lots?" Smoke rattled on. "Some dandy building sites here, but we can't sell yet. We haven't had the town surveyed. Come around next week, Wild Water, and for peace and quietness, I'll show you something swell, if you're anxious to live over here. Next week, sure, it will be surveyed. Good-by. Sorry I can't ask you inside, but Shorty—well, you know him. He's peculiar. He says he came over for peace and quietness, and he's asleep now. I wouldn't wake him for the world."

As Smoke talked he shook their hands warmly in farewell. Still talking and shaking their hands, he stepped inside and closed the door.

They looked at each other and nodded significantly.

"See the knees of his pants?" Saltman whispered hoarsely.

"Sure. An' his shoulders. He's been bumpin' an' crawlin' around in a shaft." As Wild Water talked, his eyes wandered up the snow-covered ravine until they were halted by something that brought a whistle to his lips. "Just cast your eyes up there, Bill. See where I'm pointing? If that ain't a prospect-hole! An' follow it out to both sides—you can see where they tramped in the snow. If it ain't rim-rock on both sides I don't know what rim-rock is. It's a fissure vein, all right."

"An' look at the size of it!" Saltman cried. "They've got something here, you bet."

"An' run your eyes down the slide there—see them bluffs standin' out an' slopin' in. The whole slide's in the mouth of the vein as well."

"And now just *keep* a-lookin' on, out on the ice there, on the trail," Saltman directed. "Looks like most of Dawson, don't it?"

Wild Water took one glance and saw the trail black with men clear to the far Dawson bank, down which the same unbroken string of men was pouring.

"Well, I'm goin' to get a look-in at that prospect-hole before they get here," he said, turning and starting swiftly up the ravine.

But the cabin door opened, and the two occupants stepped out.

"Hey!" Smoke called. "Where are you going?"

"To pick out a lot," Wild Water called back. "Look at the river. All Dawson's stampeding to buy lots, an' we're going to beat 'em to it for the choice. Right, Bill?"

"Sure thing," Saltman corroborated. "This has the makin's of a Jim-dandy suburb, an' it sure looks like it'll be popular."

"We're not selling lots in that section where you're heading," Smoke answered. "Over to the right there, and back on top of the bluffs are the lots. This section, running from the river and over the tops, is reserved. So come on back."

"That's the spot we've gone and selected," Saltman argued.

"Nothing doing," Smoke said sharply.

"Any objections to our strolling, then?" Saltman persisted.

"Decidedly. Your strolling is getting monotonous. Come on back down from there."

"I just reckon we'll stroll anyways," Saltman replied stubbornly. "Come on, Wild Water."

"I warn you, you're trespassing," was Smoke's final word.

"Nope, just strollin'," Saltman gaily retorted, turning his back and starting on.

"Hey! Stop in your tracks, Bill, or I'll sure bore you!" Shorty thundered, drawing and leveling two Colt forty-fours. "Step another step in your steps an' I let eleven holes through your danged ornery carcass. Get it?"

Saltman stopped, perplexed.

"He sure got it," Shorty whispered to Smoke. "If he goes on I'm up against it hard. I can't shoot. What'll I do?"

Saltman himself came to the rescue. "Look, Shorty, listen to reason," he begged.

"Come here to me an' we'll talk reason," was Shorty's retort.

And they were still talking reason when the head of the stampede emerged from the zigzag trail and came upon them.

"You can't call a man a trespasser when he's on a town-site lookin' to buy lots," Wild Water was arguing, and Shorty was objecting: "But they's private property in townsites, an' that there strip is private property, that's all. I tell you again, it ain't for sale."

"Now we've got to swing this thing on the jump," Smoke muttered to Shorty. "If they ever get out of hand—"

"You've sure got nerve, if you think you can hold them," Shorty muttered back. "They's two thousan' of 'em an' more a-comin'. They'll break this line any minute."

The line ran along the near rim of the ravine, and Shorty had formed it by halting the first arrivals when they got that far in their invasion. With the crowd had come half a dozen Northwest Mounted Police with a lieutenant. With the latter Smoke conferred in undertones.

"They're still piling out of Dawson," he said. "Before long there will be five thousand here. The danger is if they start jumping claims. Those claims were recorded this morning and can't be jumped."

"Right-o," said the lieutenant. "I'll get my men together. We can't have any trouble here, and we won't have. But you'd better get up and talk to them."

"There must be some mistake, fellows," Smoke began in a loud voice. "We're not ready to sell lots. The streets are not surveyed yet. Next week we shall have the grand opening sale."

He was interrupted by an outburst of impatience and indignation.

"We don't want lots," a young miner cried out. "We don't want what's on top of the ground. We've come for what's under the ground."

"We don't know what we've got under the ground," Smoke answered. "But we do know we've got a fine townsite on top of it."

"Sure," Shorty added. "Grand for scenery an' solitude. Folks lovin' solitude come a-flockin' here by thousands. Most popular solitude on the Yukon."

Again the impatient cries arose, and Saltman, who had been talking with the later comers, came to the front.

"We're here to stake claims," he opened. "We know what you've did—filed a string of five quartz claims on end, and there they are over there running across the townsite on the line of the slide and the canyon. Only you misplayed. Two of them entries is fake. Who is Seth Bierce? No one ever heard of him. An' you filed a claim in the name of Harry Maxwell. Harry Maxwell ain't in the country. He's down in Seattle. Went out last fall. Them two claims is open to relocation."

"Suppose I have his power of attorney?" Smoke queried.

"You ain't," Saltman answered. "If you have, you got

to show it. Anyway, here's where we relocate. Come on, fellows."

Saltman, stepping across the deadline, had turned to encourage a following, when the Mountie lieutenant's voice rang out and stopped the forward surge of the great mass.

"Hold on there! You can't do that, you know!"

"Can't, eh?" said Bill Saltman. "The law says a fake location can be relocated, don't it?"

"Thet's right, Bill! Stay with it!" the crowd cheered from the safe side of the line.

"It's the law, ain't it?" Saltman demanded truculently of the lieutenant.

"It may be the law," came the steady answer. "But I won't allow a mob of five thousand men to attempt to jump two claims. It would be a riot, and we're here to see there is no riot. Here, now, on this spot, the Northwest Mounted Police are the law. The next man who crosses that line will be shot. Saltman, step back."

Saltman obeyed reluctantly. But an ominous restlessness became apparent in the mass of men, irregularly packed and scattered over a landscape that was mostly up-and-down.

Smoke shuddered and got up. "I'm willing to play fair, fellows. If you insist on town lots, I'll sell them to you, one hundred dollars apiece, and you can raffle locations when the survey is made." With raised hand he stilled the movement of disgust. "Don't move, anybody. If you do, there'll be hundreds of you shoved over the bluff. The situation is dangerous."

"Just the same, you can't hog it," a voice went up. "We don't want lots. We want to relocate."

"But there are only two disputed claims," Smoke argued. "When they're relocated where will the rest of you be?"

He mopped his forehead with his shirt-sleeve, and another voice cried out:

"Let us all in, share and share alike!"

Nor did those who roared their approbation realize that the suggestion had been made by Breck, primed to make it the moment he saw Smoke mop his forehead.

"Take your feet out of the trough an' pool the townsite," Breck went on. "Pool the mineral rights with the townsite, too."

"But there isn't anything in the mineral rights, I tell you," Smoke objected.

"Then pool them with the rest. We'll take our chances on it."

"Fellows, you're forcing me," Smoke said. "I wish you'd stayed on your side of the river."

With a mighty roar the crowd swept him on to agreement. But Saltman and others in the front rank demurred.

"Bill Saltman, here, and Wild Water don't want you all in," Smoke informed the crowd. "Who's hogging it now?"

And at that, Saltman and Wild Water became profoundly unpopular.

"Now how are we going to do it?" Smoke asked. "Shorty and I ought to keep control. We discovered this townsite."

"That's right!" many cried. "It's only fair!"

"Three-fifths to us," Smoke suggested, "and you fellows come in for two-fifths. And you've got to pay for your shares."

"Ten cents on the dollar!" was a cry.

"Ten cents on the dollar will help start things. You buy two-fifths of the stock, hundred dollars par, at ten dollars.

That's the best I can do. There's about five thousand of you, which will make five thousand shares," Smoke worked the problem aloud. "And five thousand is two-fifths of twelve thousand, five hundred. Therefore the Tra-Lee Townsite Company is capitalized for one million two hundred and fifty thousand dollars, there being twelve thousand, five hundred shares, hundred par, you fellows buying five thousand of them at ten dollars apiece. And I don't care a whoop whether you accept it or not. And I call you all to witness that you're forcing me against my will."

With the assurance of the crowd that they had caught him with the goods in the form of two fake locations, a committee was formed and the rough organization of the Tra-Lee Townsite Company effected. Scorning the proposal of delivering the shares next day in Dawson, because of the objection that the portion of Dawson not engaged in the stampede would ring in for shares, the committee, by a fire on the ice at the foot of the slide, issued a receipt to each stampeder in return for ten dollars in dust duly weighed on two dozen gold-scales brought over from Dawson.

By twilight the work was accomplished and Tra-Lee was deserted, save for Smoke and Shorty, who ate supper in the cabin and chuckled at the list of shareholders, four thousand eight hundred and seventy-four strong, and at the gold-sacks, which contained forty-eight thousand seven hundred and forty dollars.

"But you ain't swung it yet," Shorty objected.

"He'll be here," Smoke asserted with conviction. "He's a born gambler. When Breck whispers the tip to him not even heart disease would stop him."

Within the hour came a knock at the door, and Wild Water entered, followed by Bill Saltman. Their eyes swept the cabin eagerly, coming to rest on the windlass elaborately concealed by blankets.

"But suppose I do want to buy twelve hundred more shares," Wild Water was arguing half an hour later. "With the other five thousand sold today it'd make only sixty-two hundred shares. That'd leave you and Shorty with sixty-three hundred. You'd still control."

"But what d'you want with that much townsite?" Shorty queried.

"You can answer that better 'n me," Wild Water replied. "An' between you an' me," his gaze drifted over the blanket-draped windlass, "it's a pretty good-looking townsite."

"But Bill wants some, too," Smoke said grudgingly. "We simply won't part with more than five hundred shares."

"How much you got to invest?" Wild Water asked Saltman.

"Five thousand. It's all I could scare up."

"Wild Water," Smoke went on, in the same grudging, complaining voice, "if I didn't know you so well, I wouldn't sell you a single besotted share. Shorty and I won't part with more than five hundred, and they'll cost you fifty dollars apiece. That's the last word, and if you don't like it, good night. Bill can take a hundred and you can have the other four hundred."

Next day Dawson began its laugh. It started early in the morning, just after daylight, when Smoke went to the bulletin board outside the A. C. Company store and tacked up a notice. Men gathered and were reading and snickering over his shoulder before he had driven the last tack. Soon the board was crowded by hundreds who could not get near enough to read. Then a reader was appointed by acclamation, and thereafter, throughout the day, many men were acclaimed to read in loud voice the notice Smoke Bellew had nailed up. And there were numbers of men who stood in the snow and heard it read several times in order to memorize the succulent items that appeared in the following order:

The Tra-Lee Townsite Company keeps its accounts on the wall. This is its first account and its last.

Moneys Received and Disbursed

From 4874 shares at $10.00	$48,740.00
To Dwight Sanderson for Townsite of Tra-Lee	10,000.00
To incidental expenses, to wit: powder, drills, windlass, gold commissioner's office, etc.	1,000.00
To Dawson General Hospital	37,740.00
Total	$48,740.00

(Any shareholder who objects to donating ten dollars to the Dawson General Hospital may obtain his ten dollars on personal application to Wild Water Charley, or, failing that, will absolutely obtain it on application to Smoke Bellew.)

From Bill Saltman, for 100 shares privately purchased at $50.00	$ 5,000.00
From Wild Water Charley, for 400 shares privately purchased at $50.00	20,000.00
Total	$25,000.00

To Bill Saltman, in recognition of services
as volunteer stampede promoter $5,000.00
To Dawson General Hospital   3,000.00
To Smoke Bellew and Jack Short, balance
in full on egg deal and morally owing   17,000.00

           Total $25,000.00

Shares remaining to account for 7126. These shares, held by Smoke Bellew and Jack Short, value nil, may be obtained gratis, for the asking, by any and all residents of Dawson desiring change of domicile to the peace and solitude of the town of Tra-Lee.

(NOTE: *Peace and solitude always and perpetually guaranteed in town of Tra-Lee*)

           SMOKE BELLEW, *President*
             JACK SHORT, *Secretary*

CHAPTER 11

Wonder of Woman

SMOKE turned his steaming, stick-propped moccasins in front of the campfire. "We've got to rest over tomorrow and make moccasins for the dogs," he vouchsafed. "That crust is playing the devil with their feet."

"We oughta keep goin' somehow," Shorty objected. "We ain't got grub enough to turn back with, and we gotta strike that run of caribou or them 'white Indians' almighty soon or we'll be eaten' the dogs, sore feet an' all. Now who ever seen them white Indians anyway? Nothin' but hearsay. How can a Indian be white? Smoke, we just oughta travel tomorrow. The country's plumb dead of game. We ain't seen even a rabbit-track in a week, you know that. An' we gotta get out of this dead streak into somewhere that meat's runnin'."

"They'll travel all the better with a day's rest for their feet and moccasins all around," Smoke counseled. "If you get a chance at any low divide, take a peep over at the country beyond. We're likely to strike open rolling country any time now. That's what La Perle told us to look for."

"Huh! It was ten years ago that La Perle come through

this section, an' he was that loco from hunger he couldn't
know what he did see. He said himself he never seen any
white Indians—that was Anton's yarn. An', besides, Anton kicked the bucket two years before you an' me come
North. But I'll take a look tomorrow. Mebbe I might pick
up a moose. What d' you say we turn in?"

Smoke spent the morning in camp, sewing dog-mocca-
sins and repairing harnesses. At noon he cooked a meal for
two, ate his share, and began to look for Shorty's return.
An hour later he strapped on his snowshoes and went out
on his partner's trail. The way led up the bed of the
stream, through a narrow canyon that widened suddenly
into a moose pasture. But no moose had been there since
the first snow of the preceding fall. The tracks of Shorty's
snowshoes crossed the pasture and went up the easy slope
of a low divide. At the crest Smoke halted. The tracks continued down the other slope. The first spruces, in the creek
bed, were a mile away, and it was evident that Shorty had
passed through them and gone on. Smoke looked at his
watch, remembering the oncoming darkness, the dogs, and
the camp, and reluctantly decided against going farther.
But before he retraced his steps he paused for a long look.
All the eastern sky-line was saw-toothed by the snowy
backbone of the Rockies. The whole mountain system,
range upon range, seemed to trend to the northwest, cutting athwart the course to the open country reported by
La Perle. The effect was as if the mountains conspired to
thrust back the traveler toward the west and the Yukon.
Smoke wondered how many men in the past, approaching
as he had approached, had been turned aside by that forbidding aspect. La Perle had not been turned aside, but,
then, La Perle had crossed over from the eastern slope of
the Rockies.

Until midnight Smoke maintained a huge fire for the guidance of Shorty. In the morning, waiting with camp broken and dogs harnessed for the first break of light, Smoke took up the pursuit. In the narrow pass of the canyon, his lead-dog pricked up its ears and whined. Then Smoke came upon the Indians, six of them, coming toward him. They were traveling light, without dogs, and on each man's back was the smallest of pack outfits. Surrounding Smoke, they immediately gave him several matters for surprise. That they were looking for him was clear. That they talked no Indian tongue of which he knew a word was also quickly obvious. They were not white Indians, though they were taller and heavier than the Indians of the Yukon basin. Five of them carried the old-fashioned, long-barreled Hudson's Bay Company musket, and in the hands of the sixth was a Winchester rifle which Smoke knew to be Shorty's.

Nor did they waste time in making him a prisoner. Unarmed himself, Smoke could only submit. The contents of the sled were distributed among their own packs, and he was given a pack composed of his and Shorty's sleeping-furs. The dogs were unharnessed, and when Smoke protested, one of the Indians, by signs, indicated a trail too rough for sled-travel. Smoke bowed to the inevitable, cached the sled end-on in the snow on the bank above the stream, and trudged on with his captors. Over the divide to the north they went, down to the spruce which Smoke had glimpsed the preceding afternoon. They followed the stream for a dozen miles, abandoning it when it trended to the west and heading directly eastward up a narrow tributary.

The first night was spent in a camp which had been occupied for several days. Here was cached a quantity of dried salmon and a sort of pemmican, which the Indians added to their packs. From this camp a trail of many snowshoes led off—Shorty's captors, was Smoke's conclusion; and before darkness fell he succeeded in making out the tracks Shorty's narrower snowshoes had left. Questioning the Indians by signs, they nodded affirmation and pointed to the north.

Always, in the days that followed, they pointed north; and always the trail, turning and twisting through a jumble of up-standing peaks, trended north. Everywhere, in this bleak snow-solitude, the way seemed barred, yet ever the trail curved and coiled, finding low divides and avoiding the higher and untraversable chains. The snowfall was deeper than in the lower valleys, and every step of the way was snowshoe work. Furthermore, Smoke's captors, all young men, traveled light and fast; and he could not forbear pride in the knowledge that he easily kept up with them. They were travel-hardened and trained to snowshoes from infancy; yet such was his condition that the traverse bore no more of ordinary hardship to him than to them.

In six days they gained and crossed the central pass, low in comparison with the mountains it threaded, yet formidable in itself and not possible for loaded sleds. Five days more of tortuous winding, from lower altitude to lower altitude, brought them to the open, rolling, and merely hilly country La Perle had found ten years before. Smoke knew it with the first glimpse. It was a sharp cold day, the thermometer forty below zero, the atmosphere so clear that he could see a hundred miles. Far as he could see rolled the open country. High in the east the Rockies still thrust their snowy ramparts heavenward. To the south and west extended the broken ranges of the project-

ing spur-system they had crossed. And in this vast pocket
lay the country La Perle had traversed—snow-blanketed,
but assuredly fat with game at some time in the year, and
in the summer a smiling, forested, and flowered land.

Before midday, traveling down a broad stream, past
snow-buried willows and naked aspens, and across heavily
timbered flats of spruce, they came upon the site of a large
camp, recently abandoned. Glancing as he went by, Smoke
estimated four or five hundred fires, and guessed the population to be in the thousands. So fresh was the trail, and
so well packed by the multitude, that Smoke and his captors took off their snowshoes and in their moccasins struck
a swifter pace. Signs of game appeared and grew plentiful
—together with tracks of wolves and lynxes. Once, one of
the Indians cried out with satisfaction and pointed to a
large area of open snow, littered with fang-polished skulls
of caribou, trampled and disrupted as if an army had
fought upon it. And Smoke knew that a big caribou killing had been made by the hunters since the last snow
flurry.

In the long twilight no sign was manifested of making
camp. They held steadily on through a deepening gloom
that vanished under a sky of light—great, glittering stars
half veiled by a greenish vapor of pulsing aurora borealis.
Smoke's dogs first caught the noises of the camp, pricking
their ears and whining in low eagerness. Then it came to
the ears of the humans, a murmur, dim with distance, but
not invested with the soothing grace common to distant
murmurs. Instead, it was in a high, wild key, a beat of
shrill sound broken by shriller sounds—the long wolf-
howling of many wolf dogs, a screaming of unrest and
pain, mournful with hopelessness and rebellion. The men
about him quickened. The legs that had lifted through a

dozen strenuous hours lifted in a still swifter pace that
was half a run and mostly a running jog. Through a dark
spruce-flat they burst upon an abrupt glare of light from
many fires and upon an abrupt increase of sound. The
great camp lay before them.

And as they entered and threaded the irregular runways of the hunting camp, a vast tumult, as in a wave,
rose to meet them and rolled on with them—cries, greet-
ings, questions and answers, jests and jests thrust back
again, the snapping snarl of wolf dogs rushing in furry
projectiles of wrath upon Smoke's stranger dogs, the scold-
ing of squaws, laughter, the whimpering of children and
wailing of infants, the moans of the sick aroused afresh to
pain, all the pandemonium of a camp of primitive wilder-
ness folk.

Striking with clubs and the butts of guns, Smoke's party
drove back the attacking dogs, while his own dogs, snapping and snarling, awed by so many enemies, shrank in
among the legs of their human protectors, and bristled
along stiff-legged in menacing prance.

They halted in the trampled snow by an open fire.
Shorty and two young Indians were squatting on their
hams, broiling strips of caribou meat. Three other young
Indians, lying in furs on a mat of spruce boughs, sat up.

The old familiar grin twisted on Shorty's face. "When
did they catch you?" he asked.

"Day after you left."

"Hum," Shorty said, the light of whimsy dancing in his
eyes. "Well, I'm doin' fine, thank you most to death. This
is the bachelor's camp." He waved his hand to embrace
its magnificence, which consisted of a fire, beds of spruce
boughs laid on top of the snow, flies of caribou skin, and
windshields of twisted spruce and willow withes. "An'

these are the bachelors." This time his hand indicated the
young men, and he spat a few spoken gutterals in their
own language that brought the white flash of acknowledgment from eyes and teeth. "They're glad to meet you,
Smoke. Set down an' dry your moccasins, an' I'll cook up
some grub. I'm gettin' the hang of the lingo pretty well,
ain't I? You'll have to come to it, for it looks as if we'll be
with these folks a long time. They's another white man
here. Got caught six years ago, over Great Slave Lake way.
Danny McCan is what he goes by. He's settled down with
a squaw. Got two kids already, but he'll skin out if ever
the chance opens up. See that low fire over there to the
right? That's his camp."

Apparently this was Smoke's appointed domicile, for
his captors left him and his dogs, and went on deeper into
the big camp. While he attended to his footgear and de-
voured strips of hot meat, Shorty cooked and talked.

"This is a sure peach of a pickle, Smoke—you listen to
me. An' we got to go some to get out. These is the real,
blowed-in-the-grass, wild Indians. They ain't white, but
their chief is. He talks like a mouthful of hot mush, but if
he ain't full-blood Scotch they ain't no such thing as Scotch
in the world. He's the hi-yu, skookum top chief of the
whole caboodle. What he says goes. You want to get that
from the start-off. Danny McCan's been tryin' to get away
from him for six years. Danny's all right, but he ain't got
go in him. He knows a way out—learned it on huntin'
trips—to the west of the way you an' me came. He ain't
had the nerve to tackle it by his lonely. But we can pull
it off, the three of us. Whiskers is the real goods, but he's
mostly loco just the same."

"Who's Whiskers?" Smoke queried, pausing from wolf-
ing down a hot strip of meat.

"He's the top geezer—the Scotcher. He'll see you tomorrow an' show you clear as print what a measly shrimp you are on his stompin' grounds. These grounds belong to him. You got to get that into your noodle. They ain't never been explored, nor nothin', an' they're his'n. An' he won't let you forget it. He's got about twenty thousand square miles of huntin' country here all his own. He's the white Indian, him an' the skirt. Huh! Don't look at me that way. Wait till you see her. Some looker, an' white, like her dad —he's Whiskers. An' say, caribou! I've saw 'em. A hundred thousan' of good running meat, an' ten thousan' wolves an' cats a-followin' an' livin' off the stragglers an' the leavin's. The herd's movin' to the east, an' we'll be after 'em any day now. We eat our dogs, an' what we don't eat we smoke 'n' cure for the spring before the salmon run gets its sting in. Say, what Whiskers don't know about salmon an' caribou nobody knows, take it from me."

It was morning, and the bachelors were squatting over a breakfast of caribou meat, which they ate as they broiled. Smoke glanced up and saw a small and slender man, skin-clad like any savage, but unmistakably white, striding in advance of a sled team and a following of a dozen Indians. Smoke cracked a hot bone, and while he sucked out the steaming marrow gazed at his approaching host. Bushy whiskers and yellowish gray hair, stained by camp smoke, concealed most of the face, but failed wholly to hide the gaunt, almost cadaverous, cheeks. It was a healthy leanness, Smoke decided, as he noted the wide flare of the nostrils and the breadth and depth of chest.

"How do you do," the man said, slipping a mitten and holding out his bare hand. "My name is Snass."

"Bellew," Smoke returned, gazing into the keen-searching black eyes.

"Getting plenty to eat, I see."

Smoke nodded and resumed his marrow bone, the purr of Scottish speech strangely pleasant in his ears.

"Rough rations. But we don't starve often. And it's more natural than the hand-reared meat of the cities." He turned abruptly away, and, recollecting himself, remarked casually over his shoulder:

"I'll see you later, Mr. Bellew. The caribou are moving east, and I'm going ahead to pick out a camp. You'll all come on tomorrow."

Later in the morning Smoke went for a stroll through the camp, busy with its primitive pursuits. A big body of hunters had just returned, and the men were scattering to their various fires. Women and children were departing with dogs harnessed to empty toboggan-sleds, and women and children and dogs were hauling sleds heavy with meat fresh from the killing and already frozen. An early spring cold-snap was on, and the wildness of the scene was painted in a temperature thirty below zero. Woven cloth was not in evidence. Furs and soft-tanned leather clad all alike. Boys passed with bows in their hands, and quivers of bone-barbed arrows; and many a skinning knife of bone or stone Smoke saw in belts or neck-hung sheaths. Women toiled over the fires, smoke-curing the meat, on their backs infants that stared round-eyed and sucked at lumps of tallow. Dogs, full kin to wolves, bristled up to Smoke to endure the menace of the short club he carried and to whiff the odor of this newcomer whom they must accept by virtue of the club.

Segregated in the heart of the camp, Smoke came upon what was evidently Snass's fire. Though temporary in

every detail, it was solidly constructed. A great heap of
bales of skins and outfit was piled on a scaffold out of reach
of the dogs. A large canvas fly, almost half-tent, sheltered
the sleeping and living quarters. To one side was a silk tent
—the sort favored by explorers and wealthy big-game
hunters. Smoke had never seen such a tent, and stepped
closer. As he stood looking, the flaps parted and a young
woman came out. So quickly did she move, so abruptly did
she appear, that the effect on Smoke was as that of an ap-
parition.

She was dressed entirely in skins, but such skins and
such magnificently beautiful furwork Smoke had never
dreamed of. Her parka, hood thrown back, was of some
strange fur of palest silver. The mukluks, with walrus-hide
soles, were composed of the silver-padded feet of many
lynxes. The long-gauntleted mittens, the tassels at the
knees, all the varied furs of the costume, were pale silver
that shimmered in the frosty light; and out of this shimmering silver, poised on slender, delicate neck, lifted her
head, the rosy face blonde as the eyes were blue, the ears
like two pink shells, the light chestnut hair sparkling with
frost dust.

All this and more, as in a dream, Smoke saw; then, recollecting himself, his hand fumbled for his cap. At the
same moment the wonder-stare in the girl's eyes passed
into a smile, and she slipped a mitten and extended her
hand.

"How do you do," she murmured gravely, with a queer,
delightful accent, her voice, silvery as the furs she wore,
coming with a shock to Smoke's ears, attuned as they were
to the harsh voices of the camp squaws.

Smoke could only mumble phrases awkwardly reminis-
cent of his best society manner.

"I am glad to see you," she went on slowly and gropingly, her face a ripple of smiles. "My English you will please excuse. It is not good," she gravely assured him. "My father 'he is Scotch. My mother she is dead. She is French, and English, and a little Indian, too. Her father was a great man in the Hudson's Bay Company. Brrr! It is cold." She slipped on her mitten and rubbed her ears, the pink of which had already turned to white. "Let us go to the fire and talk. My name is Labiskwee. What is your name?"

And so Smoke came to know Labiskwee, the daughter of Snass.

Much Smoke learned in the days that followed, as the hunting camp moved on in the trail of the caribou. These were real wild Indians—the ones Anton had encountered and escaped from long years before. This was nearly the western limit of their territory, and in the summer they ranged north to the tundra shores of the Arctic, and eastward as far as the Luskwa. What river the Luskwa was Smoke could not make out, nor could Labiskwee tell him, nor could McCan. On occasion Snass, with parties of strong hunters, pushed east across the Rockies, on past the lakes and the Mackenzie and into the Barrens. It was on the last traverse in that direction that the silk tent occupied by Labiskwee had been found.

"It belonged to the Millicent-Adbury expedition," Snass told Smoke.

"Oh! I remember. They went after musk oxen. The rescue expedition never found a trace of them."

"I found them," Snass said. "Dead."

"The world still doesn't know. Word never got out."

"Word *never* gets out," Snass assured him pleasantly.

"You mean if they had been alive when you found them—?"

Snass nodded. "They would have lived with me and my people."

"Anton got out," Smoke challenged.

"I do not remember the name. How long ago?"

"Fourteen or fifteen years," Smoke answered.

"So he pulled through, after all. Do you know, I've wondered about him. We called him Long Tooth. He was a strong man, a strong man."

"La Perle came through here ten years ago."

Snass shook his head.

"He found traces of your camps. It was summer time."

"That explains it," Snass answered. "We are hundreds of miles to the north in the summer."

Strive as he would, Smoke could get no clue to Snass's history in the days before he came to live in the northern wilds. Educated he was, yet in all the intervening years he had read no books, no newspapers. What had happened in the world he knew not, nor did he show desire to know. He had heard of the miners on the Yukon, and of the Klondike strike, but gold miners had never invaded his territory. The outside world to him did not exist. He tolerated no mention of it.

Nor could Labiskwee help Smoke with earlier information. She had been born on the hunting grounds. Her mother had lived for six years after. Her mother had been very beautiful—the only white woman Labiskwee had ever seen. She said this wistfully, and wistfully, in a thousand ways, she showed she knew of the great outside world on which her father had closed the door. But this knowledge was her secret. She had early learned that mention of it threw her father into a rage.

As a source of information, Danny McCan was impossible. He did not like adventure. Wild life was a horror, and he had had nine years of it. Shanghaied on a whaleship in San Francisco, he had deserted at Point Barrow with three companions. Two had died, and the third had abandoned him on the terrible traverse south. Two years he lived with the Eskimos before raising courage to attempt the south traverse, and then, within several days of a Hudson's Bay Company post, he had been gathered in by a party of Snass's young men. He was a small, stupid man, afflicted with sore eyes, and all he dreamed or could talk about was getting back to San Francisco.

"You're the first intelligent man we've had." Snass complimented Smoke one night by the fire. "Except old Four Eyes. The Indians named him so. He wore glasses and was shortsighted. He was a professor of zoology. He died a year ago. My young men picked him up strayed from an expedition on the upper Porcupine. He was intelligent, yes; but he was also a fool. That was his weakness —straying. He knew geology, though, and working in metals. Over on the Luskwa, where there's coal, we have several creditable hand forges he made. He repaired our guns and taught the young men how. He died last year, and we really missed him. Strayed—that's how it happened—froze to death within a mile of camp."

It was on the same night that Snass said to Smoke:

"You'd better pick out a wife and have a fire of your own. You will be more comfortable than with those young bucks. The maidens' fires—a sort of feast of the virgins, you know—are not lighted until full summer and the salmon, but I can give orders earlier if you say the word."

Smoke laughed and shook his head.

"Remember," Snass concluded quietly, "Anton is the

only one that ever got away. He was lucky, unusually lucky."

"Once we hit out we'll sure have some tall runnin'," Shorty said dismally.

"The place is a big trap," Smoke agreed.

From the crest of a bald knob they gazed out over Snass's snowy domain. East, west, and south they were hemmed in by the high peaks and jumbled ranges. Northward, the rolling country seemed interminable; yet they knew, even in that direction, that half a dozen transverse mountain chains blocked the way.

"At this time of the year I could give you three days' start," Snass told Smoke that evening. "You can't hide your trail, you see. Anton got away when the snow was gone. My young men can travel as fast as the best white man; and, besides, you would be breaking trail for them. And when the snow is off the ground, I'll see to it that you don't get the chance Anton had. But it's a good life here, and soon the world fades. I have never quite got over the surprise of finding how easy it is to get along without the world."

"What's eatin' me is Danny McCan," Shorty confided to Smoke. "He's a weak brother on any trail. But he swears he knows the way out to the westward, so we got to put up with him."

"We're all in the same boat," Smoke answered.

"Not on your life. It's a-comin' to you straight down the pike."

"What's coming? What are you talking about?"

"You ain't heard the news?"

Smoke shook his head.

"The bachelors told me. They just got the word. To-

night it comes off, months ahead of the calendar. Danny's
wife told the bachelors," Shorty paused impressively. "An'
the bachelors told me, that the maidens' fires is due to be
lit tonight. That's all. How do you like it?"

"I don't get your drift, Shorty."

"Don't, eh? Why, it's plain open and shut. They's a skirt
after you, an' that skirt is goin' to light a fire, an' that
skirt's name is Labiskwee. Oh, I've been watchin' her
watch you when you ain't lookin'. She ain't never lighted
her fire. She wouldn't marry a Indian. An' now, when she
lights her fire, it's a cinch it's my poor old friend Smoke.
Hey! Listen to that!"

Three ancient squaws had halted midway between the
bachelors' camp and the camp of McCan, and the oldest
was declaiming in shrill falsetto.

Smoke recognized the names, but not all the words, and
Shorty translated with melancholy glee.

"Labiskwee, the daughter of Snass, the Great Chief,
lights her first maiden's fire tonight. Maka, the daughter
of Owits, the Wolf-Runner—"

The recital ran through the names of a dozen maidens,
and then the three heralds tottered on their way to make
announcement at the next fires.

The bachelors, who had sworn youthful oaths to speak
to no maidens, were uninterested in the approaching cere-
mony. To show their disdain they made preparations for
immediate departure on a mission set them by Snass upon
which they planned to start the following morning. Not
satisfied with the hunters' estimates of the caribou, Snass
had decided that the run was split. The task set the bachelors was to scout to the north and west in quest of the
second division of the great herd.

Smoke, troubled by Labiskwee's fire-lighting, announced he would accompany the bachelors. But first he talked with Shorty and with McCan.

"You be there on the third day, Smoke," Shorty said. "We'll have the outfit an' the dogs."

"Remember," Smoke cautioned, "if there is any slip-up in meeting me, keep on going and get out to the Yukon. That's final. If you make it, come back for me in the summer."

McCan, standing by his fire, indicated silently with his eyes a rugged mountain where the high western range out-jutted on the open country.

"That's the one," he said. "A small stream on the south side. We go up it. On the third day you meet us. We'll pass by on the third day. Anywhere you tap that stream you'll meet us—or our trail."

But the chance did not come to Smoke on the third day. The bachelors had changed the direction of their scout, and while Shorty and McCan plodded up the stream with their dogs, Smoke and the bachelors were sixty miles to the northeast picking up the trail of the second caribou herd. Several days later, through a dim twilight of falling snow, they came back to the big camp. A squaw ceased from wailing by a fire and darted up to Smoke. Harsh-tongued, with bitter, venomous eyes, she cursed him, waving her arms toward a silent, fur-wrapped form that still lay on the sled which had hauled it in.

What had happened, Smoke could only guess, and as he came to McCan's fire he was prepared for a second cursing. Instead, he saw McCan himself, industriously chewing a strip of caribou meat.

"I'm not a fightin' man," he whiningly explained. "But Shorty got away, though they're still after him. He put up a hell of a fight. They'll get him, too. He ain't got a

chance. He plugged two bucks that'll get around all right.
An' he croaked one square through the chest."

"I know," Smoke answered. "I just met the widow."

"Old Snass'll be wantin' to see you," McCan added.
"Them's his orders. Soon as you come in you was to go
to his fire. I ain't squealed. You don't know nothing. Keep
that in mind. Shorty went off on his own along with me."

At Snass's fire Smoke found Labiskwee. She met him
with eyes that shone with such softness and tenderness as
to frighten him.

"I'm glad you didn't try to run away," she said. "You
see, I—" She hesitated, but her eyes didn't drop. They
swam with a light unmistakable. "I lit my fire, and of
course it was for you. I like you better than everybody else
in the world. Better than my father. It is very strange."

Smoke had never been proposed to in his life, and he
was unable to meet the situation. Worse, it was not even
a proposal. His acceptance was taken for granted. Labiskwee prattled on, chanting the happy burden of her love,
while he strove to grip himself in the effort, somehow, to
wound her with the truth. This, at the very beginning,
was the golden opportunity.

And then Snass strode in to the fire through the falling snowflakes, and Smoke's opportunity was lost.

"Good evening," Snass burred gruffly. "Your partner has
made a mess of it. I am glad you had better sense."

"You might tell me what's happened," Smoke urged.

The flash of white teeth through the stained beard was
not pleasant. "Certainly, I'll tell you. Your partner has
killed one of my people. That sniveling shrimp, McCan,
deserted at the first shot. He'll never run away again. But
my hunters have got your partner in the mountains, and
they'll get him. He'll never make the Yukon basin. As for

you, from now on you sleep at my fire. There'll be no more scouting with the young men. I shall have my eye on you."

Smoke's new situation at Snass's fire was embarrassing. He saw more of Labiskwee than ever. In its sweetness and innocence, the frankness of her love was terrible. Her glances were love glances; every look was a caress. A score of times he nerved himself to tell her of Joy Gaskell, and a score of times he discovered that he was a coward.

"Listen to me," said McCan. "The spring thaw is here, an' the crust is comin' on the snow. It's the time to travel, exceptin' for the spring blizzards in the mountains. I know them. I would run with no less a man than you."

"But you can't run," Smoke contradicted. "You can keep up with no man. Your backbone is limber as thawed marrow. If I run, I run alone. The world fades, though, and perhaps I'll never run. Caribou meat is very good, and soon will come summer and the salmon."

Said Snass: "Your partner is dead. My hunters did not kill him. They found the body, frozen in the first of the spring storms in the mountains. No man can escape."

And Labiskwee: "I watch you. There is trouble in your eyes, in your face. Oh, I know all your face. There is a little scar on your neck, just under the ear. When you are happy, the corners of your mouth turn up. When you think sad thoughts they turn down. Is the world so good that you, too, are hungry for it?" She sighed and shook her head. "If you lived here always would you die hungry for the world? Do you want to run away to the world?"

Smoke could not speak, but by his mouth-corner lines she was convinced.

Minutes of silence passed, in which she visibly struggled, while Smoke cursed himself for the unguessed weak-

ness that enabled him to speak the truth about his hunger
for the world while it kept his lips tight on the truth of
the existence of another woman.

Again Labiskwee sighed.

"Very well. I love you more than I fear my father's
anger, and he is more terrible in anger than a mountain
storm. You told me what love is. This is the test of love. I
shall help you to run away, back to the world."

Smoke awakened softly and without movement. Warm
small fingers touched his cheek and slid gently to a pressure on his lips. Fur, with the chill of frost clinging in it,
next tingled his skin, and the one word, "Come," was
breathed in his ear. He sat up carefully and listened. The
hundreds of wolf dogs in the camp had lifted their noc-
turnal song, but under the volume of it, close at hand, he
could distinguish the light, regular breathing of Snass.

Labiskwee tugged gently at Smoke's sleeve, and he knew
she wished him to follow. He took his moccasins and socks
in his hand and crept out into the snow. Beyond the glow
from the dying embers of the fire, she indicated to him to
put on his footgear, and while he obeyed, she went back
under the fly where Snass slept.

It was about one in the morning and quite warm, not
more than ten below zero. Labiskwee rejoined him and
led him on through the dark runways of the sleeping
camp. Walk lightly as they could, the frost crunched
crisply under their moccasins, but the sound was drowned
by the clamor of the dogs, too deep in their howling to
snarl at the man and woman who passed.

"Now we can talk," she said, when the last fire had been
left half a mile behind.

And now, in the starlight, facing him, Smoke noted for

the first time that her arms were burdened with his snow-shoes, a rifle, two belts of ammunition, and his sleeping-robes.

"I have everything fixed," she said, with a happy little laugh. "I have been two days making the cache. There is meat, even flour, and skis, which go best on the hard crust and, when they break through, the webs will hold up longer. Oh, I do know snow travel, and we shall go fast."

Smoke checked his speech. That she had been arranging his escape was surprise enough, but that she had planned to go with him was more than he was prepared for. Unable to think, he gently, one by one, took her burdens from her. He put his arm around her and pressed her close, and saw all his memory of the bright world and the sun-lands reel and fade.

"We will go back, Labiskwee," he said. "You will be my wife, and we shall live always with the Caribou People."

"No! no!" She shook her head. "I have thought much. The hunger for the world would come upon you, and in the long nights it would devour your heart. All men from the world hunger for it. We will go on across the snow mountains on the south traverse."

"We must go back," he urged.

"We shall go *on*, to the cache," she said with decision. "It is three miles from here. Come."

He held back, almost tempted to tell her of the other woman beyond the south traverse.

"It would be a great wrong to you to go back," she said. "I—I am only a wild girl, and I am afraid of the world; but I am more afraid for you. You see, I love you more than anybody else in the world. I love you more than my-self. The Indian language is not a good language. The English language is not a good language. The thoughts in

my heart for you, as bright and as many as the stars—
there is no language for them. How can I tell them?"

Smoke could no longer resist. So firm was the crust,
frozen during the night after the previous day's surface
thaw, that they slid along rapidly on their skis.

"Just here, in the trees, is the cache," Labiskwee told
Smoke.

The next moment she caught his arm with a startle of
surprise. The flames of a small fire were dancing merrily,
and crouched by the fire was McCan.

"I was minded you'd run without me," McCan explained, his small peering eyes glimmering with cun-
ning. "So I kept an eye on the girl, an' when I seen her
caching skis an' grub, I was on. I've brought my own skis
an' webs an' grub. The fire? Sure, an' it was no danger.
The camp's asleep an' snorin', an' the waitin' was cold.
Will we be startin' now?"

"McCan, you are a dog," Labiskwee hissed, and her
eyes were savage with anger. "I know it is in your heart
to wake the camp if we don't take you. Very well. We
must take you. But you know my father. I am like my
father. You will do your share of the work. You will obey.
And if you play one dirty trick, it would be better for
you if you had never run."

McCan looked up at her, his small pig-eyes hating and
cringing, while in her eyes, turned to Smoke, anger melted
into luminous softness.

"Is it right, what I have said?" she queried.

Daylight found them in the belt of foothills that lay
between the rolling country and the mountains. McCan
suggested breakfast, but they held on. Not until the after-

noon thaw softened the crust and prevented travel would they eat.

The foothills quickly grew rugged, and the stream, up whose frozen bed they journeyed, began to thread deeper and deeper canyons. The signs of spring were less frequent, though in one canyon they found foaming bits of open water, and twice they came upon clumps of dwarf willow upon which were the first hints of swelling buds.

Labiskwee explained to Smoke her knowledge of the country and the way she planned to baffle pursuit. There were but two ways out, one west, the other south. Snass would immediately dispatch parties of young men to guard the two trails. But there was another way south. True, it did no more than penetrate halfway into the high mountains—then, twisting to the west and crossing three divides, it joined the regular trail. When the young men found no traces on the regular trail they would turn back in the belief that the escape had been made by the west traverse, never dreaming that the runaways had ventured the harder and longer way around.

Glancing back at McCan, in the rear, Labiskwee spoke in an undertone to Smoke. "He is eating," she said. "It is not good."

Smoke looked. The Irishman was secretly munching caribou suet from the pocketful he carried.

"No eating between meals, McCan," he commanded. "There's no game in the country ahead, and the grub will have to be shared in equal rations from the start."

By one o'clock the crust had thawed so that the skis broke through, and before two o'clock the web-shoes were breaking through. Camp was made and the first meat eaten. Smoke took stock of the food. McCan's supply was

a disappointment. So many silver foxskins had he stuffed
in the bottom of his meat bag that there was little space
left for meat.

"I didn't know there was so many," McCan explained.
"I done it in the dark. But they're worth good money. An'
with all this ammunition we'll be gettin' game a'plenty."

"The wolves will eat you a'plenty," was Smoke's hopeless comment, while Labiskwee's eyes flashed their anger.

Enough food for a month, with careful husbanding, was
Smoke's and Labiskwee's judgment. Smoke apportioned
the weight and bulk of the packs, yielding in the end to
Labiskwee's insistence that she, too, should carry a pack.

Next day the stream shallowed out in a wide mountain
valley, and they were already breaking through the crust
on the flats when they gained the harder surface of the
slope of the divide.

"Ten minutes later and we wouldn't have got across the
flats," Smoke said, when they paused for breath on the
bald crest of the summit. "We must be a thousand feet
higher here."

But Labiskwee, without speaking, pointed down to an
open flat among the trees. In the midst of it, scattered
abreast, were five dark specks that scarcely moved.

"The young men," said Labiskwee.

"They are wallowing to their hips," Smoke said. "They
will never gain the hard footing this day. We have hours
start on them. Come on, McCan. Buck up. We don't eat
till we can't travel."

McCan groaned, but there was no caribou suet in his
pocket, and he doggedly brought up the rear.

In the higher valley in which they now found themselves, the crust did not break till three in the afternoon,
at which time they managed to gain the shadow of the

mountain where the crust was already freezing again. Once only they paused to get out McCan's suet, which they ate as they walked. It crumbled in their mouths and eased the palpitating faintness in their stomachs.

Black darkness, with an overcast sky, came on after a long twilight, and they made camp in a clump of dwarf spruce. McCan was whining and helpless. The day's march had been exhausting, but in addition, despite his nine years' experience in the arctic, he had been eating snow and was in agony with a parched and burning mouth. He crouched by the fire and groaned, while they made the camp.

Labiskwee was tireless, and Smoke could not but marvel at the life in her body, at the endurance of mind and muscle. Nor was her cheerfulness forced. She had ever a laugh or a smile for him, and her hand lingered in caress whenever it chanced to touch his. Yet, always, when she looked at McCan, her face went hard and pitiless and her eyes flashed frostily.

In the night came wind and snow, and through a day of blizzard they fought their way blindly, missing an important turn of the trail as it led up a small stream and crossed a divide to the west. For two more days they wandered, lost, crossing other and wrong divides, and in those two days they dropped spring behind and climbed up again into the abode of winter.

"The young men have lost our trail, an' what's to stop us restin' a day?" McCan begged.

But no rest was accorded. Smoke and Labiskwee knew their danger. They were lost in the high mountains, and they had seen no game nor signs of game. Day after day they struggled on through an iron configuration of landscape that compelled them into labyrinthine canyons and valleys that led rarely to the west. Once in such a canyon, they could only follow it, no matter where it led, for the cold peaks and higher ranges on either side were unscalable and unendurable. The terrible toil and the cold ate up energy, yet they cut down the size of the ration they permitted themselves.

One night Smoke was awakened by a sound of struggling. Distinctly he heard a gasping and strangling from where McCan slept. Kicking the fire into flame, by its light he saw Labiskwee, her hands at McCan's throat and forcing from his mouth a chunk of partly chewed meat. Even as Smoke saw this, her hand went to her hip and flashed with the sheath knife in it.

"Labiskwee!" Smoke cried.

The hand hesitated.

"Don't," he said, coming to her side.

She was shaking with anger, but the hand, after hesitating a moment longer, descended reluctantly to the sheath. As if fearing she could not restrain herself, she crossed to the fire and threw on more wood. McCan sat up, whimpering and snarling, between fright and rage spluttering an inarticulate explanation.

"Where did you get it?" Smoke demanded.

"Feel around his body," Labiskwee said.

It was the first word she had spoken, and her voice quivered with the anger she could not suppress.

McCan strove to struggle, but Smoke gripped him cruelly and searched him, drawing forth a strip of caribou meat. A quick exclamation from Labiskwee drew Smoke's attention. She had sprung to McCan's pack and was opening it. Instead of meat, out poured moss, spruce needles, chips—all the light refuse that had taken the place of the meat and given the pack its due proportion minus its weight.

Again Labiskwee's hand went to her hip, and she flew at the culprit, only to be caught in Smoke's arms, where she surrendered herself, sobbing with the futility of her rage.

"It is not the food," she panted. "It is you, your life. The dog! He is eating you, he is eating you!"

"We will yet live," Smoke comforted her. "Hereafter he shall carry the flour. He can't eat that raw, and if he does I'll kill him myself, for he will be eating your life as well as mine." He held her closer. "Killing is men's work. Women do not kill."

"You would not love me if I killed the dog?" she questioned in surprise.

"Not so much," Smoke temporized.

She sighed with resignation. "Very well," she said. "I shall not kill him."

The pursuit by the young men was relentless. By miracles of luck, the young men picked up the blizzard-blinded trail and clung to it. When the snow flew, Smoke and Labiskwee took the most improbable courses, turning east when the better way opened south or west, rejecting a low divide to climb a higher. Being lost, it did not matter. Yet they could not throw the young men off. Sometimes they gained days, but always the young men appeared again. After a storm, when all trace was lost, they would cast out like a pack of hounds, and he who caught the later trace made smoke signals to call his comrades on.

Smoke lost count of time, of days and nights and storms and camps. Through a vast mad phantasmagoria of suffer-

ing and toil he and Labiskwee struggled on, with McCan
somehow stumbling along in the rear. Great peaks, pitiless
and serene in the chill blue, towered about them. They
fled down black canyons with walls so precipitous that the
rock frowned naked, or wallowed across glacial valleys
where frozen lakes lay far beneath their feet. And one
night, between two storms, a distant volcano glared the
sky. They never saw it again, and wondered whether it
had been a dream.

Crusts were covered with yards of new snow, that
crusted and were snow-covered again. There were places,
in canyon drifts, where they crossed snow hundreds of feet
deep, and they crossed tiny glaciers, in drafty rifts, wind-
scurried and bare of any snow. They crept like silent
wraiths across the faces of impending avalanches, or
roused from exhausted sleep to the thunder of them. They
made fireless camps above timber line, thawing their meat
rations with the heat of their bodies before they could eat.
And through it all Labiskwee remained Labiskwee. Her
cheer never vanished, save when she looked at McCan,
and the greatest stupor of fatigue and cold never stilled the
eloquence of her love for Smoke.

Like a cat she watched the apportionment of the meager
ration, and Smoke could see that she grudged McCan
every munch of his jaws. Once she distributed the ration.
The first Smoke knew was a wild harangue of protest from
McCan. Not to him alone, but to herself, had she given a
smaller portion than to Smoke. After that, Smoke divided
the meat himself. Caught in a small avalanche one morning after a night of snow, and swept a hundred yards down
the mountain, they emerged half-stifled and unhurt, but
McCan emerged without his pack in which was all the
flour. A second and larger snow-slide buried it beyond

hope of recovery. After that, though the disaster had been
through no fault of his, Labiskwee never looked at McCan,
and Smoke knew it was because she dared not.

It was a morning, stark still, clear blue above, with
white sun-dazzle on the snow. The way led up a long, wide
slope of crust. They moved like weary ghosts in a dead
world. No wind stirred in the stagnant, frigid calm. Far
peaks, a hundred miles away, studding the backbone of
the Rockies up and down, were as distinct as if no more
than five miles away.

"Something is going to happen," Labiskwee whispered.
"Don't you feel it?—here, there, everywhere? Everything
is strange."

"I feel a chill that is not of cold," Smoke answered.
"Nor is it of hunger."

"It is in your head, your heart," she agreed excitedly.
"That is the way I feel it."

A quarter of an hour later they paused for breath.

"I can no longer see the far peaks," Smoke said.

"The air is getting thick and heavy," said Labiskwee.
"It is hard to breathe."

"There be three suns," McCan muttered hoarsely, reeling as he clung to his ski-pole for support.

There was a mock sun on either side of the real sun.

"There are five," said Labiskwee; and as they looked,
new suns formed and flashed before their eyes.

"By Heaven, the sky is filled with suns beyond all
countin'," McCan cried in fear.

Which was true, for look where they would, half the
circle of the sky dazzled and blazed with new suns
forming.

McCan yelped sharply with surprise and pain. "I'm
bit!" he cried out, then yelped again.

Then Labiskwee cried out, and Smoke felt a prickling stab on his cheek so cold that it burned like acid. It reminded him of swimming in the salt sea and being stung by the poisonous filaments of Portuguese Men-of-War. The sensations were so similar that he automatically brushed his cheek to rid it of the stinging substance that was not there.

And then a shot rang out, strangely muffled. Far down the slope were the young men, standing on their skis, and one after another opened fire.

"Spread out!" Smoke commanded. "And climb for it! We're almost to the top. They're a quarter of a mile below, and that means a couple of miles head start on them going down the other side."

With faces prickling and stinging from invisible atmospheric stabs, the three scattered widely on the snow surface and toiled upward. The muffled reports of the rifles were weird to their ears.

"Thank the Lord," Smoke panted to Labiskwee, "that four of them are muskets, and only one a Winchester. Besides, all these suns spoil their aim. They are fooled. They haven't come within a hundred feet of us."

"It shows my father's temper," she said. "They have orders to kill."

"How strange you talk," Smoke said. "Your voice sounds far away."

"Cover your mouth," Labiskwee cried suddenly. "And don't talk. Now I know what it is. Cover your mouth with your sleeve, and do not talk."

McCan fell first, and struggled wearily to his feet. And after that all fell repeatedly before they reached the summit. Their wills exceeded their muscles, they knew not why, save that their bodies were oppressed by a numbness and heaviness of movement. From the crest, looking back, they saw the young men stumbling and falling on the upward climb.

"They will never get here," Labiskwee said. "It is the white death. I know it, though I have never seen it. I have heard the old men talk. Soon will come a mist—unlike any mist or fog or frost-smoke you ever saw. Few have seen it and lived."

McCan gasped and strangled.

"Keep your mouth covered," Smoke commanded.

A pervasive flashing of light from all about them drew Smoke's eyes upward to the many suns. They were shimmering and veiling. The air was filled with microscopic fire-glints. The near peaks were being blotted out by the weird mist; the young men, resolutely struggling nearer, were being engulfed in it. McCan had sunk down, squatting, on his skis, his mouth and eyes covered by his arms.

"Come on, make a start," Smoke ordered.

"I can't move," McCan moaned.

His doubled body set up a swaying motion. Smoke went toward him slowly, scarcely able to will movement through the lethargy that weighed his flesh. He noted that his brain was clear. It was only the body that was afflicted.

"Let him be," Labiskwee muttered harshly.

But Smoke persisted, dragging McCan to his feet and facing him down the long slope they must go. Then he started him with a shove, and McCan, braking and steering with his pole, shot into the sheen of diamond-dust and disappeared.

Smoke looked at Labiskwee, who smiled, though it was all she could do to keep from sinking down. He nodded for her to push off, but she came near to him, and side by side, a dozen feet apart, they flew down through the stinging thickness of cold fire.

Brake as he would, Smoke's heavier body carried him past her, and he dashed on alone, a long way, at tremendous speed that did not slacken till he came out on a level, crusted plateau. Here he braked till Labiskwee overtook him, and they went on, again side by side, with diminishing speed which finally ceased. The lethargy had grown more pronounced. The wildest effort of will could move them no more than at a snail's pace. They passed McCan, again crouched down on his skis, and Smoke roused him with his pole in passing.

"Now we must stop," Labiskwee whispered painfully, "or we will die. We must cover up—so the old men said."

She did not delay to untie knots, but began cutting her pack-lashings. Smoke cut his, and, with a last look at the fiery death-mist and the mockery of suns, they covered themselves over with the sleeping-furs and crouched in each other's arms. They felt a body stumble over them and fall, then heard feeble whimpering and blaspheming drowned in a violent coughing fit, and knew it was McCan who huddled against them as he wrapped his robe about him.

Their own strangling began, and they were racked and torn by a dry cough, spasmodic and uncontrollable. Smoke noted his temperature rising in a fever, and Labiskwee suffered similarly. Hour after hour the coughing spells increased in frequency and violence, and not till late afternoon was the worst reached. After that the mend came slowly, and between spells they dozed in exhaustion.

McCan, however, steadily coughed worse, and from his groans and howls they knew he was in delirium. Once,

Smoke made as if to throw the robes back, but Labiskwee
clung to him tightly.

"No," she begged. "It is death to uncover now. Bury
your face here, against my parka, and breathe gently and
do no talking—see, the way I am doing."

They dozed on through the darkness, though the decreasing fits of coughing of one invariably aroused the
other. It was after midnight, Smoke judged, when McCan
coughed his last. After that he emitted low and bestial
moanings that never ceased.

Smoke awoke with lips touching his lips. He lay partly
in Labiskwee's arms, his head pillowed on her breast. Her
voice was cheerful and usual. The muffled sound of it had
vanished.

"It is day," she said, lifting the robes. "We have lived
through; and we no longer cough. Let us look at the world,
though I could stay here thus forever and always. This last
hour has been sweet."

"I do not hear McCan," Smoke said. "And what has
become of the young men that they have not found us?"

He threw back the robes and saw a normal and solitary
sun in the sky. A gentle breeze was blowing, crisp with
frost and hinting of warmer days to come. All the world
was natural again. McCan lay on his back, his unwashed
face, swarthy from camp smoke, frozen hard as marble.
The sight did not affect Labiskwee.

"Look!" she cried. "A snowbird! It is a good sign."

There was no evidence of the young men. Either they
had died on the other side of the divide or had turned back.

There was so little food that they dared not eat a hun-
dredth part of what they desired, and in the days that followed, wandering through the lone mountainland, the

sharp sting of life grew blunted and the wandering
merged half into a dream. Smoke would become abruptly
conscious, to find himself staring at the never-ending
hated snowpeaks, his senseless babble still ringing in his
ears. And the next he would know, after seeming centuries, was that again he was roused to the sound of his
own maunderings. Labiskwee, too, was lightheaded most
of the time. In the main their efforts were unreasoned,
automatic. Ever they worked toward the west, and ever
they were baffled and thrust north or south by snowpeaks
and impassable ranges.

"There is no way south," Labiskwee said. "The old men
know. West, only west, is the way."

The young men no longer pursued, but famine crowded
on the trail.

Came a day when it turned cold, and a thick snow, that
was not snow but frost crystals of the size of grains of
sand, began to fall. All day and night it fell, and for three
days and nights it continued to fall. It was impossible to
travel until it crusted under the spring sun, so they lay in
their furs and rested, and ate less because they rested. So
small was the ration they permitted that it gave no ap-
peasement to the hunger pang that was much of the
stomach, but more of the brain.

Labiskwee, delirious, maddened by the taste of her tiny
portion, sobbing and mumbling, yelping sharp little animal cries of joy, fell upon the next day's portion and
crammed it into her mouth. Then it was given to Smoke
to see a wonderful thing. The food between her teeth
roused her to consciousness. She spat it out, and with a
great anger struck herself with her clenched fist on the
offending mouth.

It was given to Smoke to see many wonderful things in

the days yet to come. After the long snowfall came a great wind that drove the dry and tiny frost particles as sand is driven in a sandstorm. All through the night the sand-frost drove by, and in the full light of a clear and wind-blown day, Smoke looked with swimming eyes and reeling brain upon what he took to be the vision of a dream. All about towered great peaks and small, lone sentinels and groups and councils of mighty Titans. And from the tip of every peak, swaying, undulating, flaring out broadly against the azure sky, streamed gigantic snow-banners, miles in length, milky and nebulous, ever waving lights and shadows and flashing silver from the sun.

"I dream, Labiskwee," he said. "Look. Do you, too, dream within my dream?"

"It is no dream," she replied. "This have the old men told me. And after this will blow the warm winds, and we shall live and win west."

Smoke shot a snowbird, and they divided it. Once, in a valley where willows budded standing in the snow, he shot a snowshoe rabbit. Another time he got a lean, white weasel. This much of meat they encountered, and no more, though, once, half-mile high and veering toward the west and the Yukon, they saw a wild duck wedge drive by.

"It is summer in the lower valleys," said Labiskwee. "Soon it will be summer here."

Labiskwee's face had grown thin, but the bright, large eyes were brighter and larger, and when she looked at him she was transfigured by a wild, unearthly beauty.

The days lengthened, and the snow began to sink. Each day the crust thawed, each night it froze again; and they were afoot early and late, being compelled to camp and rest during the midday hours of thaw when the crust

could not bear their weight. When Smoke grew snow-
blind, Labiskwee towed him on a thong tied to her waist.
And when she was blinded, she followed behind a thong
tied to his waist. Starving, in a deeper dream, they struggled on through an awakening land bare of any life save
their own.

Exhausted as he was, Smoke grew almost to fear sleep,
so fearful and bitter were the visions of that mad, twilight
land. Always were they of food, and always was the food,
at his lips, snatched away by the malign deviser of dreams.
He attended Gargantuan feasts, where multitudes fed on
innumerable bullocks roasted whole, prying them out of
smoldering pits and with sharp knives slicing great strips
of meat from the steaming carcasses. He stood, with mouth
agape, beneath long rows of turkeys which white-aproned
shopmen sold. And everybody bought save Smoke, mouth
still agape, chained by a leadenness of movement to the
pavement. A boy again, he sat with spoon poised high
above great bowls of bread and milk. He pursued shy
heifers through upland pastures and centuries of torment
in vain effort to steal from them their milk, and in noi-
some dungeons he fought with rats for scraps and refuse.
There was no food that was not a madness to him, and he
wandered through vast stables, where fat horses stood in
mile-long rows of stalls, and sought but never found the
bran-bins from which they fed.

Once, only, he dreamed to advantage. Famishing, ship-
wrecked or marooned, he fought with the big Pacific surf
for rock-clinging mussels, and carried them up the sands
to the dry flotsam of the spring tides. Of this he built a fire,
and among the coals he laid his precious trove. He
watched the steam jet forth and the locked shells pop
apart, exposing the salmon-colored meat. Cooked to a

turn—he knew it; and this time there was no intruding presence to whisk the meal away. At last—so he dreamed within the dream—the dream would come true. This time he would eat. Yet in his certitude he doubted, and he was steeled for the inevitable shift of vision until the salmon-colored meat, hot and savory, was in his mouth. His teeth closed upon it. He ate! The miracle had happened! The shock aroused him. He awoke in the dark, lying on his back, and heard himself mumbling little piggish squeals and grunts of joy. His jaws were moving, and between his teeth meat was crunching. He did not move, and soon small fingers felt about his lips, and between them was inserted a tiny sliver of meat. And in that he would eat no more, rather than that he was angry, Labiskwee cried and in his arms sobbed herself to sleep. But he lay on awake, marveling at the love and the wonder of woman.

The time came when the last food was gone. The high peaks receded, the divides became lower, and the way opened promisingly to the west. But their reserves of strength were gone, and, without food, the time quickly followed when they lay down at night and in the morning did not arise. Smoke weakly gained his feet, collapsed, and on hands and knees crawled about the building of a fire. But try as she would Labiskwee sank back each time in an extremity of weakness. And Smoke sank down beside her, a wan sneer on his face for the automatism that had made him struggle for an unneeded fire. There was nothing to cook, and the day was warm. A gentle breeze sighed in the spruce trees, and from everywhere, under the disappearing snow, came the trickling music of unseen streamlets.

Labiskwee lay in a stupor, her breathing so imperceptible that Smoke thought her dead. In the afternoon the

chattering of a squirrel aroused him. Dragging the heavy rifle, he wallowed through the crust that had become slush. He crept on hands and knees, or stood upright and fell forward in the direction of the squirrel that chattered its wrath and fled slowly and tantalizingly before him. He had not the strength for a quick shot, and the squirrel was never still. At times Smoke sprawled in the wet snow-melt and cried out of weakness. Other times the flame of his life flickered, and blackness smote him. How long he lay in the last faint he did not know, but he came to, shivering in the chill of evening, his wet clothing frozen to the re-forming crust. The squirrel was gone, and after a weary struggle he won back to the side of Labiskwee. So profound was his weakness that he lay like a dead man through the night, nor did dreams disturb him.

The sun was in the sky, the same squirrel chattering through the trees, when Labiskwee's hand on Smoke's cheek awakened him.

"Put your hand on my heart, lover," she said, her voice clear but faint and very far away. "My heart is my love, and you hold it in your hand."

A long time seemed to go by, before she spoke again.

"Remember always, there is no way south. That is well known to the Caribou People. West—that is the way—and you are almost there—and you will make it."

And Smoke drowsed in the numbness that is near to death, until once more she aroused him.

"Put your lips on mine," she said. "I will die so."

"We will die together," was his answer.

"No." A feeble flutter of her hand checked him, and so thin was her voice that scarcely did he hear it. Her hand fumbled and groped in the hood of her parka, and she drew forth a pouch that she placed in his hand. "And now

your lips, my lover. Your lips on my lips, and your hand on my heart."

And in that long kiss darkness came upon him again, and when he was conscious again he knew that he was alone and he knew that he, too, was to die. He was wearily glad that he was to die.

He found his hand resting on the pouch. With an inward smile at the curiosity that made him pull the drawstring, he opened it. Out poured a tiny flood of food. There was no particle of it that he did not recognize, all stolen by Labiskwee from Labiskwee—bread fragments saved far back in the days before McCan lost the flour; strips and strings of caribou-meat, partly gnawed; crumbles of suet; the hindleg of the snowshoe rabbit, untouched; the hindleg and part of the foreleg of the white weasel; the wing of the snowbird dented still by her reluctant teeth—pitiful remnants, tragic renunciations, crucifixions of life, morsels stolen from her terrible hunger by her incredible love.

With maniacal laughter Smoke flung it all out on the hardening snowcrust and went back into the blackness.

He dreamed. The Yukon ran dry. In its bed, among muddy pools of water and ice-scoured rocks, he wandered, picking up fat nugget-gold. The weight of it grew to be a burden to him, till he discovered that it was good to eat. And greedily he ate. After all, of what worth was gold that men should prize it so, save that it was good to eat?

He awoke to another sun. His brain was strangely clear. No longer did his eyesight blur. The familiar palpitation that had vexed him through all his frame was gone. The juices of his body seemed to sing, as if the spring had entered in. Blessed well-being had come to him. He turned to awaken Labiskwee, and saw, and remembered. He looked for the food flung out on the snow. It was gone. And he knew that in delirium and dream *it* had been the Yukon nugget-gold. In delirium and dream he had taken heart of life from the life sacrifice of Labiskwee, who had put her heart in his hand.

He was surprised at the ease of his movements, astounded that he was able to drag her fur-wrapped body to the exposed thawed gravel bank, which he undermined with the ax and caved upon her.

Three days, with no further food, he fought west. On the third day he fell beneath a lone spruce beside a wide stream that ran open and which he knew must be the Klondike. Before blackness conquered him, he unlashed his pack, said good-by to the bright world, and rolled himself in the robes.

Chirping, sleepy noises awoke him. The long twilight was on. Above him, among the spruce boughs, were ptarmigan. Hunger bit him into instant action, though the action was infinitely slow. Five minutes passed before he was able to get his rifle to his shoulder, and a second five minutes passed before he dared, lying on his back and aiming straight upward, to pull the trigger. It was a clean miss. No bird fell, but no bird flew. They ruffled and rustled stupidly and drowsily. A second shot was spoiled by the involuntary wince he made as he pulled the trigger. His shoulder pained him. Somewhere, in the last three days, though he had no recollection how, he must have fallen and injured it.

Still the ptarmigan had not flown. He doubled and re-doubled the robe that had covered him, and humped it in the hollow between his right arm and his side. Resting the butt of the rifle on the fur, he fired again, and a bird fell. He clutched it greedily—and found that he had shot most

of the meat out of it. The large-caliber bullet had left little
else than a mess of mangled feathers. Still the ptarmigan
did not fly, and he decided that it was heads or nothing.
He fired only at heads. He reloaded and reloaded the
magazine. He missed; he hit; and the stupid ptarmigan,
that were loth to fly, fell upon him in a rain. There had
been nine of them, and in the end he clipped the head of
the ninth, and lay and laughed and wept.

The first he ate raw. Then he rested and slept, while
his life assimilated the life of it. In the darkness he awoke,
hungry, with strength to build a fire. And until early
dawn he cooked and ate, crunching the bones to powder
between his long-idle teeth. He slept, awoke in the darkness of another night, and slept again to another sun.

He noted with surprise that the fire crackled with fresh
fuel and that a blackened coffeepot steamed on the edge
of the coals. Beside the fire, within arm's length, sat
Shorty, smoking a brown-paper cigarette and intently
watching him. Smoke's lips moved, but a throat paralysis
seemed to come upon him, while his chest was suffused
with the menace of tears. He reached out his hand for the
cigarette and drew the smoke deep into his lungs again
and again.

"I have not smoked for a long time," he said at last, in a
low calm voice. "For a very long time."

"Nor eaten, from your looks," Shorty added gruffly.

Smoke nodded and waved his hand at the ptarmigan
feathers that lay all about.

"Not until recently," he returned. "Do you know, I'd
like a cup of coffee. It will taste strange. Also flapjacks and
a strip of bacon."

"And beans?" Shorty tempted.

"They would taste heavenly. I am quite hungry again."

While the one cooked and the other ate, they told briefly what had happened to them in the days since their separation.

"The Klondike was breakin' up," Shorty concluded his recital, "an' we just had to wait for open water. Two polin' boats, six other men—you know 'em all, crackerjacks—an' all kinds of outfit. An' we've sure been a-comin' —polin', linin' up, and portagin'. But the falls'll stick 'em a solid week. I left 'em a-cuttin' a trail over the tops of the bluffs for the boats. I just had a sure natural hunch to keep a-comin'. So I fills a pack with grub an' starts. I knew I'd find you a-driftin' an' all in. Now we stay right here an' rest an' feed you up for a couple of days."

Smoke shook his head.

"What! If you could just see yourself," Shorty protested.

And what he saw was not nice. Smoke's face, wherever the skin showed, was black and purple and scabbed from repeated frostbite. The cheeks were fallen in, so that, despite the covering of beard, the upper rows of teeth ridged the shrunken flesh. Across the forehead and about the deep-sunk eyes, the skin was stretched drum-tight, while the scraggly beard, that should have been golden, was singed by fire and filthy with camp smoke.

"Pack up anyway," Smoke said.

"But you're feeble as a kid baby. What's the rush?"

"Shorty, I am going after the biggest thing in the Klondike, and I can't wait. That's all. It's bigger than lakes of gold and mountains of gold, bigger than adventure, and meat-eating, and bear-killing."

Shorty sat with bulging eyes. "In the name of the Lord, what is it?" he queried huskily. "Or are you just simple loco?"

"No, I'm all right. Perhaps a fellow has to stop eating in order to see things. I have seen things I never dreamed were in the world. I know what a woman is—now. And there's one woman I want to see right away."

"Huh! I don't need no hunch to guess *her* name. The rest of 'em has gone up to the drainin' of Surprise Lake, but Joy Gastell wouldn't go. She's stickin' around Dawson, waitin' to see if I come back with you. An' she sure swears, if I don't, she'll sell her holdin's an' hire a whole army of gun-fighters, an' go into the Caribou Country an' knock the everlastin' stuffin' outa old Snass an' his whole gang. An' if you'll hold your horses a couple of shakes, I reckon I'll get packed up an' ready to hike along with you."

WORLD *Junior* LIBRARY

Exciting, action-filled, inspiring and always engross-
ing, WORLD JUNIOR LIBRARY books will delight
all boys and girls who love good reading. These are
quality books by famous authors, in handsome, cloth-
bound library editions.

TITLES NOW AVAILABLE

JILL'S VICTORY *by Elisa Bialk*

THE SUN-DOG TRAIL *by Jack London*

SMOKE BELLEW *by Jack London*

JEAN CRAIG GRADUATE NURSE
by Kay Lyttleton

PAT'S HARMONY *by Page Cooper*

GHOST GABLES *by Mildred A. Wirt*

THE PAINTED SHIELD *by Mildred A. Wirt*

WILD STALLION *by Bud Murphy*

BULLARD OF THE SPACE PATROL
by Malcolm Jameson

FAVORITE DOG STORIES
edited by Marguerite Bloch

COMANCHE *by David Appel*

MONKEY SHINES *by Earl S. Miers*

THE WORLD PUBLISHING COMPANY

CLEVELAND AND NEW YORK

Date Due

EAU CLAIRE PUBLIC LIBRARY